BERSERKER

EMMY LAYBOURNE

BERSERKER

FEIWEL AND FRIENDS
NEW YORK

A Feiwel and Friends Book
An imprint of Macmillan Publishing Group, LLC
175 Fifth Avenue, New York, NY 10010

Our books may be purchased in bulk for promotional, educational, or business use. Please
contact your local bookseller or the Macmillan Corporate and Premium Sales Department
at (800) 221-7945 ext. 5442 or by e-mail at MacmillanSpecialMarkets@macmillan.com.

Library of Congress Cataloging-in-Publication Data

Names: Laybourne, Emmy, author.
Title: Berserker / Emmy Laybourne.
Description: First edition. | New York : Feiwel and Friends, 2017. | Summary: Hanne and her
    siblings flee Norway after her "gift" causes her to commit murder, and on the American
    frontier Owen, a cowboy, leads them toward their uncle who may help them learn control.
Identifiers: LCCN 2016058769 (print) | LCCN 2017029374 (ebook) | ISBN
    9781250135230 (Ebook) | ISBN 9781250055200 (hardcover)
Subjects: | CYAC: Ability—Fiction. | Supernatural—Fiction. | Brothers and
    sisters—Fiction. | Frontier and pioneer life—Fiction. | Immigrants—Fiction. |
    Norwegian Americans—Fiction. | Mythology, Norse—Fiction.
Classification: LCC PZ7.L4458 (ebook) | LCC PZ7.L4458 Ber 2017 (print) | DDC
    [Fic]—dc23
LC record available at https://lccn.loc.gov/2016058769

Book design by Liz Dresner

Feiwel and Friends logo designed by Filomena Tuosto

First edition, 2017

10 9 8 7 6 5 4 3 2 1

For Ellie

BERSERKER

CHAPTER ONE

The hog snorted at the two young trespassers in his pen. He kept his massive flank pressed to the oak beams of the fence, staying as far away from them as he could.

The girl, Hanne, kept her eyes on the boar, hiding the knife she held against the folds of her skirt. It was a long, slender blade; old, honed often, and very, very sharp. Her milky-blond hair was plaited in a crown around her head. She wore her oldest work dress and a coarse homespun apron stained rust at the hem. Though she was two years his senior, her brother Knut dwarfed her. He was six feet six inches tall. Barrel-chested but, at fourteen years old, barefaced.

Behind the siblings stood a large round tub, empty and waiting, and a long-handled wooden spoon. Hanne was glad for the cold October air. It tamped down the stench of the pig's mud.

The boar shifted his weight, pawing at the ground. With a sudden scrape and a bang, the door to the old farm cabin swung open.

The bowlegged farmer hurried toward the pigpen.

"Stop!" he called. "Girl! Get out of there!"

Hanne kept her gaze fixed on the hog.

Their father, Amund, came hobbling out of the farmhouse behind the farmer. "Hush now! You'll startle the pig!"

Their father's part in the butchering was to keep the farmer inside until the work of killing was finished. He always brought a jug containing a few pulls of apple wine to share. Neither Amund nor his children wished to be found out by their neighbors, for they were Nytteson.

"Calm down," Amund called to the farmer. "You'll spoil the kill."

"I didn't know you meant to have a girl aid in the butchering," the farmer protested, his face red with fear and anger. "I never would have agreed to it!"

"She's just there to help collect the blood. Don't worry."

The hog snorted and fretted. He did not like this commotion, and he did not like the two silent blond siblings staring at him from inside his own pen.

Amund caught up to the farmer. He raised his right hand, the hand with only two fingers and a thumb remaining, bidding the farmer to slow down. The sight of Amund's deformity was enough to still the man for a moment.

"You won't be sorry you hired us. Now come, let's go have a drink," Amund told the farmer.

"He'll kill her—he mauled my son," the farmer said. "That's why I hired the work out in the first place."

Amund began to speak again, but the farmer changed tactics,

calling to the girl, "Young miss, come out of there! Don't be foolish. I'll not let you be killed, not on my land."

But Hanne continued to ignore him. She could feel the anger of the hog growing, his irritation at the farmer's voice edging him toward action. His breath was steaming in the air.

"Knut," Hanne said. "The pig's taking too long. You'll have to provoke him some."

"I don't want to," her brother said softly. Hanne knew Knut would have liked to hold her hand. The bigger beasts scared him. But he wouldn't dare reach for her hand in the sight of their father.

"Get on with it, children," Amund called.

"Come out, I say!" the farmer shouted.

The boar snorted and wheeled around. He was becoming confused.

Hanne didn't want that. She wanted him mean and focused. "You've got to make him charge you," she hissed to Knut. "Come on, now! He must attack you."

Knut made a weak movement toward the hog.

"You must do better than that! Hey!" she yelled. She picked up a clump of mud and threw it at the animal's head.

The boar snorted and pawed the ground.

"Yell, Knut!" she ordered.

"Yah! Pig!" Knut yelled. He feigned a dart forward, startling the animal.

The hog lowered his head and, finally, charged Hanne's brother.

A cry went up from the farmer, who rushed forward to help.

Amund held out his crutch to restrain him, smacking the man across the chest.

Moving as fast as a lightning strike, Hanne put herself between the hog and her brother. The reek hit her as the beast's tremendous bulk bore down on her. She threw herself forward, grabbing the pig around the neck. Her body was yanked parallel to the ground by the momentum, and her legs snapped up. The hog swerved around Knut, trying to run away from Hanne, but she hooked a leg over the pig's side.

Her sense of the animal's anatomy sharpened, as it always did before the kill. Her pupils were fully wide, as if she had black eyes, not blue; and she knew without looking where the jugular vein lay.

With one arm clutching the pig's neck, she used her other hand to sink the thin blade into the flesh under the pig's ear. The knife seemed to move on its own, slicing through the fatty meat until Hanne's wrist was buried deep in the pig's throat. There. The jugular was severed, and the blood began to fountain. Hanne's hand was pushed out by the geyser of hot, slippery liquid.

The hog came to a skid, body jerking, legs still trying to charge.

"Get the bucket!" Hanne called to Knut. The farmer wanted the blood collected. If it wasn't stirred while it was hot, much of the sweetness would be lost and the sausage wouldn't taste as good.

Knut wiped tears away from his eyes with his sleeve as he hustled over. He was shaken by the killing—he always was. But he brought over the blood pan and set it down.

Hanne pushed off the hog's slick back. She dropped the knife into the wide front pocket she'd sewn in for this purpose. She wiped her hands on her apron.

Knut now did his part. He grabbed the boar by its hind feet and lifted it up. He grunted and strained, his face becoming red as he angled the beast's head to send the blood into the waiting tub.

"Ah!" the farmer cried out in wonder. To lift a hog that way was impossible for most men. Even two or three men would have to drag a beast that size on the ground. How could this boy lift it?

The farmer began to recite the Lord's Prayer. Amund snorted. "You'll see," he said, waving his stump at the pan of blood. "Best blood sausage you'll ever make. And the meat! Delicious."

Hanne knelt in the dirt beside the tub. She brushed off her hands and reached into the tub to locate the spoon. She pulled it out and began to stir. The blood splashed, then slowed to a steady flow. It ran like syrup, but the width of the stream swelled rhythmically with the final heartbeats of the swine.

The pig's eye was glossed over, even though his forehooves still twitched.

Knut's muscles strained and shook. He was sweating freely now, steam rising from his broad back like mist off morning waters.

Hanne became aware of the hunger building in her belly. Her father had brought her two loaves of brown bread and a half round of cheese in an old gunnysack. He knew the price she would pay for using her Nytte, her gift.

Knut hefted the boar up again, resettling his grip on its hocks.

The stream of blood was thinning now. Soon Knut could rest the hog, and then the butchering would begin.

5

Hanne saw the carcass begin to stiffen. Sometimes, when her father was not watching, she would sing to the beast as it died. This made Knut feel better, and if Hanne allowed herself to admit it, it comforted her as well.

Today, their father watched, leaning against his crutch. He had an eye on his children while the farmer brought a cauldron of boiling water outside with shaky hands. Amund spoke to the farmer quietly, promising a discount if the farmer kept Hanne and Knut's working methods to himself.

Today the hog went without a blessing.

THEY HAD TRAVELED to Norheimsund by foot. The road was nothing but a cart track, and the journey had taken them two hours.

Their path homeward to Øystese was downhill, but Hanne felt so tired. It was as if she were wading through mud with leaden skirts. By the time they reached the outskirts of their town, the light was beginning to go blue, and Hanne tucked her hands into her armpits to warm them. She ought to have brought her mittens. The lanolin from the good lambs' wool would have soothed her chapped fingertips. The mittens were the last thing her mother had made for her, and she was trying to preserve them. They wouldn't last forever.

Hanne was thinking of what she might barter for some nice, soft yarn. Her sister, Sissel, needed mittens, and Knut needed new socks. She could send Knut to work for the Pedersens one morning early, before their father awoke. Amund didn't like loaning out the services of his children, unless the coins came directly to his pocket. But Knut's work as a farmhand was what was keeping Hanne and her siblings fed for the most part. The stingy allowance Amund gave Hanne to cover groceries and dry goods was never enough. Never half enough.

Her older brother, Stieg, could use another pair of socks as well, to take with him to America. He said there was no more room in his bag, but Hanne could fit in one more pair of socks. Stieg was planning on taking his books with him and Hanne thought he wouldn't need books as much as he would need socks.

Hanne was thinking about Mrs. Pedersen's good black wool when they walked around the bend of a hill and came upon another party. Climbing up toward them were three students returning to their homes. She remembered them from school. Oskar Oleson, his little brother, and Linnea Solberg.

Oskar's bright eyes sparked as he recognized her, and he grinned that old, side-cracked grin she had loved to see at school.

"Good evening!" he said to them.

"Yah, yah," Amund said. "Give us the path. We've been working all day."

The three students stood to the side.

Hanne kept her eyes on the ground. Amund hobbled past them. Hanne saw Linnea's soft, pale hand clutching Oskar's arm. Two sets of books were bundled together, hanging from a book strap in Oskar's hand.

Knut lumbered past them, giving them a nod and a shy hello.

Oskar's little brother skipped ahead, his smile happy and carefree.

"Are you well, Hanne?" Oskar asked as she walked by him.

Hanne glanced up, startled, meeting his eye. She saw Linnea's nose wrinkle in distaste. Hanne realized how she must smell. Raw pork and offal.

"I'm well enough," Hanne said. She did not ask after his health.

"We see your brother Stieg at school. And Sissel, but you and Knut do not come. Why is this?" he asked.

Oskar's eyes followed her father's retreating shape. Amund's wretched, bent form did nothing to deny his bad temper.

"I'm needed at home these days, and Knut is not much for book learning," she said.

Oskar placed his hand on Hanne's arm. She jerked away from his touch. He dropped his hand to his side and spoke in a low voice. "But, Hanne, are you all right? Are you . . . treated well?"

Hanne darted her eyes to her father, hobbling down the darkening path. She didn't dare stop any longer.

"I am fine, Oskar. Thank you for asking."

She looked up at his face, his brows knit with concern for her, and remembered how he had hung around in the schoolroom at recess instead of playing with the other boys outside, how he used to bring hawthorn leaves into the schoolroom and stick them in her braids, just to tease her. He was a kind young man and smart.

And out of reach for her, now until forever.

Linnea tightened her grip on Oskar's arm.

Hanne tore her eyes from Oskar's face and stumbled behind her father and her brother.

"You're slower than me, for heaven's sake," her father groused when she had caught up. "The next time we work, as soon as the door to the farmhouse closes, get the animal moving! What were you waiting for?"

"I'm sorry, Father," she said.

"You want people to know what we are? To come hunt us out with pitchforks the way they did our ancestors?"

"No, Father."

She must have scowled or made an unpleasant face because her father stopped and pointed his walking stick at her.

"I didn't make you a Berserker, girl," he snarled. "It's not my fault Odin 'blessed' our forefathers with the Nytte."

Hanne did not like to speak of the Nytte at all, much less outside and so close to town. She nodded, keeping her head lowered. After a moment, her father resumed the slow walk home.

The Nytte was an ancient blood-gift, a pagan, Viking gift, from Odin to his three favorite kings, to be carried in their lineage. A child with the Nytte on both sides of his or her family might manifest one of six eerie powers at puberty—or might receive no Nytte at all.

Odin had bestowed the Nytte upon these kings, Hanne's aunt Aud had told her once, to create unstoppable raiding parties. Shipwright, Oar-Breaker, and Storm-Rend—these gifts were meant to help the Vikings cross the seas. Once ashore, the Berserkers and the Shield-Skinned warriors were nearly undefeatable. They massacred the enemy while the Ransackers found and looted any treasure to be had.

What good was it now, to be one of the Nytteson? They were not Vikings. They did not sail to foreign lands to plunder and pillage. They were just commoners, trying to hide their differences and earn a living.

Hanne looked back over her shoulder. She saw the silhouettes of her former schoolmates approaching the top of the hill.

Pity how that family's gone to seed since their mother left, Linnea might be saying to Oskar. *You'd think Hanne would be able to keep up with the laundry, at least. I'd never be seen in a dress that dirty!*

For one moment Hanne allowed herself to imagine what it would be like to be Linnea Solberg. To have a head full of history or mathematics and be walking home arm in arm with Oskar. She imagined how it would feel to be striding over the hill to a fine, strong home and not down to a dark, damp stone house that was slowly falling to pieces.

Linnea would sleep on clean sheets and, in the morning, put her feet into stockings that would be mended with elegant darning, if they had any holes to begin with. As for Hanne, her heel was scraped raw where her sock had worn through.

Hanne walked on, hating her dirty dress; her old, mended shoes; her coarse wraps. She hated her jealousy, and she hated who she was, for her Nytte, her "gift," was the reason their mother had finally given up and gone away.

CHAPTER TWO

Sissel had decorated the table by placing some branches of elm into one of the milk pitchers. There were autumn leaves clinging to the branches, the way elm leaves did. They had dried golden and were meant to reflect the candlelight, but to Hanne they just looked dead—her elder brother, Stieg, was going away.

The money Amund had received for Hanne and Knut's work slaughtering the pig was quickly drunk away, so Hanne had had to call in favors from their neighbors so they could give Stieg a proper farewell. She knew she should have felt excited for him. He had saved for three years to make the voyage to America, but she had dreaded every krone he'd put in the can. He was leaving Øystese in the morning.

Stieg spent the day outside, working with Knut. They were walking the farm, Stieg reminding Knut of everything he must do now that he would be running the farm himself.

Stieg had also stayed outside so as not to be in his sisters' way. They were preparing a celebration dinner for him. A grand farewell. Hanne knew he wanted, even needed, her to pretend to be happy for him. She would try her best to be convincing.

Sissel was humming as she laid the table. Hanne had used the tabletop to roll out the *tynnlefse* dough hours earlier. The table was from her father's side of the family, very old, the work of a Shipwright, no doubt. The legs were two broad panels in the shape of an X, each carved with intricate knot work. At the foot of each thick leg, the patterns ended in the flat face of a dragon. When Hanne was little, she would crouch under the table while her mother sang church hymns, rolling out dough. Hanne had liked to trace the snout of each dragon. The flat, round eyes. The curved fangs. She liked to imagine the beasts were her friends and answered only to her.

The top of the table was polished smooth by hundreds of years of hard use. Now Sissel set out their mother's prettiest napkins, the ones with the red stitching. Hanne stirred the lamb and cabbage stew—Stieg's favorite—and watched her sister limp around the table.

Sissel was too thin; everyone said so. Her hair was so blond it was white. It hung lifelessly in two thin braids that Sissel pinned up across her head, the ends tucked in, so that no one could see how straggly and fine they were. She had the habit of patting her head to make sure the ends were not sticking out. Every time she did it Hanne wondered—who was there to see?

Sissel was not a good worker—she complained often of being tired, cold, hungry. Her bad leg always ached from the dog bite she'd received when she was ten.

But Sissel was excited about the going-away party for her

brother. She could set a table well enough, Hanne noted, even if she claimed to be too weak to work to make the meal that would be served on it.

When their mother left nearly two years ago, Hanne had been forced to assume her work. Hanne did the work. She did not do it well. She did not keep a house that was sparkling clean. The wooden beams of the ceiling housed spiders and their webs, old and new. The floor was swept, but not twice daily and never sprinkled with spruce boughs, to give the house a lovely scent. Clothes were washed and mended. Not as quickly or as well as Hanne would have liked, but there was so much to do, she simply could not keep up.

If Hanne had taken on the physical work of a mother, then Stieg had taken on the emotional work. He was the one who encouraged them, who scolded them to do their chores, who heard their lessons in the winter, and who kept any hope at all kindled in their hearts.

Stieg could make learning anything interesting. The veins of a leaf. The way crumbs clump together if the bread is good. The idea of electricity. He loved to learn and loved to teach.

Once he'd set his mind on going to America, he'd brought English into the house, with its wonderfully silly round *B* and *P* sounds and the clunking *D*s.

The only new memories Hanne had worth keeping since her mother had left were the ones of Stieg teaching them English around the table on winter nights when their father went to town to drink.

"You're good at this," Stieg had told her once. She had read a paragraph from Stieg's copy of *Great Expectations*. "Hanne, you're bright."

She had flushed at the compliment. Then he had said, "You should come back to school."

Hanne had risen abruptly from the table. She crossed over to the washbasin to finish scrubbing the soup pot.

"And who would do the washing and the mending and the cooking?" She'd felt like throwing the pot through the window. "What use is there in educating a girl, after all?" she'd groused.

"The reasons to educate a girl are the same as to educate a boy! Because learning leads to a fulfilling and productive life."

"I should not bother to learn English. You'll never send for us."

"I *will* send for you!" Stieg insisted.

Hanne had been scrubbing the pot, her body bent over the task, when Stieg grabbed her by the arm. She'd been startled by his urgency.

"You must stop blaming yourself for what happened," he'd said. "Mother chose to leave us. That is her fault. And you did not choose to be a Berserker, Hanne."

"Be quiet!" she had shouted. That was the last time they had spoken of the Nytte aloud.

Stieg's plan was to find a teaching job once he reached America, then send money back for their journey.

Together they would file on a claim in Minnesota or Dakota— one of the American territories where the government was practically giving away land to encourage settlement. Stieg had copied down the contents of a flyer that had been passed around their town. It was from an American railway company and described the Great Plains, ready and ripe for planting. The ground was nearly free of stones. It had to be true, for it was printed there in the pamphlet.

Already there were towns there filled with Norwegians, with Norwegian churches and schools.

During the dark winter, Stieg had kept them fed with stories about the life that awaited them all in America. But that life was at least two or three years away. It would take time to find a teaching job, and then he must save up for their fares. Each of them must first travel to England, to a city called Liverpool, to catch the steamers headed toward New York City. The steamship fare alone was 250 kroner, not to mention the expense of the "feeder" ships to get to England.

To make it worse, he would have to save up until he had enough to send for the three of them together. They could not travel separately. Knut wasn't clever enough to travel on his own—he became confused in busy, loud places—and Sissel was too weak. Hanne was terrified by the thought of the long journey. What if someone tried to hurt her or one of her siblings? What might she do to them? She had never hurt a person. She'd never had cause to, and she prayed to keep it that way.

No, Hanne did not see them emigrating. Stieg was leaving them behind forever. Knut and Sissel might marry and move, but Hanne was stuck on the farm. She would have to care for their father. His woodworking days were over, but it hardly mattered, as his drinking had ruined the name he had built for himself. Their income was whatever they could make butchering, and whatever they could get for their excess grain and vegetables.

Knut was not a smart boy, but he was bighearted and gentle. Sissel was terribly lazy, but she was still young and had been babied. She would likely straighten out, once she undertook real work, and might make a good wife.

But Hanne would not allow herself to marry, lest she bear

children with the Nytte. Any man she married might have the Nytte in his bloodline and not know it. The gift was dormant in many. Had Hanne's mother known, she would likely not have married Amund.

No, Hanne knew she and her father would die on the farm, after a life of farming and butchering and hiding their "gifts" from their neighbors.

THE LAMB AND CABBAGE STEW was done. Hanne used the leather mitt to push it to the back of the stove. The *lefse* was finished and waiting in its large round basket. Hanne put a dish of butter on the table. Stieg liked the sweet butter, but there'd been none available to trade for. The potatoes were ready. The meal was complete.

Stieg and Knut came in, laughing, cheeks rosy.

"Ah! What delicious smells!" Stieg said.

"Yes, and see the table," Sissel said.

"It is lovely. Just as lovely as you, little sister!" Stieg bowed to her and she curtsied back, giggling.

"And how fares the big sister?" Stieg asked.

Hanne turned her face to the stove. "Fine."

"The father?" Stieg asked.

"Down at Johan's," Hanne said.

Amund was visiting with their neighbor, a sour-smelling man who lived alone in a cottage at the waterfront. He made his living repairing fishnets and liked company while he worked. Especially when the company brought a bottle.

"Oh, Father won't be late, will he? He can't be late tonight! He can't ruin this dinner!" Sissel said.

Then the door swung open and there was their father, shuffling in on his crutch. He gave off the smell of flat ale and old seawater.

"Move in, you great ox," he said to Knut. "Make some room."

The living room had felt cozy before his entrance. But now that their father was home, it felt dark and claustrophobic, as if someone had dimmed all the lamps at once.

Hanne hurried to her father's side as he shucked off his coat. His bristly face rubbed against Hanne's cheek for a moment. Their eyes met askance. They had both remembered their old ritual at the same time.

Back when he had all his digits, back when he was a renowned shipbuilder and Hanne was his little girl, she would come running to greet him at the door at the end of the day. She would jump into his arms, and they would rub faces together, his brown-and-red beard tickling her smooth cheeks.

That was before Hanne's Nytte had made itself known. They had both hoped, assumed, even, that she would be a Shipwright, like her father. She had been his favorite child—he made it clear for all to see. And she had adored him.

Hanne had always been able to calm him when his temper rose, just with a smile or a joke. They could work together for hours in a companionable silence.

But then Hanne had flowered into a young woman, and her Nytte had revealed itself. She was a Berserker, cursed to fly into action whenever anyone she loved was in danger. A killer who would be compelled to murder elegantly, viciously, and without remorse. Until she regained her senses.

Now she and her father looked away from each other.

Amund's eyes were yellowed and bloodshot. "Is that lamb stew I smell?"

"Yes, Father. It's for Stieg's going away," Sissel said.

"Ah yes," he said, hobbling to his seat at the table.

"Come to the table, then," Hanne said to her siblings. "Sit down."

They all took their usual seats. Amund had made a chair special for Knut three years ago. It was thick and wide, to accommodate his great size.

Hanne dished out the servings, and they ate in silence.

"It's good," Amund said.

"Yes, very," Stieg agreed. Amund silenced him with a look.

After a while, Stieg cleared his throat. "I would like to say a few words."

Amund snorted a laugh. He shoveled another bite of stew into his mouth. "When do you not?"

"We do not usually speak of the Nytte openly, but tomorrow I leave, and this is something I must say to you," Stieg said. "You always told us to keep our gifts a secret, and I see the reason for that, Father. But that secrecy has created shame. And I believe we are not meant to feel shame about these gifts."

Hanne's blood was pounding in her ears. No! This was not something to speak of so directly. She did not want to discuss the Nytte in front of her father. Never!

Stieg looked at Hanne. "We must not be ashamed, Sister. Our gifts are meant to give glory to the Gods."

"Glory?" Their father grunted. "The Nytte was given to the Vikings so they could rape and pillage!"

"That's not what Aunty Aud has told me. She says that the different types of Nytte are each an art."

"What is artful about your brother's brute strength? Or your sister's ability to gut a pig? Your lofty ideas are nothing but vanity!"

"What about your ability to carve and make beautiful boats? Boats that can nearly fly—"

"QUIET!" Amund yelled. "What do you know? You have the weakest Nytte of all. A Storm-Rend! You can do nothing. Make the winds twist a little. Blow hot air out of your mouth like a bellows—"

"We are not meant to feel bad about our gifts. They are not something ugly to hide away."

"Not ugly?" their father said. He unwound the cloth that covered the stump of his left hand, revealing the fingerless palm. The nubs of the finger stumps were chapped and chafing, the skin red and scabby. "Have you ever seen something as ugly as this hand?" Amund stood, his chair falling down behind him with a clatter.

"If the Nytte is a gift, and not a curse, then why must we pay such a dear price for using it? Why did I have to lose most of my fingers so that I can no longer build the damn boats my Nytte shows me?"

"Father," Stieg said, his voice gentle and full of sympathy. "We know how hard it has been for you—"

Then, *WHAP!* Amund reached across the table and struck Stieg with the back of his left hand. Stieg's head snapped back, and Hanne was seized with clear, direct energy.

She was up and over the table and had her father by the throat in a heartbeat. His eyes bugged out as he beheld her, her hand gripping

19

the collar of his shirt tight. A butter knife was in her other hand, the dull blade aimed at his eye.

Amund began to make a dry, rasping sound. Was she choking him? No. He was laughing.

Hanne realized now that Knut had one of his giant arms around her waist.

"Let me go," she said. Knut let her go, and she in turn released her father. He fumbled for his crutch, which lay against the wall.

"Your Nytte reveals your affections, Hanne," he said. "At least I know where I stand."

He took stock of them, standing around the table. The plates broken, stew spilled on the table.

"What a family I have," Amund spat. "A *gift*, indeed."

CHAPTER THREE

CHOUTEAU COUNTY, MONTANA TERRITORY

Owen Bennett tried to stay as far away from the trail boss as he could. The cowboys were pleased with their progress except for the boss, Harold Mandry, and his lanky, lisping yes-man, an unpleasant fellow everyone called Whistler.

The team of ten men had brought the Herefords, nearly twelve hundred of them, down from Bullhook Bottoms, Montana, at a respectable pace, grazing along the way. They'd lost only three, and those had started the journey with bellies crawling with gut worms.

Nevertheless, each night, as they gathered up at the chuck wagon to collect the day's portion of chicken stew or rabbit stew or the stewed version of whatever game they'd scared up along the way, Mandry would be in a foul mood.

Mandry didn't like Owen; that much was clear. The rancher Wilson, a friend of Owen's father, had forced Mandry to hire him, but Owen knew there had to be more to it because Mandry disliked Owen with a vengeance.

Owen couldn't figure it out. He was quiet and kept to himself. Didn't complain. He was a good cowboy, knew how to calm the cattle, and handled his rope well. He kept his Winchester handy and frequently handed over a rabbit or some grouse to the chuck wagon. True, Owen did prefer the company of his dog, Daisy, to that of men, but she was a trusted friend, and these men were all new to him.

Owen held the bowl from his kit out to Old Eben, the cook. Old Eben gave Owen a generous portion of dried venison stew. "Take some biscuits, too," Old Eben said. "Only let 'em soak a bit. Fire got the best of me." He winked.

This had become a running joke around the evening campfire. Old Eben was an admittedly lousy cook. He'd only signed on because he wanted to get down to Helena, to meet up with his brother.

Besides the boss Mandry and Old Eben, all the other men were drovers. At eighteen, Owen wasn't the youngest. The youngest was a kid named Billy who would have been handsome but for his two front teeth, both gray from a goat-butt to the face.

"Dear Lord, you gone and burned the biscuits again?" Whistler cried, grabbing a biscuit off the stack Old Eben had on a tin serving plate. "Is burnin' them a part of your damn recipe?"

Whistler looked around, closed one eye, and chucked the biscuit at Daisy, who was minding her own business, sitting near the lodgepole pine where Owen had dropped his saddle and his bedroll. Daisy flinched as the missile landed near her.

Owen frowned. Daisy padded forward and sniffed at the biscuit. She gave Owen a look: *Can I eat it?*

"Leave it," he instructed. He liked her to eat off a plate or from his hand, not just go eating any old thing. Daisy sighed.

"Now, don't you harass Daisy," the next guy in line said. He was a wide, brawny guy named Hoakes. He was friendly to everyone, and easygoing in a way Owen much admired. Hoakes winked at Owen. "That bitch does more work in an hour than you do all day, Whistler."

Owen took his plate and two biscuits and headed away from the men, toward Daisy. She watched him sit and then put her head on her paws, regarding the lone biscuit sitting off in the dirt in a forlorn way.

"Here you go, girl," Owen said, trying to break one of his biscuits in two. It wasn't easy. He had to put down his tin bowl in order to do it. He set one half in his bowl to soak and gave Daisy the other half.

Daisy gnawed at her portion with gusto.

Owen hoped Whistler would let him and Daisy alone. His strategy, when harassed, was to become as uninteresting as possible. He had three half brothers. He'd used this strategy frequently.

Owen's mother had died in childbirth. Catherine Ryan had been the cook at the ranch, a spirited if plain dark Irish girl. She had been hired and brought all the way from Chicago by Mr. Bennett on one of his business trips to the stockyards. He'd hired the girl as a surprise for Mrs. Bennett—a young woman to help in the kitchen and keep her company.

Mrs. Bennett had been surprised, and even more so when, one year later, she learned her husband had gotten a bastard on the Irish cook.

At the time, Catherine had gone to Mrs. Bennett, begging her mercy and for an advance on her pay that she might return to her people in Ireland. Mrs. Bennett provided neither and dismissed her from service. When Catherine Ryan died in childbirth some months later, the doctor, a kind and discreet man, brought the newborn child to the Bennett household.

Mrs. Bennett saw, in that bundled quilt, a solemn dark-haired boy peering at her like a wizened sage. She also saw an opportunity.

The infant was given the name Owen Bennett, he was raised with Mrs. Bennett's three sons, and whenever her husband set a toe out of line, or found himself with the slightest complaint about the way his wife managed household affairs on the ranch, all she had to do was press her lips together and glance Owen's way. Owen was a living reprimand to his father.

From the start, Owen had been made aware of his position of half privilege. To all outsiders, he was a full Bennett brother, but in the privacy of the ranch house, his status was clear.

He wore handed-down clothes of his half brothers, played with their discarded toys, and was even encouraged to eat their leftover food, in the kitchen with the new cook, who was exceptionally homely and gruff but kind, before he helped her do the dishes.

It was a strange situation for a boy, and it was made stranger by the fact that he resembled his father more than any of his half brothers did. They were all fair, sandy haired, and gray eyed, like Mrs. Bennett. But Owen had his father's big brown eyes, olive complexion, and lean frame, together with his mother's near-black hair.

Owen's resemblance to his father curried no favor with Mr. Bennett. He could barely stand to be in the same room with Owen, and only seemed comfortable around him when he could treat him like any other ranch hand.

Owen had worked the ranch, and worked hard, and on his seventeenth birthday his father had given him a new saddle and Owen's favorite horse. They were all he could expect in terms of an inheritance, and he was grateful enough for them. He also got to take his gun, a '73 Winchester he'd been carrying for so long he could clean and oil it blindfolded.

His brothers all stayed on at the ranch, vying for their father's attention. But Owen had never had much of a shot at that, so he'd left.

No one outside the family knew his story, or that he was a bastard. It was a funny feeling. Liberating, if slightly disorienting. Who was he, when not examined in contrast to his rowdy blond "brothers"? Who was he, when not the subject of his father's shame or his stepmother's annoyance?

He was tired, that was for sure. He was looking forward to turning in for the night. He'd done everything he could to stay out of Mandry's way that day. There was no reason for him to assign Owen another half night of guard duty. He'd had it nine nights in a row. Each cowboy was expected to watch the cattle at night when his turn came.

Owen leaned over and made a grab for his bedroll.

"I swear, Old Eben, this food's so bad we should say a prayer *after* we eat."

There were laughs from the other cowboys.

"I like your cookin', Old Eben," said Billy.

"What do you know about it? You got rotten teeth, prob'ly make your food taste all rotten."

Owen wanted dearly not to enter the conversation, but Billy's face fell and he looked so ashamed.

"I say Eben's a fine cook," Owen ventured.

"Now we got our other greenhorn weighin' in," said Whistler. "This one's sweet on his dog."

His teeth whistled on the *sw* sound, and Hoakes laughed.

"*Thweeet*, indeed," Hoakes teased. "Whistler, you're awfully musical tonight."

Whistler leaped up to charge Hoakes. Several men rushed in to keep them apart.

"Break it up, you morons," Mandry roared. "You just earned yourself a place sitting guard tonight, Hoakes. You can have the first shift, along with Owen Bennett and his blasted dog."

Owen tried not to show a darn thing on his face. Not surprise. Not anger. Nothing at all.

"Hey now, Mandry, that don't seem quite fair," a guy named Jimmy protested.

Hoakes joined in. "Ain't it Whistler's turn tonight?" he asked. "He ain't set out but one night, and that was the first week!"

"You don't like sitting up, Hoakes?" Mandry said. "I guess you don't like the sitting-up portion of your pay, neither. I'm happy to dock it for you."

"Now, I'm happy to do my share, but you know you had Owen Bennett on guard every night for more than a week. He's a boy. Needs a full night's rest."

"Well, all right, then. Old Eben, you can sit up for Owen." Mandry turned on the cook. Old Eben hadn't even heard him. He was nearly deaf. "Hear that, you old bastard? You're on the watch tonight."

"Yes, sir," Old Eben mumbled. He looked as surprised as the rest of them felt. "You mean for me to watch the cattle, you say?"

Old Eben wasn't a cowboy. He'd been a miner. He didn't know how to keep the cattle calm. There was a trick to it—lots of tricks to it.

Owen told himself to shut up, but he couldn't. "Excuse me, Mr. Mandry, I'll take the watch."

Mandry smiled like he'd known Owen would volunteer.

"See there, Hoakes," Mandry said. "He's happy to do the watch. He wants to do it. He wants to do a double shift, don't you, Owen Bennett?"

Mandry's eyes glittered with malice. Whistler had a big smile on his ugly face.

Not for the first time, Owen wished himself an easygoing, lighthearted type of person. If he were, he could make some joke, get Mandry to laugh it off, and get out of this moment. As it was, he felt cornered and angry.

He looked Mandry in the eye. "I can do it," he said. "Sure enough."

OWEN HAD PLENTY of time to regret his stubbornness, over the long night. He was on at first with Hoakes. They walked their horses in a circle around the herd, opposite each other.

Hoakes liked to sing to the cattle, and it did seem to keep them nice and calm. Owen knew because he'd done guard duty with most of the other fellows, in turns, too. Some of them didn't like to sing. But any insurance against a stampede was worth taking. Some herds got jumpy, and any sound could set them off—a big noise like thunder, or a little noise like a careless cook gonging a pan on a rock. A beef could lose fifty pounds in a hot stampede and a cowboy could lose his life.

"*Oh bury me not on the lone prairie.*" Hoakes's voice came wavering over the heads of the cattle. His voice was mellow and deep.

"*These words came low and mournfully | From the pallid lips of a youth who lay | On his dying bed at the close of day.*"

If Owen had not been so self-conscious, he might have sung back. He certainly knew the words to all eight verses by now, for though Hoakes liked to sing, he didn't know a great many songs. Owen could not bring himself to lift his voice in return. He felt too shy.

"*Oh bury me not on the lone prairie | Where the coyote howls and the wind blows free | In a narrow grave just six by three | Bury me not on the lone prairie.*"

Owen shivered. He wore a wool poncho over his oilskin canvas coat. He pulled it up somewhat on his neck. It was getting colder now. They'd be lucky to make it to Helena before the first snowfall.

CHAPTER FOUR

One moment Hanne was deep in the feather bed, cuddled near her sister, her body heavy with the rich sleep of the hard worker; the next her bare feet slapped the cold floor and she was upright.

She was propelled to the door. Her hands found the latch. She pushed into the hall. There was danger in the barn. Her heart beat with such urgency and alarm, she had to *run*. She tore down the stairs, three at a time. Her nightgown caught against the rough-hewn wall, but she did not feel the fabric tear.

Then she was outside, striding toward the threat. The barn. She heard the voices of men, three of them, arguing with her father.

"We've waited long enough!" came a low voice. It was Nils Paulsen, the gambler from the pub. Hanne knew this instantly.

Her feet went across the mud.

She saw every detail of the dark farmyard. The pitchfork left out by accident. The pots with Sissel's foxglove plants and wild roses, fallow now, until the springtime. There was a matched team of chestnut-brown horses standing next to the barn, asleep on their feet and still harnessed to a wagon. Her breath made frost, but not much because she moved too fast.

"You wouldn't shoot me," she heard her father say.

The heavy barn door was thrown open; it was she who threw it, but she did not feel herself do it.

Four men turned, shocked. At first, she saw only the gun.

"Hanne, no! Hanne!" her father shouted.

Hanne stalked in. Three attackers, this was new. She had only fought animals before, and only one at a time. The man with the gun was in front, with two cronies behind him. The horses were in their stalls, huffing and stamping, displeased. The chickens roosting in the rafters were awake and clucking with alarm.

Hanne inhaled deeply. She felt wonderfully alive. She smiled.

Her mind expanded with a vision, an all-knowing sense of who was where and how the bodies of the men were made. She could feel them, feel how strong they were and where they were weak and what they might do. The man with the gun was lazy and slow. He was not the true threat—it was the skinny man behind him, the one with the cap pulled low to shadow his eyes. The skinny man wanted to kill her father. He had such a strong revulsion for Amund that he was red hot, ready to strike. The third man was calm and more deliberate. A man experienced in fighting. He would be last to join in.

"Hanne, this is between us. Go back to bed," her father was saying. He had his hands up to her, imploring, and his voice was gentle. He had not spoken to her kindly in a long time.

But Hanne's eye was on the scrawny man behind him, his hand on a knife he had hidden in his pocket.

It was thrilling, the power she felt. She was grinning, her body thrumming, taut as a bowstring. It was delicious.

"Maybe she came in for a bedtime story?" Nils, the man with the gun, said, a sneer playing on his lips. "I could tell her a good one."

"Hey now!" Amund said, spinning back to face Nils. "Leave her out of it. She's sleepwalking, is all."

Then the scrawny man leaped at Amund, knife arm raised. Hanne jumped forward, pushing her father down, then vaulted over his body to where the ax lay half sunk in the chopping stump.

The ax was in her hand, and then it was flying through the air, landing with a solid *THUNK* in the solar plexus of the scrawny man. His body flew back, and his knife hand swung up, releasing the knife into the air. Hanne crouched and sprang for the weapon.

Time was as slow as dripping honey to Hanne. She was swimming through the air, passing in front of the man with the gun. She felt her thighs brush against the front of his body. Then she picked the knife out of the air as easy as if she'd been picking an apple off a tree.

She kicked out and kneed the gunman in the throat.

The gun went off twice. *BAM! BAM!*

He was on his back and Hanne was next to him. She slashed twice, once on each side of his throat, and the blood geysered up.

The calm man, the one who knew how to fight, was backing away.

"No," he said. "Please. I want no part in this." But she was already advancing on him.

The knife was too slippery in her hand so she dropped it.

The man backed away from her. He nearly tripped over a rake left standing near the hay and then he grabbed it, arming himself.

"I don't want to fight you, girl!" he said.

Hanne pressed forward, backing him into the corner. He swung. *WHAM!* The metal teeth of the rake dug grooves into the log wall.

She ducked. He swung again. More gouge-holes in the wall on the other side.

He thought he could keep her away with a rake! Hanne darted forward. She ran right up the wall of the barn, feeling the bark of the old, rough logs under her bare feet. He swiveled to watch her, mouth agape with wonder, and let the rake drop.

Hanne took two steps on the ceiling. Then she had the man's sweaty head in her arms, and as gravity brought her back to earth, she yanked his skull to the side, breaking his neck.

Hanne opened her hands, and the man's head hit the floor with a *THUMP.* She stood, taking in the room, one foot on his chest. Her hands open and ready. Four bodies, none moving.

Her attention fell on the body of her father. The life force of her father, that which she had been called from bed to protect, was draining away. She scrambled over the warm bodies of the dying men to him.

Amund had been shot in the chest.

Hanne's eyes scanned the room for something she could use to stanch the flow of blood. She looked down. Her nightgown was sheer, clinging to her body with blood. It was already saturated—it would not help.

There came her brother Knut to the door, Stieg behind him.

"Oh! Oh!" Stieg cried. He recoiled from the sight, stumbling back.

"Father!" Knut rushed over and knelt next to Hanne, placing his great hand over their father's wound. He pushed right down over the mess of shattered ribs and torn flesh.

Hanne could hear Stieg retching outside and Sissel coming near, asking what had happened? Who had fired? Then her sister arrived and her thin screams pierced Hanne's ears.

Hanne looked around. With awkward jolts, like a sled bouncing to rest at the bottom of a long hill, time was returning to normal speed.

A gnawing began to gather in her gut. Suddenly she was ravenous. She was nothing but an empty stomach, screaming to be filled.

HANNE ATE. Barefoot, in the kitchen, she ate the whole week's baking of *flatbrød*. She'd eaten the leftover stew already. She'd eaten it with her bare hands, her knuckles scraping the kettle. Her siblings bustled around her.

"Pack your woolens!" Stieg told Knut. "We may need to stay in the hills. I don't know!"

Knut clomped around the house, gathering supplies under Stieg's direction. Tears dripped down his face as he moved. Sissel sat slumped against the wall. Her face was so pale, she might have been in shock, but there was consciousness in her eyes as she watched her sister eat.

"Sissel!" Stieg yelled. "Get up! You must pack. You must pack for Hanne and yourself."

"Look at her," Sissel said. "She's an animal."

Hanne heard, but did not break stride. She had the preserves open now. *Bringebaer* jam. She scooped it out with her fingertips.

"It's the curse that comes with her Nytte," Stieg said. "If she doesn't eat, she'll die."

Sissel did not move. She was mesmerized by her sister's feeding.

Stieg grabbed Sissel by the arms and hauled her to her feet. She began to cry.

"She killed those men," Sissel wept.

"Sissel, pack your bags and dress! If you do not, we will leave you behind and you can answer for the slaughter in the barn yourself!"

"Three men!"

Stieg dragged Sissel toward the bedroom she shared with Hanne.

Sissel took hold of Stieg's lapels. "Brother! It is her crime. Why do we flee?"

Stieg dropped her arms. She rocked back. Stieg's eyes were a cold, bleak gray.

"If you want to stay, that's your choice, Sissel. I am taking Hanne . . . away. Knut will want to come. But you can stay here. You can have this house and everything in it all to yourself."

"Stieg, no!"

"You can cover for us. Tell them that Father killed the gamblers. Tell them we were so upset, we've gone away, but that you wanted to stay behind so the truth could be told."

"Stop it—"

"You'll make a good marriage, with the farm as yours—"

"I'm coming with you."

"Then dress and pack!"

Seeing that Sissel was moving toward the cupboard where she and Hanne stored their clothes, Stieg turned and went out. Now he had to go to the barn and do his best to make it look somehow as if his father had killed three men and died in self-defense. His father, who could barely hold a knife, much less wield an ax.

BY THE TIME they were ready, Hanne had gorged herself into a stupor and had lain down in bed. Sissel had had to dress Hanne as if she were an invalid, pulling the bloodied nightgown off her and dressing her in her drab, loose-fitting work clothes, fastening her apron as best she could over Hanne's prone form. Sissel kept her eyes off her sister's greasy, sticky hands. There was still blood on them, under the jelly and the butter and the salmon fat. She had stuck Hanne's bare feet into her heavy, wooden-soled shoes. She wasn't going to pull her stockings on for her. It was too much to ask.

Knut loaded Hanne into the wagon. She lay in the back, on the rough wooden slats, legs askew. Sissel came, hoisted over the side, next. She pulled away from her sister and sat with her arms curled around her thin body. Then Knut began to load in the few possessions they had packed. A bag of linens. Stieg's fine carpetbag, plump and ready for the journey. A gunnysack with Hanne's and Sissel's clothes stuffed in. Knut's own clothes in a careless armful.

"Good, fine," Stieg said. His face was pale and he was sweating, despite the cool air. "We go, then!"

There were many hours left in the night, and a half-moon shone down from a clear sky. Stieg climbed onto the wagon seat and chirruped to the horses. Knut walked alongside, his hand on the slats of the wagon. The two horses could not be burdened with his weight.

Hanne and her siblings moved away from their little stone house and log barn on the hillside. It had belonged to their mother's family. Each of them had been born within those old walls.

Sissel took one last look at the farm over her shoulder. Tears welled in her eyes and ran down her cheeks. She dabbed them away with the hem of her shawl.

SEVERAL HOURS LATER, they reached a stream and Stieg said they could stretch.

The wagon jolted hard as the horses moved down to the stream to drink. Hanne was pitched forward. Suddenly she gasped, leaning back up straight. She stood in the tilted bed of the wagon. She looked at her hands, then at her siblings. The night sky. Her bare ankles, stained with blood, poking out from under her homespun skirt.

"Oh, Stieg!" A choking sob broke free. "Dear God . . . What did I do?"

CHAPTER FIVE

"Watch your stock!" Owen called to Daisy. Daisy circled around and caught sight of the cow cutting back behind them, toward a stand of aspens at the tree line. Daisy was covered in mud. Owen was, too. A thick, wet snow had been falling since right before sunup, the kind of wet, clumpy snow that made a cattle drive a messy prospect.

Daisy went after the straggler, winding through the skinny, ash-colored trunks. After a good nip on the heel, the cow came back, bawling.

Owen didn't blame the cow for trying to get to the trees. They were in the rocky foothills of Hedges Mountain, and the going was difficult.

The beasts streamed down narrow paths between boulders and scrub, their hooves churning the packed earth into sandy mud. Slippery. It would be wise to go slow, but Mandry had made no mention of the trail conditions at breakfast. He'd just cursed the weather and told the men that if they hurried, they could be in Helena for a hot bath by Friday.

Owen's horse, Pal, was taking his time. The other cowboys poked fun at Pal's name. Did Owen think his dark gray quarter horse with the black mane was a palomino?

In a rare moment of privilege, Howard Bennett had allowed Owen to name the colt. He'd named it Pal purely because he wanted a friend, and the scrawny, buck-kneed colt had looked like he could use one, too. It was a foolish name, and it caused Owen some embarrassment to remember it. But the horse knew his name, and Owen couldn't change it on him now.

The cattle at the back of the herd were the slower ones. Owen felt to rush them was to risk losing them. It'd be easy to slip and topple down the hill. Easier still to break a leg on the rocks.

Hoakes, also riding flank, drifted back to chat with Owen around midday.

"Hey there," he said. Melted snow was dropping off his whiskers.

Owen nodded and a little snow plopped off his hat brim, down onto his poncho. It was a good poncho, tight knit, and though it wasn't waterproof, it was wool so it stayed warm when wet. He whistled twice to Daisy—telling her to come to his side.

"Awful slick out," Hoakes said loudly, to be heard over the sounds of the herd clomping over the rocky ground.

"Yep."

"So what's gonna be the first thing you do with your pay when we get to Helena?" Hoakes asked. This was a common question circulating the camp. Thinking about the pay to come helped make the long days pass quicker.

While Owen thought for an answer, that same cow made another break for the tree line. "Watch your stock!" Owen called, and Daisy went right after her.

"Me?" Hoakes continued, as if Owen had answered. "I'm going to have a drink, then get myself a bath and a hot shave. You had a hot shave?"

"Not yet," Owen said. Owen handled his own shaving needs, such as they were, with a kit he'd purchased in Bullhook Bottoms with his first paycheck. It was a prized possession.

"It's a mighty fine thing. I'm gonna get a shave and a haircut, then I'm going to go up to stay with my sister in Great Falls. Her husband died in a mining accident. She needs some help, I guess. What you gonna do?"

"Look for some work in Helena for the winter, I suppose."

They rode on. The snow fell in clumps on the backs of the cattle.

Owen was used to keeping his own counsel, but he'd been mulling over an idea and Hoakes seemed someone a man could confide in.

"I guess I do have an idea," Owen ventured. "You want to hear it?"

"Sure I want to hear it. What else do I have to do? I'll hear any damn thing you want to tell me."

"I've got an idea to raise cattle dogs. Breed them. Train them. Then sell them."

"Well, but a man's got to train his own dog for it to stick, don't it?"

Owen shrugged. He didn't think so.

"Whistle twice," Owen said.

"What say?"

"Whistle twice for Daisy."

Hoakes let out two long, breathy whistles.

Daisy stayed put, but looked over and cocked her head as if asking, "What's wrong with you, fellow?"

Owen whistled correctly—two quick chirps. Daisy came at a bound and placed herself on his right. Perfect position.

He rewarded her with a nod.

Neither man was compelled to comment on the failure of the experiment.

They rode without speaking for a moment, Owen riding ahead of Hoakes as they went through a narrow section between a boulder and a knot of scrub oak. The trail ahead was steep and striated with descending switchbacks.

"Men have gotten by doing stranger things, I guess," Hoakes offered loudly, coming back alongside again. "But you're a mighty fine cowhand. I mean, that's a real living."

Owen nodded.

On the one hand, he wished he hadn't mentioned his idea to Hoakes. On the other, to hell with it. If he wanted to have any friends in this life, he'd have to talk sometime. And it was such a nice dream.

Owen saw himself with a little ranch. A small bit of land, just a couple acres. He wanted a couple of cows for dairy, and chickens. Then he'd just start looking for good dogs. He wanted to breed Daisy with a collie with longer legs, increase the stride some.

He knew he could make good money at it, as long as his customers were willing to learn the commands he'd teach the dogs. Men had offered him money for Daisy plenty of times.

Hoakes had moved his horse in front of Owen. The trail was narrow again, scrub oak on either side.

"Hee-yaw there!" Hoakes shouted. Owen couldn't see around the man's broad back, but he heard the sound of cattle lowing and hooves clattering on rocks.

"Stuck cow up here!" Hoakes called.

Because the path was narrow and falling steeply off to the side, Owen wheeled Pal back and went around the thicket to the left, picking his way through the brush lower down the hill to get a better view.

There was a ledge, with a sharp drop and only one path leading down from it. A steer had his leg trapped in a rock right at the only place the beef could scramble down. Seven or eight cattle were milling behind him. They couldn't get past the downed steer, and they were trapped.

It was a slick, rocky ledge they were on, with a wall on the right of about five feet and a drop to the left of a deadly fifteen.

From his vantage point below and slightly beyond the downed animal, Owen saw he had to make the cattle climb up the wall of rock behind them, to a path running above they couldn't see. They wouldn't like it, to scramble up that way, but they could do it.

He called to Daisy, "With me!" and charged Pal up at the cattle, shouting, "Ha! Ha! Get up! Get up now!"

The ground was slick and Pal balked, but Daisy nipped at his heels and together, man, horse, and dog drove up the cattle.

The beasts' eyes were wild, and it seemed, for one second, that they'd turn around and come trampling down on Owen as he and Pal scrambled up the slick bank, urging the cattle to go up to the path above them.

Daisy growled and barked and Owen shouted again and the cattle jumped up the hill.

Whistler came riding back. "What the hell, Bennett?" he yelled.

But then he got a sight of the steer and figured out what had nearly happened.

Hoakes drew up to the lowing steer and slid off his horse.

"Easy now," he said to the stuck beast, who was rolling his eyes and bawling. His leg was broken.

Owen stood catching his breath. His horse was lathered and steaming in the sleet. The cattle he'd routed were headed past Whistler, joining ones ahead.

Now Owen had to go back down and help Hoakes with the steer. They'd likely have to shoot the animal, and explain what had happened to Mandry. He wouldn't like losing a big beef like that, not fifty miles from Helena, but they could all see things could've been much worse.

Anyway, now there'd be steaks for dinner.

"Hey, Owen," Hoakes called up to him. He had his hat off and was scratching his bald head. "I'll take one of those dogs, you get 'im trained up for me. I'll pay good money for him, too. I could learn to whistle better."

CHAPTER SIX

S treaks of peach-colored sky came through the firs in the woods behind their aunt Aud's house in Tysse. It was dawn, and they had ridden through the night. Hanne felt like a wrung-out rag. Grief, shame, and horror had possessed her in alternation during the night's ride.

Time and time again she had pleaded with Stieg. She must turn back, return to their village, and turn herself in to the constables.

Stieg had stopped responding to her.

Now they were in the thick pine wood above the valley where their aunt lived. She shared a house with several other unmarried women. Some were widows, though their aunt was simply a spinster— never married.

Together the women made and sold beautiful blankets and weavings.

Aud was a Storm-Rend, gifted with the ability to create winds with her breath, and she was blind.

There was great animosity between Amund and his older sister, Aud, over something Amund had done, in the past, something Aud had never forgiven. It meant that the children saw their aunt only rarely. But Hanne had gathered from things their father had let slip that Aud's blindness was a result of overexertion from using her Nytte.

Blind or not, Aud was a marvelous spinner, with her sensitive fingers and a habit of whistling to the wool as she worked, gently warming the air near the bobbin.

"Why can't we go to her house?" Sissel complained. "I want to get warm, Stieg. And bathe. And Hanne could bathe."

Sissel's face looked drawn and pinched. She had not complained during the long, cold night. Hanne sensed that something had happened between her sister and older brother. Something must have happened. It was uncharacteristic of Sissel to suffer in silence.

"And what of her friends in the common house? They'd all see us," Stieg said. "This is the first place the police will look for us. Better for them to think we never came this way, Sissel."

"Then why come at all? If we can't go in and eat and be warm!" Sissel pouted.

"Because I don't know what to do!" he shouted. "I need her advice!"

"Stieg, there's only one thing for us to do. We go home and I confess to the constable," Hanne said.

"No," Stieg said, pacing the terrain with his long legs. "It wasn't you. It was the Nytte."

"It was me! I did it!"

"No!" he insisted. "You, Hanne Amundsdotter, would never commit such an act. You were possessed by the Nytte. And no one will understand that. No one outside our family."

"Anyway, if you think about it," Knut said in his slow, thoughtful way, "why would they believe you?"

He was standing next to the big dray horse, scrubbing it down with a handful of dry leaves and fir needles. "You're just a girl, Hanne. They would not believe you could kill three grown men. Not with such skill."

"That's right!" Stieg said. "Well done, Knut! They would not believe you!"

Knut smiled his great, bashful smile. Stieg clapped him on the shoulder. "You three wait here. I'll get Aunty Aud. She'll know what to do."

Hanne lay down on the carpet of fir needles. She thought she'd never sleep, but a maelstrom of exhaustion pulled her under.

SHE AWOKE TO Stieg shaking her. Morning had come and the sunlight shone through the branches of the fir trees.

"Hanne. Come here," her aunt called.

Aud was seated on a fallen tree. She had a brown wrap drawn over her head and shoulders. It flowed down to the log on which she sat, matching the color of the bark and making it look as if she were a growth on the trunk.

Aud was very little, with a bent back. She was older than their father, nearing fifty, but the lines and wrinkles on her face made her look even older.

Hanne rose and brushed the needles off her skirt. She stumbled over to her aunt to kneel in front of her.

Her aunt's eyes had been pale to start with. Now, in her blindness, it looked as though someone had rubbed out her eyes with an eraser—they were nearly entirely white, but for the gauzy, gray pupils.

"Are you hurt?"

"No, Aunty."

"Did you have any trouble?"

"What do you mean?"

"Killing the men who killed your father. Was it difficult to do?"

"No," Hanne said. Hanne felt her body begin to shiver. "It was easy."

"And then you ate?" Aud called off to Stieg, "Did she eat very much?"

"She ate all the food in the larder," Stieg answered.

"Good. You know my mother was a Berserker," Aud said. She patted Hanne's head. "You have the look of her, you know. I remember from before the Gods took my sight. She had the same strange set-apart eyes and pointy chin. And you have the same joyless sense of duty she had. Too serious. Too long-suffering. You hear me, child. You remember what I am saying."

"Aunty, I have committed a terrible sin," Hanne protested. "It is right I should suffer. I told Stieg I must turn myself in."

"No. You four will go to America. It is providential that Stieg already has one ticket booked. You will purchase three more. When does the boat leave?"

Her question was lost in the tumult. Knut exclaimed in surprise, while Sissel squealed, "All four of us?" clapping her hands.

Aud waved her cane. "Quiet! Do not let my friends hear you! I will not have you put them in danger! No one is to know you've come here. When does the boat leave?"

"Tomorrow," Stieg answered. "I was to catch what they call a feeder ship from Bergen to Hull, in England. From there, a train to Liverpool—"

"Good. They will find the bodies soon. You must be on a boat to England by the end of day. I have a trunk you can take, and some linens. Good wool shawls for you two—"

"But how are we to pay for the tickets?" Stieg said. "Selling the horses and the wagon, we might be able to purchase one ticket more."

"I have something for you," Aud said. She withdrew an old chamois purse from her pocket. "Come, see." She called them around.

Aud tilted the contents of the purse into her gnarled palm. There against her wrinkled hand were three old gold coins.

Sissel gasped.

"These are six hundred years old," Aud said. "I was saving them for you, for after your father died. They are all we have left of the great treasures of our bloodline. I would not give them to you when your father was alive, for I knew he would drink them up. Now that he's gone, they are for you."

She closed the pouch and reached her hand forward, confident that Stieg would take it. He did.

"Sell one of those when you get to Bergen. Only one! There is a coin dealer in town. Do not take less than four thousand kroner for it. It's worth even more."

"Thank you, Aunty," Stieg said. He was beaming with relief. Hanne could see him planning. Four thousand kroner! That would get them to America and buy them a house! He could teach school—he could even go to university himself, if he chose to do so! She could see the relief pouring out of him, like sun breaking through clouds.

"It is not the weight of the gold, but the age. Make sure you take it to a coin dealer," Aud insisted.

"Aunty, you are giving us a future. Thank you," he said.

"Yes, thank you!" Sissel said, clapping her hands in joy. Knut was looking back between Aud and Stieg, dumbfounded. Sissel limped forward and embraced Aud in her happiness. Aud pushed her away firmly.

"I'm not done!" Aud said. She held out a letter. The paper was covered in an elegant, thin scrawl.

"You have an uncle. Håkon. He's our baby brother. When he was just a boy, he went to Canada. Now he lives in the territory of Montana, in the far west. A village called Wolf Creek. That letter is from only one year ago. Go and find him."

"But I thought we should go to a city," Stieg said. "Chicago—"

"Your sister must have guidance. Håkon is a Berserker. He can show Hanne how to control the Nytte."

Hanne looked up. "Is there a way to control it?"

"Of course! Each of the Nytte can be controlled."

"Can you suppress it entirely?" Hanne asked.

Aud shook her head. "No, that's the wrong idea. To control it, you embrace it."

Hanne felt a shudder travel through her body. Embrace it? Never.

"You know, you four were not to have been born," Aud said. "Our mother was so ashamed of her powers and so sure they were an affront to the Church, she made us promise we would not create any more children to carry on the Nytte. I obeyed her. My brother Amund, your father, did not. He never told your mother of his Nytte when they were courting.

"Perhaps if he had, she would have learned of the Nytte in her own bloodline. But your father concealed it from her, and by the time she knew, you four had been born. Stieg, when your gift appeared, when you were twelve, she came weeping to me, terrified and appalled. I tried to teach her what I knew of the Nytte, the ways to welcome it and learn to work with it, but she blamed me for not telling her sooner. She wanted nothing to do with me, especially as my eyes clouded over. She saw your fate in my eyes, Stieg, and I'm sure it frightened her."

The siblings sat in the wakening forest and thought about this.

"And I cannot help you much now," she said, her voice gritty with regret. "But Håkon! He was the brightest of us all. Smart. Kind. An adventurer and a scholar. He will know how to help you, Hanne. I'm sure of it."

Birds called to one another in the deep pine wood, and Hanne's heart brightened for a moment.

"Aunty," Sissel ventured. "You said Hanne favored our grandmother." She paused, trying to find the right words. "Is there anyone I favor?"

"You are wondering if you will have a Nytte. And what it might be? It's normal to wonder," their aunt said. She gestured for Sissel to come near. Aud placed her sensitive fingers on Sissel's face and felt it all over.

"I think you will be lucky and it will skip you. I had a great-uncle who had no Nytte at all. He was thin and scrawny like you."

Sissel could hardly take this as a compliment, but was mollified nonetheless. She wanted no part of the Nytte.

"Now," Aud said. "Head south. Take the main road and move quickly. Do not worry about being seen once you hit the main road. Just make sure you are on a boat by nightfall."

"Wait," Hanne said. She grabbed her aunt's hands. "Aunty Aud, please. Listen to me. If they go with me, they will be helping me to escape from the law. But, I don't want to be above the law. I killed three men. I am guilty of the worst sin there is! I should confess. I must confess and turn myself in!"

Aud reached for Hanne's hands and held them to her heart, pulling Hanne close to her face. "I know how dark you feel, child."

"You can't," Hanne whispered.

"I know because I, too, once used my gift to kill." Hanne looked right into the woman's glassy eyes. She could see her reflection, a blue shadow on an icy pond. Aud drew her even closer and murmured, "And I, too, enjoyed how it felt."

Hanne let go and sat back, hard. She pushed away from her aunt, struggling to get to her feet.

"Embrace the Nytte," Aud said, as Hanne scrambled backward in the pine needles and dried leaves. "Open your heart to it, or it will be the ruin of you. And your siblings, too."

CHAPTER SEVEN

ØYSTESE, NORWAY

Rolf Tjossem eyed the distance to the ground with some apprehension. The Baron's horses were all rather too regal and tall. He gripped the pommel and swung his leg over, trying to lower himself to the ground with dignity, but failing as his legs went wobbly beneath him.

The townsfolk of the dead farmer were all looking at him and Ketil. They had been watching them as they rode up from the direction of town. Rolf knew this. The glossy-maned, long-legged horses themselves would have drawn attention in any small town in this part of the backcountry. These were no European horses, but Arabians. They had brought Rolf and Ketil from Bergen much faster than the short-legged Fjord horses could have.

Rolf himself was fairly inconspicuous. Age had helped accomplish this. He was near fifty now, his hair and whiskers more white than brown. His face had not grown more attractive as he'd aged; it was pitted and pockmarked from smallpox he'd suffered as a child.

Ketil, on the other hand, was a distinctly handsome man and young. He stood over six feet tall, with a mustache and blond hair he kept slicked back with pomade. He wore a well-cut suit from Oslo, and was forever fiddling with a gold pocket watch the Baron had given him. He walked with a long-limbed jangle that spoke of confidence.

Dismounting his horse, Ketil winked at several young peasant girls. They tittered in response.

Rolf sighed as he brushed off his suit. He very much wished Ketil had not been assigned to accompany him on this investigation.

News of the massacre had reached the Baron's estate at Gamlehaugen by telegraph. The Baron Fjelstad was well connected with the local authorities and paid for tips such as this one—a vicious murder with multiple victims.

Awake before Fjelstad or any of his business associates or secretaries, Rolf had been downing some smoked herring and brown bread for breakfast. He had hoped to retreat to the library before being interrupted.

Only the day before, Rolf had received the rubbings from a runestone grave marker discovered near the Lofoten Islands. The runes praised the man buried beneath, describing him as a warrior able to rip apart churches in his search for gold. This could well be a description of the rarest type of Nytteson, a Ransacker. Any new information about them was a valuable boon.

Rolf was impatient to begin building a framework for interpretation of the runes; his mind had been on the work ahead of him when a footman entered, his livery askew in the rush of being summoned so early in the morning. He told Rolf he was needed in the Baron's drawing room.

Rolf had stifled the groan he felt building. Fjelstad frequently sent Rolf afield to investigate people who might be Nytteson. Rolf had crossed Europe dozens of time in the past twenty years, searching out people rumored to be exceptionally good with wood or investigating reports of odd weather patterns that might be the work of a Storm-Rend. Fjelstad even sent him to carnivals, hoping to spot Oar-Breakers performing as strongmen.

Over those twenty years, Rolf had found only two dozen of the Nytteson. Of those, only three females. The gift was dying out. This was why the Baron Fjelstad offered every Nytteson Rolf was able to locate a good job at the estate at Gamlehaugen. In a way, Fjelstad collected Nytteson, that they might be protected.

Fjelstad had been waiting in his study with several of his assistants, including Ketil. Fjelstad informed Rolf that there had been a triple murder in the small town of Øystese, and that the man who'd done the killing was said to be a carpenter of local renown, who had been shot dead during the fight.

"I'd like you to go today," Fjelstad had said. "Right away. If you hurry, you might get there before they remove the bodies."

"I will go, of course," Rolf had said.

The Baron must have heard some resignation in his voice because he'd looked up, a twinkle in his eye. "Yes, old friend, I know you're eager to hide away with your new pressings.

"I realize that you view the recruitment of Nytteson as a chore. And that is why you will take with you young Ketil here! He's been working at my estate in Greenland, and I feel this would be a suitable assignment for him."

Ketil had given Rolf a wink, which Rolf had done his best to ignore.

Rolf's first impression had been that Ketil was too cocky and impatient for the assignment. It was a job that required not only detective work but humility and empathy. Finding a Nytteson was one thing; persuading him to meet the Baron was another. Rolf knew the teenagers he recruited were scared. He offered them reassurance and the promise of knowledge and training.

Ketil was a showy man, a vain man, and as far as Rolf could tell, did not respect the importance of the job. But Rolf had taken him along to appease Fjelstad. If nothing else, Rolf could teach Ketil more about the different kinds of Nytte they might encounter. All who served the Baron needed this knowledge.

"GOOD MORNING," Rolf said as he and Ketil approached one of the constables clearly charged with keeping an eye on the crowd. "We have been sent by the Baron Fjelstad. He was concerned about the news. May we speak to the chief constable?"

The young officer crossed his arms. "No one may pass through. I have orders."

"Ah yes," Rolf said, and Ketil tried to jump in, but Rolf continued on. "But perhaps you would let us in. The Baron has an interest in seeing peace observed in the towns near his estate."

The officer shook his head. Ketil reached forward to straighten the lapels of the man's uniform, and flashed him sight of the fifty-kroner note he had concealed in his palm. Ketil gave the man a small, conspiratorial nod.

"You can arrange it, can't you?" Ketil asked. "A man of your standing? The truth is, we don't need to speak to the constable, only to get a quick peek at the bodies."

The young officer gulped. Fifty kroner was more than a month's salary for him. Nearly double a month's salary.

"The Baron wants to make sure it's no one he knows," Ketil whispered. Then again he winked.

"Hmmm. Very well," the officer said loudly, for the benefit of the townsfolk. "I understand the Baron's concerns. Especially due to the nature of these murders. You may proceed."

Ketil shook the officer's hand and pressed the folded bill into it. The officer motioned inside, to two colleagues taking notes and measurements, and summoned them out so Rolf and Ketil had the barn, and its sad, dead inhabitants, to themselves.

Taking in the scene of the slaughter, a fragment of a poem Rolf had been working on translating came to mind. He spoke the words aloud, first in Old Norse, then in Norwegian: "*Fields drink blood / Crops are slaughtered / But in Valhalla souls feast.*"

Rolf had meant it to be a solemn observation, but Ketil nodded and laughed. "I like it."

Ketil leaned over the body of a large man, who'd been beheaded, the ax stuck fast into the packed earth. "It's a Berserker who did this. No doubt at all. We've got a Berserker here!"

Rolf agreed, though he did not care to comment. He had seen the killing work of a Berserker before, but that did not make him any less queasy seeing it now.

"Ax work," Ketil went on. "Not very tidy, but an effective blow. I put our boy at twenty if not older."

Rolf paced the distance between the ax-murdered corpse and the next one, who lay curled on his side. From what Rolf could see, he'd been cut at the throat.

"What?" Ketil said. "What do you see?"

"I just wondered why the Berserker wouldn't have pulled the ax out to kill this man," Rolf said. "I think he's younger. Lacking in strength."

The third body lay close to the back wall.

"He broke this one's neck very cleanly," Ketil said. "I'd say he's plenty strong."

Rolf looked at the way the straw had been kicked at on the ground. The rake handle had gouged and scraped the walls and in one place, poked clean through. There had been at least a moment of struggle.

But Rolf kept his tongue. He hardly needed to win an argument with Ketil. The young man seemed to hate being wrong.

"You're right," Rolf said. "At least twenty. And strong."

"The Baron will be pleased. A new Berserker, right here in Southern Bergenhus County." Ketil looked around the barn with a satisfied grin. Rolf had never met a man so comfortable with the results of slaughter.

Rolf stopped to examine the last corpse. He was badly gut-shot.

"He might not be so happy to learn there was a Shipwright here all this time," Rolf said, taking in the sight of the man's fingerless hand pressed into the gore at his belly. "Poor soul. If we had heard of him earlier, we could have helped him."

Ketil looked down at the dead Shipwright.

"I've never seen one so old," Ketil said. "He must be near forty. Look at how he's rotted away. Didn't have a finger to scratch his ass. And those idiots outside believe he killed these men?" Ketil indicated the corpses with his chin. "How stupid."

"Who knows what they will figure out," Rolf said. "We know it was a Berserker who killed these men. And we must find him."

OUT IN THE COURTYARD, Ketil nodded to the young officer, who then began issuing orders to the other men to finish their measurements so the bodies could be carted away.

Ketil made a move toward their horses, but Rolf walked toward the villagers.

"We should get back and report the news," Ketil said.

"I'd like to see if I can find out any more information," Rolf said.

"Good idea," Ketil admitted. Rolf rolled his eyes, but out of Ketil's view.

Rolf walked near a small group of women but then turned out to face the courtyard, as if he'd decided to watch the proceedings. Ketil came to stand near his side.

Ketil started to speak, but Rolf held up his hand unobtrusively—*Wait*. The townswomen had seen him and Ketil arrive. Their natural curiosity would bring them to ask the men what they'd seen.

But Ketil did not wait.

"Good afternoon, my lady," he said, addressing the tallest of the three, a woman with an expression like she'd smelled bad cheese. "And what a lovely apron you are wearing. Who did the embroidery?"

The woman boggled at him.

"I say, I did it myself! Who else would do it?" She was nearly indignant from having been complimented. She looked to her friends, and the three of them frowned in the same way, deciding whether or not to move away.

A little boy sat on the fence next to the women, clearly interested in the men.

"Ah, so sad," Rolf said. "What we saw inside . . ."

The tall woman could not withstand the bait. "They say it's three bodies in there. Is that so?"

Rolf shook his head and sighed. "I'm afraid it was four."

"Not counting Amund, I meant," said the woman.

"Do you know who they are? The others?" asked another of the women. She was pregnant and had a lazy eye, which was looking so far back into her head it showed all white. "We know Nils Paulsen never came home last night. Was he one of them? And he was out with Little Black Berg, a crook from Oslo."

"They'd all been drinking," added the third woman, who was young and plump. She smiled shyly at Ketil.

He grinned back. He was obnoxiously good looking, Rolf decided.

"We don't know the men," Ketil said. "But we're from Baron Fjelstad's household, so we don't know all the townspeople in these parts."

The women's eyes widened. They were impressed. Now Ketil was in his element.

"How did the Baron come to hear about the murders?" one of them asked.

"He takes an interest in all the goings-on in his county," Ketil said.

"Did the farmer Amund have children?" Rolf asked, but was ignored.

"Oh, what is the world coming to, that we should suffer such crimes here, in Øystese," moaned the woman with the lazy eye.

"It is a terrible shame." Ketil sighed. The plump woman sighed, too. She was watching Ketil's mouth with a hungry air.

"Amund had children, I suppose?" Rolf asked.

Ketil and the women ignored his question.

"What's he like, the Baron?" the young girl asked.

"I'll tell you, he throws great, grand parties," Ketil said. He leaned against the railing, and the women drew closer.

Rolf walked away, trying to hide his displeasure. He would find out the information they needed so that they could get back to Gamlehaugen.

Rolf closed his eyes and placed his hand on the rune stone he kept in his pocket. A small, round stone, inscribed with the rune for Odin. The stone had changed the course of his life.

"There's four of them," piped up a small voice. A hand tugged at the hem of Rolf's coat. "Amund had four children."

It was the boy who had been listening in on the conversation at the fence. He was barefoot and kept placing one foot up on his thin calf, to warm it, then hopping to the other. Rolf dug into his pocket and brought out a krone. "This is for you if you can tell me their names and ages."

And Rolf learned that Stieg was the oldest at eighteen; then came Hanne, Knut, and Sissel, all spaced neatly, two years apart.

Rolf tossed the coin to the child. He caught it handily. The boy's grin nearly cracked his little, dirty face in two.

"I've got another if you have any idea where they might have gone," Rolf said.

The boy's face fell. "I couldn't imagine," he said.

Rolf smiled at the boy. He tousled his hair.

Rolf's mind began to play out what might happen next. He would report his findings to Fjelstad. He would want to send Rolf after the Berserker, especially since the Berserker had sisters. Girls with the Nytte—Nyttesdotters—were more rare and thus more important than boys. The Baron would want to ascertain if any of the girls had the Nytte.

But he thought of the rubbing of the rune stone waiting at Gamlehaugen. Perhaps Rolf could bow out and let Ketil take the trip. The children would probably head to the home of their nearest relative.

Rolf was lost in thoughts about how Fjelstad might take the news of the Berserker in their midst when the boy interrupted him again.

"Oh, sir," the child said, tugging on Rolf's coat. "I was thinking . . . Stieg was leaving tomorrow for America. So maybe he took them all with him."

CHAPTER EIGHT

Owen had been in a saloon before, but this was his first time drinking. When they'd walked in, Owen hadn't wanted to partake, but Mandry had insisted they all have a drink together to celebrate a successful drive. Mandry had kept his gaze leveled at Owen, and it felt almost like a dare. Then Owen had a shot of whiskey in his hand and that was that.

The Bennett ranch was run bone dry. There was not a bottle of spirits to be found on the place, even for medicinal purposes. Mrs. Bennett liked to claim the victory for this, but it was the cook, Lucy, who made it clear drinking would not be tolerated. If Lucy smelled whiskey on the breath of a ranch hand come mealtime, he would not get fed. It was as simple as that.

The whiskey, Owen discovered, burned like blazes going down, but once the fire of it hit his gut, he rather liked the feeling. In fact he *very much* enjoyed the feeling. He found himself chatty and confident, being warm and easily social—the way he'd always wanted to be.

Mandry had given Owen his pay, thirty dollars for the month's work. Owen slapped a dollar down on the bar. That bought him plenty more shots of the stuff.

Owen started telling Old Eben and Billy, who was still sipping his first glass of whiskey, about his plans to breed cattle dogs. He gestured to Daisy, who they could see on the boardwalk outside the door, staying right where he'd told her to stay.

"She's a good dog. Oh, she's a beauty," Owen said loudly. "Let's drink to Daisy, everyone! How much is it, bartender, to buy a round of drinks? 'Cause we should drink to my dog. She's saved my life plenty of times, there's no doubt about it!"

"Hold your pouring arm," Hoakes told the barkeep. "My young friend's had enough to drink now."

"But, Hoakes, look at her, just lying there waiting. We gotta drink to her!"

"Say, bud," said a short man Owen didn't know. He was chewing on the end of a cigar. "You in the mood for a game of cards?"

"Mebbe," Owen said. "I'm a pretty good hand at whist."

The man found that pretty funny and laughed so hard he had to excuse himself. Hoakes shooed him off.

"Well, I know he meant poker," Owen told Hoakes. "I was saying I'm awful good at whist so I'd probably be good at poker."

"You know, Owen, some cowboys blow their wages pretty quick right out of the saddle. What say you and I head back to the boarding-house. You've had a good share of fun now."

"Aw no, Hoakes. Hey, you should sing a song! Hear the piano playing? Come on, Hoakes, sing for the people. They're not as pretty as the beefs, but they likely won't stampede." Owen thought that was a pretty funny one. Old Eben and Billy gave a good laugh, but Hoakes tried to steer Owen out the door.

Owen's legs weren't working the way he was accustomed to. His feet seemed distant and his legs pleasantly numb. The floor was covered in sawdust, set down to absorb chaw spit and spilled liquor. His feet slid on it.

He was surprised to find Hoakes's arm supporting him.

Hoakes led Owen toward the door, but Owen stumbled and careened into Whistler. Whistler's whiskey splashed down on his boots, and he straightened up, angry.

"Bennett! You did that on purpose."

Whistler grabbed Owen by the front of his shirt and pulled him up to his face. Whistler's breath stank of drink and mutton. He looked like he was going to hit Owen, but then he laughed.

Outside the door, Daisy began to bark. She couldn't see through the steamed-up windows, but she could sense Owen's distress.

"Can't hold your drink, none, can you? Ha! Mandry, he's half Indian, like I said!"

"Shut up, Whistler! Don't harry the boy!" Hoakes said. Hoakes pulled Owen away and headed him again toward the exit.

"He ain't half Indian, he's half *Irish*," Mandry said, and spat a stream of tobacco juice on the floor. "I heard it from his older brother. That boy's Bennett's bastard, got on an Irish housemaid!"

It took a moment for Owen to parse the sentence; his brain was all fogged up by the liquor. Mandry smiled at him. Took a sip of whiskey, and then Owen swung.

Mandry neatly ducked the first blow, and punched Owen twice in rapid succession. Then Owen got one good punch in, a heavy blow to Mandry's kidneys, but Whistler got into the fight and Owen went down. Whistler had kicked him three times—"Dirty." "Irish." "Bastard."—before Hoakes and the bartender could pull him off.

WHEN OWEN OPENED his eyes, the first thing he saw was Daisy's pink tongue. It was broad daylight, and he was laid out on the wooden walkway, close to a building. Daisy wriggled with joy, seeing Owen responsive. She licked him all over his face.

It was cold. Someone had laid an old horse blanket over him. Daisy had been pressed against his feet, as was her custom, probably to help keep him warm.

"All right, girl, I'm alive," he said. She made a joyful whimper. Owen pushed her off with his arm, which gave him a sharp pain in the side. He felt like he'd been caught on the cattle hoof side of a stampede.

Passersby clucked and shook their heads.

Owen prodded his teeth with his tongue. They seemed to be intact, though the inside of his cheek was all cut up. Tenderly, he touched his face.

With a stiff neck, Owen looked around for his hat and saw it over on the walkway at the other side of the doorway, where his friend Hoakes was laid out. Owen's hat was covering Hoakes's face.

Owen looked up and squinted, trying to see what building they were leaned up against. Daisy's tail thumped against the wooden boards of the walkway.

A man opened the door. He wore a fine black suit, spectacles, and had a neat, trimmed beard.

"Come in when you're up. I'll see if there's anything I can do for you. And if you'd be so kind to bring in my blankets."

Owen saw now that the sign above the door was of a winged staff with two snakes curling up around it—it was a doctor's office.

"Shhh," said Hoakes from under Owen's hat. The doctor shook his head and closed the door.

"Hoakes," Owen said. "I'm glad you're not dead."

"I might be," Hoakes answered. "Daisy, go fetch us some water."

Daisy perked up her ears. She looked over to Hoakes and back to her master.

"Why are we sleeping on the street?" Owen croaked.

"I dragged you over here last night, you ingrate." Hoakes lifted the hat brim and glanced at Owen. "Figured I ought to get you out of Whistler's way. Then I got awful tired and it seemed like a good place to rest and here we are."

Owen sat up slowly. The street was spinning in a disquieting way. One of his teeth felt loose in the socket, but at least it was still in place. Owen spat out a mouthful of foul rust-colored saliva.

"Say, I hope you weren't depending on your good looks to get a winter gig, son. 'Cause you look a fright," Hoakes offered.

Owen suddenly felt for his pay. There was a pocket sewn inside his vest, especially made to keep money close.

It was gone. Every cent of the thirty dollars he'd earned was gone, along with the thirteen dollars he had saved doing odd jobs back home.

He cussed.

"What is it?" Hoakes said, sitting up with a grimace.

Owen couldn't answer for a moment, he was so angry. Forty-three dollars! That was to be his seed money! All gone. And he couldn't even go after Mandry or Whistler for it. He'd been lying, passed out, on the public walkway all night and half the morning. *Anyone* could have taken it.

Owen cussed again. A stringy woman carrying two live chickens head down in each hand stopped and cocked her head to listen.

"Listen to you, carrying on! If you was my own, I'd thrash you good!" she said, with a brittle southern accent. "Someone oughta call the sheriff on you. Laying about in the street, sleeping off a drunk. This is a decent town we got here. Helena's gonna be the state capital, once we get ratified!"

"I've been robbed," Owen said. His voice came out with a crack in it, and even to his own ears, he sounded foolish and younger than he wanted to be.

"Well, if I were you, I'd count that as a lesson learned!" She turned on her heel and walked away.

Owen swallowed. He'd never felt such anger and despair. Daisy licked at his face, but he pushed her away.

"I'm sorry about your money, Owen," Hoakes said. "You should go see the sheriff. He might be able to help."

Owen shook his head.

"Look, I can stake you five dollars out of my pay," Hoakes said.

"No." Owen wouldn't take his money.

"Consider it a loan."

"No," Owen said. He didn't want to look at Hoakes. He didn't want to see the pity in his eyes. "I don't intend to go into debt one month after I leave home."

"What'll you do?"

"I'll find work that comes with room and board for the winter. Get signed up on a drive come spring." He struggled to his feet. The whole street swam.

"How're your ribs? Anything feel broke?" Hoakes held out Owen's hat, and Owen took it.

"Nope. Just sore, is all."

"Aw, take the five bucks, kid. You don't have to pay me back. You might have a hard time getting work, your face all smashed up."

"I'm not taking charity," Owen said. "Thanks just the same."

"Well, stop and think for a minute. Why don't you come with me to Great Falls? My sister's got a big place and two little'uns. I bet she could use us both."

"Thank you, Hoakes, but no. I'll make my own way."

Owen swayed on his feet.

Now, he knew he ought to fold the blanket and return it to the doctor, but more than that he wanted to get out of Hoakes's sight as fast as he could. He was going to vomit, and he didn't want Hoakes to feel any worse for him than he already did. Kicking the blanket aside, Owen walked stiffly away, his hat clutched in his left hand, Daisy padding faithfully on his right.

CHAPTER NINE

The SS *Helvetia* accommodated seventy-two first class passengers and twelve hundred in steerage. It had both sails and steam engines and could cut across the ocean at a top speed of ten knots. The journey from Liverpool to New York, which would take up to a month on a sailing vessel, took merely ten to twelve days now.

Hanne walked the deck, where so many languages from so many countries were spoken at the same time that it sounded more like chickens squawking than human conversation. From the hatware alone one could tell that many European nations were represented on board. Some ladies wore woolen wraps, like hers; others had frilly bonnets or silken caps perched on their heads, held on with hatpins. Some men had on funny fur caps.

Sissel was sick, constantly bringing up the biscuits and gruel Hanne forced her to eat. Hers was not the only vomit to streak the sleek sides of the steamship. She clung to Hanne, moaning and complaining almost all the time. Hanne accepted it. It was fair Sissel should complain and curse her. After all, Hanne was the cause of all their misfortune.

Only Stieg and Knut weren't suffering at all. They were delighted, gleeful, even. This bothered Hanne. She felt somehow that they should be miserable and feel terribly ashamed about their sister's crimes, or worried about the future. But they were happy at sea.

Each day, Stieg taught English in a small space at the back of the deck. It was for the children, but more and more adults gathered to listen as the days passed. Most were Norwegians and Swedes, and some were Germans, too. The ship also held many English. They had no need for Stieg's lessons, of course. Some bad boys came to tease the first day, but Knut had looked their way and they'd scrambled off.

During the lessons, Hanne and Sissel sat leaning against the railing, both wan and listless for their private reasons, while Stieg entertained and educated.

Stieg lectured on common verbs and nouns, drilling the children. But the favorite moments were the skits he enacted with members of the crowd. One morning Stieg borrowed Hanne's wrap and tied it over the head of a bright young man from Oslo, under his chin, like an old peasant.

"Good afternoon, miss," Stieg said in English, bowing to the boy. Everyone giggled.

"Gut afternoon, sir," the boy replied.

"Did you go to the market today?"

"Ya."

"Yes," Stieg corrected. "And what did you buy?"

"Er . . . *brød*."

"Ah! Bread! Yum!" Laughs from the deck. "*Brød*. Bread." The children watched in delight, the wind toying with the wisps of their hair. The boys held their caps in their little hands.

"What else?"

"Bread?"

"Yes. We know of the bread. What else did you buy? Apples?"

"Ya. Yes, apples." The boy nodded, grinning.

"And sugar? Butter? Then we can make some cookies for Christmas. Come, children, pick up your bowl and your spoon."

Now Stieg would lead them in a pantomime, making cookies.

Hanne watched him instructing these children of different countries. Everyone knew how to make cookies, of course. Boy or girl, they had all helped their mothers with baking. And now they learned the English words for *stir*, *spoon*, *bowl*, *peel*, *chop*.

With every span of the ship they put between them and the shore, Stieg seemed to grow more confident. It should have made her happy. Her brother was a gifted teacher. He would do so well in America. But even seeing her brother command the attention of a whole flock of children with their parents gathered behind them could not lighten her heart.

Before killing the men, she had used her Nytte to butcher livestock. She had had to trigger her Nytte by putting herself or one of her siblings in danger, but still, she thought of it as a tool, something she could choose to bring to hand.

Now she saw how naive she had been. The quicksilver power to kill was waiting in her body at all times, even when she slept. She was like a drawn bow, with a deadly arrow quivering, singing to be set free.

She had thought herself to be a good girl. She *had* been good! But that was before the Nytte came.

Her back to the rails and her face in the wind, Hanne remembered how she used to race home from school, going directly to her father's workshop where he would show her the day's work. He had taught her his craft, so sure was he that she would be a Shipwright, like him. He said it didn't matter that Hanne was a girl. And though he had lost digits, and was continuing to lose them, he had faith Hanne would carry on his work. Once her Nytte came into bloom, she'd be as good with the wood as he was. Her nimble, capable fingers would articulate his designs. Together, they would build ships known around the world.

And then she had come of age. Their mother had explained to Hanne how to change the cloths to catch her monthly bleeding. Privately, Sissel had asked Hanne if it hurt. Did she mind terribly, now that she could no longer run and play with the boys at recess, but must stay inside with the older girls?

Hanne had not minded at all. She was happy to become a young woman. She knew it meant that if she had a Nytte, it would soon reveal itself.

Then their neighbor Johan's dog had attacked them.

It was a nasty dog, a yellow mongrel with black chops. Johan kept him tied up, and whenever the children passed his house, the dog barked and snarled, foam flying from his muzzle.

Hanne, Stieg, and Sissel were coming home from school. Knut

was at home, helping their mother with the farmwork. He was not good at school; he was confused by sums and writing. So he stayed home, and their mother taught him how to work a farm.

Hanne had been walking ahead with Stieg, their little sister trailing behind. Sissel was a pest, always whining and weak. No fun at all. Hanne and Stieg were talking about a lesson from school, about mathematics—was it preferable to do the math in your head or to do it on a slate, where you could check the work? They were ignoring their sister, and she had stopped to cry. Standing there bawling in the middle of the lane that led through the meadow to town.

Suddenly Hanne's gut went cold. She was running before her mind could even register that Sissel's whining had turned to SCREAMING.

Johan's vicious yellow dog was *free*, had gnawed through the rope. Its massive jaws were sunk into Sissel's leg, and it was dragging her into the woods. Hanne's knuckles brushed against the ground seeking a weapon. Her hand selected the sharpest stick. A stout stick. It had nearly glowed, calling to her.

She was running, full speed, and then her knee dropped onto the dog's neck. It let go of Sissel.

Hanne drove the stick into the dog's eye. Through the bone and out the other socket. She pinned the hound to the ground with that stick.

The dog howled. Its limbs scrambled in vain.

Stieg only then arrived, skidding to a stop in the fir needles. Sissel was sobbing, blood pouring from her torn calf, dirt and spittle muddying the wound. Stieg had moved into action, tearing off his jacket and wrapping it around Sissel's leg.

"Hanne? Are you all right?" he had asked.

Hanne was still on top of the dog, her arm pushing down though the dog was dead. She trembled, her body vibrating with adrenaline. The energy that had possessed her drained away as the blood of the dog coursed into the dirt. Her hand finally released the stick.

"Come, Hanne, we must get Sissel home," Stieg said. Sissel was sobbing. She screamed as Stieg lifted her. "Hanne! Come!"

But Hanne stayed. It took a while for her to return to herself. A fierce hunger overtook her, and then her belly demanded she get home.

She walked and then she ran. She ran because she was so hungry she had the desire to lick the dog blood off her hands.

When Hanne arrived home, breathless, Sissel was lying on the kitchen table, weeping, curled on her side. Water was set to boil on the stove, and their mother had laid out rolls of bandages along with the herbal salve she kept in the root cellar.

"Mama, I'm so hungry," Hanne had said.

Hanne could still see their mother's expression. Her thin face taking in the sight of Hanne standing there in the door, her hands covered with blood. Blood on her school smock. Their mother's eyes filled with tears, and the tears spilled over, streaming down her face.

Hanne crossed to the cabinet and seized the loaf of new bread, cooling inside. She sunk her teeth into the thick crust.

Stieg and Knut were off to the side, watching. They had clearly been shooed away by their mother. Hanne saw a sad understanding in Stieg's eyes. Knut only looked confused, as if he might cry.

Suddenly their mother picked up the butter bell and threw it at Hanne. It crashed into the cabinet door, the pottery shattering. Stieg, Knut, Hanne, Sissel—each child was astonished.

"This I cannot bear!" their mother had screamed. "No!"

Then she returned to binding Sissel's wound.

"First your father's fingers rot away. Then Stieg becomes a Storm-Rend, and I learn of this Nytte, this disease that haunts my family line."

She wrapped the bandages too tight and made Sissel cry harder.

"And now, Hanne, your Nytte reveals itself, and you . . . you are a—" She choked on the word. Couldn't say *Berserker*. "You are a killer!"

Hanne sank to the floor. Not in shame. The shame would come later. She knelt down for the butter, took it in her hand, and ate it, spitting out slivers of pottery.

"God help me, what will become of my sweet Knut and you, dear Sissel. Oh dear God, what will become of us!"

And their stoic, even-tempered mother put her head down onto her youngest child's thin chest and wept.

Amund's reaction had been different. He had heard the news, then inspected Sissel's bandaged leg, then walked out of the house to go get drunk. He never spoke of his disappointment to Hanne, but when she came shyly to the door of his workshop a few days later, he did not invite her in, only asked her to fetch him some ale from the house.

Their mother left not a month later. She had said she was going to visit her cousin in Bergen, but she had packed like she was going away forever.

When she said good-bye, she hugged Knut the longest. Big, shy Knut had always been her favorite. Hanne barely got a squeeze. Her mother could not stand to look at her, not even when it was her last look.

Hanne had to wonder, who would love you if your own mother could not?

HANNE SAT ON the deck, watching Stieg entertain his students. He was such a good teacher.

Even after she learned she was cursed to be a Berserker, Hanne couldn't resist Stieg's lessons. The English he studied during the long winters called to her. He had read to Sissel and studied aloud, knowing the English was seeping into Hanne's mind. She couldn't help but pick up the strange and wonderful words.

She resented it then, and she still resented it. Even now, with the ship lumbering up and down, plowing through the waves toward God only knew what in America, Stieg was cheerful and beckoning to her. Even now, with her a killer of men, Stieg winked and directed his jokes to her. He still wanted her to be alive, and it rankled Hanne, because the only way she had survived her mother's departure and their father's rapid descent into cruelty and drunkenness was to go dead at the heart.

"Children, share your cookies. Yes, put one on a plate. Now go run and give it to your mother or your father. Then come back in an hour, and we'll begin the afternoon lesson!"

Stieg held out his own imaginary plate of whatever he had conjured, sirup-snappers or krumkakker, over the heads of his small swarming charges to Hanne.

Hanne stood abruptly and turned away. She pushed through the crowd that had gathered around her brother and made her way to the back of the ship.

As she watched the water churning, she thought of what it would be like to throw herself overboard, to escape from the guilt that weighed her heart down so relentlessly. Exchange her shame for a body of water soaking her skirts, dragging her down to perdition.

"You must find a way to forgive yourself," Stieg said, appearing at her elbow. It was as if he could read her thoughts from the way she looked at the dark, roiling wake with longing.

Hanne made a low, scoffing sound. "I cannot."

"If you can't do it for yourself, for your own happiness, then you must do it for us."

"You don't understand—" she began.

"The news of what happened at home will spread. They will look for us. They may even track us to America. We are in danger.

"You got us into this situation, Hanne. I know you are deeply aware of that, and I know it grieves you. But now I charge you to get over your grief. You must keep us safe. No one can do it the way you can."

Hanne tore her gaze away from the water to regard her brother. His brow was furrowed, his blue eyes forceful but not unkind.

"You have a job now. Get yourself together, and see that you do it."

Her brother marched away to prepare for the afternoon class. Hanne sighed and began to think of how she might persuade Sissel to eat some supper.

CHAPTER TEN

No one in Helena would hire Owen Bennett. Between his smashed-up face and the rumors Mandry and Whistler were spreading in the ranching circles, and the fact that half the town had seen him passed out in front of the doctor's office, no one would even hear Owen out.

He started giving a different name when he asked for work. If his shameful reputation somehow found its way back to the ranch, it would anger his father to hear Owen had been publicly drunk.

Owen sold his oilskin coat to the owner of a general store. He only got one dollar fifty for it. He must have looked pretty down in the mouth, selling his coat, because the owner threw in a couple of days' worth of hardtack and some jerky for free. Owen found it acceptable to take this small measure of charity. The coat was only a year old and still quite water repellent.

Since the sky looked like snow, and since he wasn't eager to run into any members of his former outfit, most of whom were still enjoying the pleasures Helena had to offer, Owen set out for Winston in the afternoon.

He camped in the woods that night, beside a smoky fire. He split a piece of hardtack with Daisy and then slept deeply, warm enough in his bedroll with Daisy at his feet.

Winston was smaller than Helena, and the residents even less eager to offer a job to a beat-up drifter.

Owen had given himself a frigid bath in a stream, and tried to clean up. He'd never gotten to send his clothes to the Chinese laundry Hoakes had told him about in Helena. Now he couldn't imagine parting with a dime for such a luxury. He knew he looked bad. His hair was matted down into a greasy ring around his head. The bruises were ripening along his jaw, and his left eye had been thoroughly blackened. But by the time those bruises faded, he'd have to sell his saddle or his horse, and he couldn't bear to part with either. There was a title for a cowboy without a proper rig: It was *farmhand*.

Standing outside the Florence Hotel, he wished he looked a bit more spruce. His plan was to spend fifteen cents on luncheon, impress the cook with how polite and well mannered he was, then ask for a job.

Daisy was following at his heel. "Down," he told her. "Stay."

He pushed the door open and came face-first into a wall of smells so delicious that he saw spots for a moment. On the right was a large room which served as the dining hall.

Two long tables were set with platters of food. Rough men sat on backless benches pulled up to the tables. At the ends were a couple of proper chairs.

Two harried serving girls brought out platters heaped with food from the kitchen. Owen smelled biscuits and gravy and a stew, venison maybe.

"I'm all full up, dear," said a fat woman carrying a plate of fried potatoes. She had a thick Scottish accent. "I'm sorry, love. Canna fit another body to table."

A man with stringy hair and a badly horse-bit face sitting at the near end of the table eyed Owen. He nudged the man to his left and indicated Owen with a nod. His comrade was large and beefy, a redheaded man with a ruddy, beery complexion.

"I was wondering—" Owen found the courage to say, but the woman had already hustled away. He stood there holding the brim of his hat with both hands.

The redheaded man looked up from a scroll of dirty papers he was carrying. The sheaf of papers curled up around one another, having long been wrapped that way. The man leafed through a couple of the pages and shook his head. Owen realized with a start that the papers were wanted posters. A sheaf of wanted posters!

The Scottish lady bustled back again, this time with a tureen of beans.

"I was wondering—" Owen said again. But she didn't hear him. The smells were making him dizzy. He staggered a little and put his hand against the wall to steady himself. He hadn't eaten anything besides hardtack and jerky since supper two days ago, their last meal on the trail.

"Are you hungry, boy, or drunk?" the horse-bit man said.

"Better let that one sit down afore he falls down," a kind-looking man seated at the center of the table said to the lady.

"No room!" she said, removing an empty platter from the table.

"Aw, come on, Mrs. Dunlop, you can fit him in somewhere!" the man said good-naturedly.

"He don't have the money to buy a plate," said the horse-bit man. "Look at him. Clear as day he's come to beg for work. Go on, kid. GET!" He gave a half lunge at Owen, making all the men howl with laughter. Owen couldn't let that kind of an insult stand. He took a step toward the ugly man.

"No, no, no," Mrs. Dunlop clucked. She took Owen by the arm and led him down the table and away from the bounty hunters.

"Emery. Harper, shove over," she said. "We can fit one more in down here."

Two men scooted over, and Owen lifted one boot over the bench and got settled. A plate and fork appeared. Then rich venison stew was ladled onto his plate. To either side, the men were eating fast and with purpose. The biscuits came around, and were they ever good! Light and fluffy and golden brown. Owen slipped one into his pocket for Daisy.

WHAP! He felt the back of a wooden spoon on his shoulder.

"No squirreling away victuals, there!" said Mrs. Dunlop. The men at the table laughed. Owen felt his neck go red.

"Sorry, ma'am." And here he was, trying to make a good impression. "It was for my dog."

"That your dog, there?" she asked, nodding out the window at Daisy. "Ah, she's a bonny thing. Makes me think of ours back home.

You come to the kitchen after the meal, and I'll give you some bones for her."

"Thank you, ma'am," Owen said. He relaxed then, and ate with gusto. It'd be the perfect opening to ask about work.

But later, in the kitchen, Mrs. Dunlop said she had nothing for him.

"I'm sorry, Owen Bennett. You do seem a nice sort of boy, but I've got no work these girls can't do for me," she said.

Behind her back, the two kitchen girls exchanged a resigned look. One of them sighed. They couldn't be much older than fourteen.

Owen nodded and looked down at his hands.

"Are you a good worker?"

He nodded.

"Are you a good cowboy?"

Again, Owen nodded.

"Do you drink?"

"The one time I drank, which was the day before yesterday, I got beat up. I ruined my good name and got robbed of my pay for a month on the trail," Owen said, meeting her eye. "I'm not inclined to ever drink again, ma'am."

"I believe you, son. I'll give you a lead. My brother's the railway stationmaster down in Livingston. Jerry Walsh is his name. You go on down there and tell him I've sent you a good reference. Tell him you remind me of our uncle Oliver. That way he'll know 'twas really myself what sent you. He knows everyone down that way. He'll help you find something good."

"Thank you, ma'am."

Then she gave him a package wrapped in brown paper. "Here's

for your dog. And, Betsy, give me the rest of the day's biscuits for the boy."

Owen stood and put his hat on. He wasn't used to the company of women. He knew Mrs. Bennett. He knew Lucy, the cook at the ranch. She was slightly off in the head and kept up a continual conversation with herself, mostly about the weather.

Outside of them, he'd only spoken to a handful of women in his whole life. But he knew he needed to find some good, rich words to show his appreciation.

"Ma'am, you have done me a great kindness today and I appreciate it. I thank you most sincerely."

Mrs. Dunlop's whole countenance softened. She put a hand to her heart.

"Ach, you do remind me of Oliver, though. He was a good man. Quiet and polite, but he held his own in a fight."

Here she reached out her plump arms and drew Owen into a warm hug. The kitchen girls looked at each other in surprise.

Owen stood there, experiencing the embrace. His stepmother, if she could be called that, had rarely touched him at all, and while Lucy had hugged him a few times, she was lean and bony.

It felt awfully nice, to be hugged by a mother. Even if she didn't belong to him.

Mrs. Dunlop released him, and Owen stepped back. He hadn't realized he'd been leaning in, but he had.

"You're a good boy. You'll be all right," she said. She cleared her throat and took stock of the dirty kitchen, the sink stacked with plates. "Now take your beef bones and go."

"Yes, ma'am. Thank you again, ma'am," he said.

"Girls, let's get a start on the biscuits. Supper will be here before long!"

Owen looked around the kitchen as the three women began their work. Mrs. Dunlop's kitchen had an abundance of warmth and practical kindness. He rather wished he could stay. But she had no work for him. Out he must go.

CHAPTER ELEVEN

The trip across the ocean by steamship from Liverpool to New York City had only taken eleven days. The immigration processing at Castle Garden seemed to take eleven more.

First they had anchored at the quarantine point. After waiting a day and a half, officials finally boarded the ship. Sissel was excited to see her first American, even if the three men who arrived were, to a man, short, fat, and mustachioed. They wore crisp suits, and their shoes shone like lacquer.

After marching over every inch of the deck and checking the throats, eyes, and hands of a good number of random passengers, they declared the ship to be free of cholera, typhoid, yellow fever, and smallpox.

Passing this inspection meant that the ship was allowed to draw closer to New York City—to America!—and dock in the harbor. Then came more waiting. The first class passengers, of whom Hanne and her siblings had not seen much during the trip, were then free to disembark. Steerage passengers, however, had to wait to be "processed."

There were customs forms to fill out. The issue of surname came up. In Norway, patronymic surnames were in use. Thus, Hanne was Hanne Amundsdotter, "Amund's daughter," while Knut's last name was Amundsson.

The customs official explained that this could not be so in America. They must all use one name. Stieg saw a chance to better hide from those who might seek them out.

"We shall be the Hemstads," he told the agent.

"But why?" Sissel asked. "We are not from Hemstad—"

Hanne stepped on her sister's foot, and Sissel shut her mouth. She glared at Hanne.

"Stieg Hemstad," Stieg said, trying the name out in his mouth and liking it. "Yes, that will do. And you are Sissel Hemstad."

Hanne wished to herself it might be so easy to change as to simply call yourself something new.

Hanne Hemstad. Who was that?

Regrettably, she would surely discover it to be her own self.

Next came a cursory medical exam. All the "Hemstads" but for Sissel were declared hale and hearty by a tall, stringy Norwegian-speaking nurse with severe wire spectacles.

The nurse said Sissel was too thin. She prescribed iron pills and something called Lydia Pinkham's Blood Purifier, and sent them on their way to an appointment with the immigration agent.

There would be more waiting, but now, at least, they were finally permitted to leave the ship and enter the Castle Garden immigration depot. As they walked down the gangplank, Stieg clutched his carpetbag and a large flour sack that held the boys' clothing, as well as several books he'd brought from home. Knut carried the beautiful old trunk their aunty Aud had given them, with their bedding atop it, bound up in a great bundle and tied with rope. Hanne carried the girls' clothing in a valise they had purchased in England. Sissel, excused because of her limp, carried only the few provisions that remained and their wooden plates, tin mugs, and cutlery in a gunnysack.

Stieg and Knut had broad grins as they clattered down the gangplank. Sissel clung to Hanne's arm, while Hanne kept an eye out for trouble.

The sky was overcast, a wash-water gray. From the boat next to them, another stream of steerage passengers just as weary and dirty as they filed out onto the dock.

The people streamed and milled together, all heading toward large doors. There was a press now—men, women, and children all pushing, moving together.

Hanne's heart pounded. There was so much to guard against. So many people.

"Stay together," she called to Stieg. She had a good grip on Sissel's wrist. She pushed a German man to the side and put her hand on Stieg's shoulder. Knut was in front.

"You're hurting me!" Sissel whined.

"We must stay together!" Hanne said, and at that point the crowd had ferried them inside, and Hanne's jaw dropped.

Above them was a vast round ceiling. Pillars rose up and up. At the center of the ceiling there was a perfectly round window. A balcony ran around the wall, encircling the upper level.

Everywhere there were people.

People waited on long lines in front of booths near the walls and in a maze of desks and partitions at the center of the ground floor. Against the walls, on the stairways, and anywhere they could find, families waited for their turn. Children sprawled out, some playing with the dirty leaflets that littered the floor. Old men chatted with one another, while their sons waited on the long lines. Some women nursed babies without shame or modesty.

The Hemstads stood in a tight knot as strangers milled around them. They gazed up at the ceiling, as grand as any cathedral.

"It's a new life," Stieg said.

"We are in America," Knut said.

Hanne could not help but smile at the excitement on his face.

"I wish we'd come for a different reason, but it is good we are here," Hanne said. She did not wish to dampen her brothers' delight.

"My leg hurts," Sissel said.

"Yes!" Stieg said. "But it hurts in America!" He tapped Sissel playfully on the nose.

She swatted at his hand, but had a little smile on her lips.

People were coming in behind them. Hanne wondered how more people could fit into the space. It didn't seem possible. Yet more were coming, so those who were inside must make room.

Stieg led the way through the throngs, spotting a family decamping from an area near a corner.

"Hanne and Sissel, you wait here. I'll send Knut back for you when it comes our turn."

"More waiting?" Sissel said. Knut set down the trunk, and Sissel sank down to sit on it.

Hanne was glad to stand in the corner and observe. She had nursed a fear that they might be arrested on the spot when they arrived in America. But no one seemed to be paying them much attention at all.

Not long after Stieg and Knut left, a swarthy, handsome young man came around passing out leaflets. He wore a well-cut suit with a waistcoat and had snappy black eyes.

"You ladies need a map?" he asked. Hanne shook her head, but he pressed one into her hand. "Union Pacific—we can take you all the way to California."

"California!" Sissel exclaimed. The young man gave her a wink. Now *he* was the sort of American she had hoped to meet.

"It's always warm, the crops grow year round—and there's gold, for those brave enough to seek it."

"I like to go," Sissel ventured in tentative English.

"Here's a girl with good sense!" the man said loudly. "She's going to take the Union Pacific all the way to California, the land of sunshine and gold claims!"

"Now, now, Niccoluchi," said another young man, this one shorter but with a similar, boisterous, cheerful energy. "These girls look like they know how to farm. They'll want to be heading to Minnesota or the Dakota Territory. The land is as flat as a pancake, and there's no rocks in the soil! A farmer's paradise!"

"He's not mentioning the years of drought," the one named Niccoluchi said. "Fickle weather, in the center of the country."

Strangers listened now as the two young men bantered back and forth. Hanne had the feeling they'd done this many times before.

"Nonsense!" said the short one. "Why, the rain follows the plow.

It's a scientific phenomenon, known only to the Great Plains of North America. The plow metal draws the rain out."

"Well, this girl's up for an adventure," Niccoluchi said, tucking Sissel under the chin. "Aren't you, dolly?"

Sissel smiled back. She had never held the attention of such a handsome young man. Sickly, thin as a rail, and having a limp, why should she have? Now her pale eyes glittered from his attention.

Hanne stepped between them.

"We thank you for your map. Now, leave us."

People around them laughed. Hanne didn't like it.

"Ha! That's right. Older sister knows what's best. Here, miss. Come take a ride on the Northern Pacific. Why, we run all the way to Washington Territory!"

The man held out a map, and Hanne took it.

"You'll be on the coast in six short days! Fancy that!"

Nodding her thanks, she turned her back on the two men and placed the map against the wall. She studied it. NORTHERN PACIFIC, ROUTES AS OF SEPTEMBER 1883.

The map was broken up by boxes; they must be the states and territories. "Pennsylvania." "Wisconsin." "Dakota Territory." And there, at the other side of the page, "Montana Territory."

It was a big country.

ROLF WAS TIRED of waiting, and he was tired of the company of Ketil Nilsen.

They had traveled quickly, not sparing their fine horses, to reach

Gamlehaugen after they had learned all they could at the dead Shipwright's farm.

Ketil had wanted to speak with the Baron Fjelstad, but Rolf insisted on a private conversation with his friend and employer.

Fjelstad was distracted, looking out the windows onto the autumn grasses on the hills around the estate as Rolf described what they had learned about the Nytteson children.

"This is the perfect opportunity for you to do some research in America. We might find many Nytteson among the emigrants there," Fjelstad said.

"But my work, Baron Fjelstad—" Rolf protested.

"Take the rubbing with you!" Fjelstad snapped. Rolf was surprised by this outburst. The Baron prided himself on his reserve and self-discipline. Fjelstad had removed his wire-rimmed spectacles and rubbed at the bridge of his nose. "I'm sorry. Agatha is . . . unwell. Again."

Rolf knew what this meant. Agatha was Fjelstad's second wife. She'd had a miscarriage the year before. Fjelstad had been so excited to become a father. Rolf's heart sank for the Baron and his new wife. They had not been lucky with children.

"I am so sorry to hear that news, my lord," Rolf said. "Please give her my condolences."

Rolf thought for a moment, regarding his friend and employer.

Fjelstad was in his midthirties. He took pains to look the part of a nobleman. He wore elegant, understated suits that conveyed wealth and power, and kept his hair combed and dressed in a tidy, conservative style.

Rolf knew him to be ambitious in business and a fair dealer with all. Since assuming the Barony after his father's death, Fjelstad had increased the value of his holdings several times over through shrewd investments. And that meant more wealth to support his research and protection of the Nytteson.

Yet for all the Baron's appearances of success and prosperity, Rolf read defeat and resignation in the set of his friend's shoulders.

ROLF HAD BEEN a librarian working in Trondhjem, at the Gunnerus Library, the official library of the Royal Norwegian Society of Sciences and Letters, for more than twenty years when he had first met Fjelstad. It was a position he had studied for and one he cherished. He could not imagine a greater duty in life than to serve the great library and the many works whose only copies were cataloged on its shelves.

The young Fjelstad, fourteen years old, was enrolled at the Trondhjem *katedralskole*, but spent all his free time in the library at Gunnerus. He was searching for information about an old legend, the Nytte; he kept pestering librarians and pages alike, and had come to be an irritation. The master librarians foisted the young lord on Rolf but he had found the boy's boundless energy charming. He listened while Fjelstad recounted all he knew about the Nytte and the six ancient Viking superpowers it might bestow. His hair was floppy and messy, and Rolf remembered how he would push it aside and continue telling tales of the Shipwrights, who could make boats that could nearly fly on the water, or the Ransackers, who knew where treasure was buried, even from leagues away. His enthusiasm had been intoxicating and impossible to resist.

After several weeks of searching, Rolf had located a poem that referred to an Oar-Breaker. Rolf sent word to the *katedralskole*, and Fjelstad arrived before the day was through. The young lord was so elated when Rolf presented him with the poem that he'd whooped with joy, which had made Rolf laugh aloud. The librarians shushed them. The two of them stifled their laughter, but not their excitement.

Over the next months, Rolf had dedicated himself to finding any information he could about the strange myth. There was precious little to be found, but when he did find some mention of it, Rolf would send word and Fjelstad would come directly.

After one of those visits, as Rolf accompanied him to the gates of the library, the young lord had offered him a job. Fjelstad had his father's support: Rolf would be given a salary, rooms at Gamlehaugen, the Baron's estate in Bergen, and freedom to use all the best libraries in Europe.

Then Fjelstad pulled Rolf close. "We will find the Nytteson! We will prove they exist!"

Rolf had colored and looked away, out of courtesy, embarrassed for the young man.

"Yes, my lord," he'd said, stalling for time.

Researching old legends was one thing. But it was quite another to suppose that men with a divine gift existed in the present day. Rolf was considering how to let the young lord down in the most gentle and polite way possible—then Rolf's eyes had focused on the ground.

There, half covered in dirt, was a perfectly round, white stone.

He tried to ignore the stone, but it seemed to twinkle at him, winking almost.

Begging Fjelstad's pardon, Rolf bent to inspect it.

When he saw what it was—a flat, round stone deeply etched on one side with what looked like a diamond standing on two splayed legs, Rolf had begun to tremble.

It was an ancient Viking divining stone, carved with the rune of Odin All-Father. It was warm to the touch, though the day was cold.

"I accept your offer, my lord," Rolf said, in a voice that shook with wonder. "I will serve you the best that I can."

Fjelstad clapped Rolf on the shoulder. Rolf had felt suddenly important, like his small life might matter in the end. He carried that stone in his pocket to this day.

"I know you don't want to go to America," Fjelstad said. "I don't blame you. I suppose there are other ways we could try to locate them. There's a gentleman at the Norges Bank who was speaking to me of the Pinkerton Detective Agency."

How could Rolf refuse to help his old friend, who had just suffered another terrible personal loss, and who had selflessly borne the responsibility of sheltering and aiding the Nytteson?

"I will go, my lord," Rolf said.

"You will?" The Baron looked up, relief breaking over his features.

"Please forgive me for hesitating."

"Thank you! This is marvelous!" Fjelstad had said. He'd risen to shake hands with Rolf. "And I want Ketil to accompany you."

"No, no. Please. He's too young and too unformed."

"And how will he learn, if we don't teach him?" the Baron had said, his head turned down to his writing desk. "I insist you take him.

Think of him as a bodyguard. He's very strong. And this is exactly the kind of mission he needs to gain experience."

"Please, my lord, Ketil is . . . an unpleasant traveling companion," Rolf protested.

The Baron evidently considered the matter closed, for he took out his ledger and wrote Rolf a check for a large sum. He handed the slip of paper over the desk.

"Take the fastest ship and book yourselves into first class. You don't want to ride with the rabble."

"Very well," Rolf said.

"And send Ketil in. I'll speak to him about my expectations for his behavior on the journey."

"Yes, my lord."

The Baron did not go back to staring glumly out the window, but began to shuffle and sort the papers on his desk, humming. For a moment, his spirits seemed to have lifted. This, at least, made Rolf glad.

BUT TIME HAD PASSED, and Rolf had come to regret his offer.

All they had to go on was the child's description of the siblings: a tall boy; a slender girl; a great, big hulking boy; and a limping little sister.

Each week, tens of thousands of immigrants were processed in the immense rotunda at Castle Garden. Thousands arrived each day, and as many were discharged into the bowels of Manhattan Island. Finding four children among this chaos would be a near-impossible task.

"We've lost them," Ketil said to Rolf, returning from pacing the floor. "They came through and we missed them, or they never even came here, but are off hiding in the fjords."

"Be quiet and watch," Rolf said. He had studied the grounds and chosen a good place to stand and watch—near the first set of large wooden doors that the immigrants passed through as they departed Castle Garden and entered the Bowery, Manhattan's ugly lower slums. He had not ventured out himself; he did not want to let a single moment go by unmonitored. Ketil had gone out and come back, bathed, shaved, and carnally satisfied by a dockside prostitute who had "given him a ride" for free, if his account was to be trusted.

Nearly all the newcomers stopped and stared at the chaotic scene that awaited them beyond that set of doors. Low buildings and rooming houses, with the taller buildings of the financial district rising behind them. The hucksters swarmed—men and women of all nationalities, teeming for the chance to "help" the immigrants. Some of them offered decent housing and meals, some stood by to rob them at the first opportunity, but many were simply eager citizens, waiting for friends and family to arrive.

Rolf kept his eye trained on the faces of the crowd. Despite the hectic and daunting landscape that presented itself, what Rolf saw again and again, on all manner of faces, was hope.

The immigrants stood there and braced themselves for America, and though there was fear and exhaustion from the long journey, there was ambition and confidence and faith. It was moving, the dream of America. It was even moving him. It made him think of the old line of Norse poetry, "*Many bellies, many skins, one light shared in the blood.*"

He considered the line. Translating from Old Norse allowed for many interpretations. The great poets ordered words for meter and scansion, allowing many meanings at once. He played with the poem, twisting it to see what other meaning might be found.

"What will the Baron say if we've lost them?" Ketil asked Rolf, elbowing him right out of his thoughts.

"He'll understand when we tell him how large this place is."

"Well, you'll be the one to answer to the Baron. Not me."

"Yes, Ketil. I know that. Why don't you go walk the Norwegian queue again?"

Ketil leaned against the wall. "I just walked it!"

Rolf sighed. He wouldn't let the younger man irritate him. He closed his burning eyes for a moment, turning the rune stone in his pocket over and over.

"Odin, please hear me," Rolf prayed softly. Ketil was likely to mock him. However, prayer was a part of Rolf's methodology, and Ketil should know that it worked.

"If it is your will I should find the Nytteson, please send me aid."

A few moments passed.

Ketil chuckled in a mean way. "Odin, hear me, too! Send me a beer. I pray thee."

Suddenly Rolf felt warmth in his chest, a blossoming of warmth, like hot water poured into a cold bath.

He shot out his hand and touched Ketil's retreating back.

"They're here. Look closely. They're here! I know it."

THE FOREIGNER SHOUTED something at Knut in some choppy, Slavic language. He was a hairy man with a face like a boiled ham, and he carried a canvas rucksack.

Knut had done something—maybe stepped on the man's foot. Now he was threatening Knut with a dull knife.

Hanne felt her Nytte gathering, readying itself in case the man turned violent. Her heart began to pound loudly.

"Sorry! Sorry!" Stieg said in English. He had one hand out to the man, and another holding Hanne's shoulder, trying to steady her. "We apologize. No harm meant."

Hanne forced herself to breathe. The man suddenly became aware of her and shot her a mean look. Her body jumped toward him, and Stieg hauled her back.

The man retreated into the crowd, grumbling.

Stieg pulled Hanne close, and they resumed their place in the ticket line for the Northern Pacific Railroad. Hanne was trembling, but breath by breath, she got her pulse back to normal.

They did not notice two tall men get in line, three parties behind them.

Finally it was their turn.

Stieg counted out the fare in kroner. They still had an enormous sum left from exchanging the first gold coin. Hanne had sewn the other two coins into the lining of his underdrawers. No one would be pickpocketing him. Stieg bought four cross-country tickets to Helena, Montana. From there, they would hire a coach to take them to Wolf Creek.

The girl at the ticket booth spoke Norwegian with a heavy Bergen accent. There were ticket sellers of many different nationalities: Norwegian, Finnish, Swedish, German, Russian, on and on. The Norwegian ticket girl wore a flouncy white shirt, and her hair was pulled into a bun, with a great mass of hair in front, her poufy hairdo wilted. She seemed bored by her job, though to Hanne it seemed a glamorous post.

She advised them to change the rest of their kroner for dollars at the bank in the rotunda before setting out into Manhattan for the train station. Grand Central.

This seemed like a good idea. Stieg had nearly three thousand Norwegian kroner left from when he had sold the first gold coin in Bergen. They meant more than three hundred and fifty of the lovely green American bills, with their red stamps and their angels.

Stieg liked to joke that, at the very least, Hanne's abilities would keep them from getting robbed. There was no way anyone could sneak up on him with malicious motives and escape her notice.

Hanne found little to joke about in regards to her Nytte.

WHEN ROLF AND KETIL got to the head of the line and set their leather valises down, the ticket girl looked tired, but perked up when Ketil winked at her. Rolf knew that he would work her beautifully. She was just the type who flowered under his attentions—plain and bored.

"Destination, please," she said in Norwegian.

"I don't know," Ketil asked, leaning against the booth. "You tell me, where should we go?"

She huffed and looked up at him, a small smile forming on her lips as he held her gaze.

"You tell me," she responded. "You're the one paying."

"Well, where did the last ones go?" Ketil said, thumbing toward a short, old couple who'd just been to the counter. "Mr. and Mrs. Oldy Pants."

The girl giggled. "They're going to Dakota Territory, to homestead, most likely."

"I don't want to go there, do you?" Ketil asked.

The girl shook her head coyly.

She pointed at two young women, traveling alone.

"See those two? They're off to be housemaids in Minneapolis."

"Pah. No. I don't fancy Minnie-map-opops for us. What about that great big oaf? That young fellow with all the muscles? Let's go where he's going and hire him to carry our bags."

"Montana?" the girl said.

"Montana! Just where I want to go. What city?"

"Helena. And that's just about the end of the line."

"Two tickets to Helena, then," Ketil said.

The girl smiled.

"I can't really go, you know."

"I know. I'll have to take my friend here."

He nodded toward Rolf.

The girl's smile extended to Rolf for a moment.

"Where do you really want to go?" she said back to Ketil.

"Helena, Montana, please."

Her smile faltered.

"You really mean to go there on a whim?"

"Why not?"

She didn't move, processing this.

"We'll take the tickets, please," Rolf said, his eyes tracking the retreating backs of the Nytteson. "And quickly now."

Rolf counted out four American ten-dollar bills on the counter and six singles.

The girl still didn't move.

"Come, dear, we don't want the train to leave without us," Ketil said.

He tapped his knuckles on the wooden booth. The girl jumped into action and issued them their tickets, her lips pursed in puzzlement. She'd been tricked, but wasn't quite sure how.

"I still don't understand why you want to follow them," Ketil said under his breath, as they trailed Amund's children out of the depot. "Why take the risk of losing them on the long ride to Montana? Why not approach them now?"

"Because they are going to family," Rolf said. He put up a hand to silence Ketil's protest. "Which possibly means more Nytteson. It's worth the risk."

"It will be easy to lose them."

"There could be a whole hoard of Nytteson in America," Rolf said. "Who knows—there might be a Ransacker or a Shield-Skinned."

Ketil shot Rolf a measured glance.

"I suppose it's worth taking a chance," he conceded.

CHAPTER TWELVE

Hanne did not like the motion of the train; the continuous lurching felt dangerous. But it had been five wearing days of train travel, and her body had become accustomed to it. When the train stopped to take on passengers or let them off, she felt unsettled by the stillness, as if her bones had wished to keep rocking.

This was the third train they'd ridden. New York to Chicago. Chicago to St. Paul. And now this train, which would deposit them in Helena later in the day. From there, they would hire a coach, if such a thing could be done, or purchase horses, to cross the land to Wolf Creek.

The first day of train travel had felt restful, after the grimy chaos of New York City. The population of the bustling eastern American cities reminded her of a patchwork quilt. Never had Hanne imagined there were so many variations on the human form. But her fascination was dampened by her constant, nagging fear.

Now, five days later, the anxiety was a dull throb. Hanne's body ached with so much sitting still. Her rear-quarters knew every lump in the flat leather upholstery. It seemed as if she and her siblings would never have a place to put their belongings and rest.

Hanne had watched the Great Plains whir by. Empty. Golden. Nothing to see for miles in every direction but the waving autumn prairie grasses. The "Great American Desert" they had heard so much about was so unceasingly flat, it evoked astonishment, then a pronounced, mesmerizing boredom.

Once they had neared Billings, Montana, there were finally some landmarks to be seen. There were rocky hills and shrubs and actual trees. Snow lay on the caps of Montana's high, distant mountains. It showed through bare patches between the stands of pine trees and blanketed the meadows at the base of the mountains.

Hanne saw a vast herd of cattle, spread over a mountain pass like a wide, black shadow. But when she turned to show her sister, she found Sissel napping.

The other travelers in the train car busied themselves looking out the window or reading. There was a tense-looking woman traveling with three small children. Knut had played a lengthy game of peek-aboo over the seat back. A handsome young man read aloud to his mother at the back of the car. Hanne blushed when she thought of how dirty her face and hair must be. But there was nothing to be done about that until they arrived in Helena.

Stieg and Knut sat across the aisle from them. Knut dozed heavily against the window, and Stieg was rereading Dickens's *Our Mutual Friend*.

"Look, Stieg," Hanne said. "Look at the cattle!"

"Must be two thousand of them," Stieg marveled. "Have you ever imagined so many cows in one place at a time?"

Two young women Hanne's age wandered back, likely from first class. It was common for people to roam the train. Such a long journey made for many dull hours. Stieg had walked the train many times, making friends all the way.

These two girls might have been twins, with the same bright blue eyes and petite, pinched noses, except one was decidedly prettier. She wore a brown traveling dress with blue trim. The other wore a similar outfit in shades of gray and lavender.

Hanne's foot had strayed slightly into the aisle, and the first young lady stopped and stared pointedly at Hanne's shoe with pursed lips.

Hanne pulled it back, and the young lady stepped past. Hanne caught sight of her neat, buttoned-up boots under her swishing skirts.

"Poor Swedes," the girl said to her sister. "Can you imagine wearing shoes with wooden soles—"

"Clomping around like a horse," her sister finished the sentence.

Hanne's face burned. The mother with her children pretended not to hear the slight, and the girls swished by.

"Sister," Stieg said loudly in his measured English. "Have you heard what the British poet Samuel Butler said? 'It is tact that is golden, not silence.' Novel concept."

The girls turned, startled, looking back at Hanne and Stieg.

"I wonder when it will take hold in America," he added.

"Not soon enough, I think," Hanne said in return.

The girls stared like iced fish, eyes round, mouths open. It was apparently difficult to believe that people dressed like the Hemstads might speak English so well.

The tired mother stifled a little peep of delight.

Stieg was grinning.

"Beg pardon," one of them had the manners to say. Red faced, they bundled back through the car toward the safety of first class.

Stieg popped out of his seat.

"I'm going to walk a bit," he told his sister. "I'll be back shortly."

She watched Stieg walk down the aisle, noticing how dark his blond hair appeared—purely from the dirt. Hanne's pride at his witty comment leached away, leaving her feeling ashamed of her appearance, and that of her siblings. Their clothes were so sour and dirty and stiff they could stand up by themselves.

Hanne looked at Sissel's woolen wrap. It had been homespun gray to begin with, but was now sooty and soiled near to black in places. The hem was ragged. There would be no laundering the wrap. It was fit for rags and little else.

With the balance of their first gold coin, could they each buy a new wardrobe? Could they buy American boots with buttons?

Hanne knew it was wasteful thinking but she also imagined that having some new clothes, in an American style, might be a peace offering she could make to her sister. Sissel had said scarcely a word to Hanne since they'd left Norway, only speaking when necessary. It pained Hanne to have a rift between them. At home, there had not been great love between them, but they spoke, even if only to tease each other.

A dove-gray traveling dress with lavender trim would likely ease the distance. At the least, it would bring them together because Sissel would need her to do up the buttons in the back.

In a few minutes the train would come into a station at a town called Livingston. From what she could tell on the map, Livingston was a larger town than most they had passed, a hub of some kind. Hopefully there would be some food to buy at one of the train-station-side shops, or perhaps someone would board with bagged suppers for sale.

The quality of the food they had experienced on the route ranged considerably, from rancid beef and oily beans to American delicacies like cold fried chicken, buttermilk biscuits, and pie. Oh, pie! Knut could eat a whole pie himself. The flaky crusts might hold any amount of ingredients, from sweet to savory. They'd had a chicken pie. And one with pecans and sugar. The sale of the pie included the pie tin. Now they had four pie tins that they used as plates or bowls from time to time. If pressed by her brothers, Hanne would admit to having some excitement about the thought of learning to make a real American pie. She felt she'd be good at it. The crust seemed not so very unlike *tynnlefse* dough.

Stieg came back, much sooner than Hanne had expected, sliding into his seat without the bag supper she had hoped to see. He was worried about something.

"What is it?" Hanne said.

Sissel's eyes flitted open.

Stieg had a copy of *Morgenbladet*, the newspaper from home.

"Where did you get that?" Hanne whispered.

"A Norwegian woman sold it to me. She bought it in St. Paul, two days ago."

On the cover page there was a drawing and the headline COUN-TRY BOY WANTED FOR TRIPLE MURDER.

Hanne knelt beside Stieg, reading in horror.

There was a second headline: WAS IT THE WOODWORKER'S SON?

The sketch was of Knut. It was a decent likeness, but the eyes were all wrong. They had given him cross, menacing eyebrows and the squinty eyes of a killer.

> After what some say was a botched investigation, the police of Øystese in the Søndre Bergenhus municipality are officially seeking the arrest of farm boy Knut Amundsson. It is believed that the boy aided his father in killing three men who had come to collect a debt. The father was shot and killed during the fight.
>
> These grisly barn slayings have shocked our proud and peaceful nation. Though the details of the murders have been suppressed by the police, rumors say that the killings were brutal and callous beyond measure, including multiple stabbings and a dismemberment with an ax. Since the devastating murders were discovered at the farm of Amund Thorson, much speculation has occurred as to the whereabouts of Knut, as well as Thorson's other three children. The police have come under stern criticism from many for not immediately locating them.
>
> Though rumors had pointed to possible

kidnapping, the police have ruled it out now, and are searching for the siblings. Knut Amundsson is described as standing six feet six inches tall and weighing three hundred pounds. Who but a brute of such size could have the physical strength to slaughter with such rank force and violence? The police will come under strict scrutiny, indeed, if it is discovered that the children have fled the country, as is suspected.

Hanne felt like all the blood in her body had drained away.

The train began to slow as it drew into the station, and her stomach lurched along with it.

"What's that?" Knut said, waking up. He yawned. His yellow hair was sticking up where his head had lain against the window. He looked, sleeping and waking, like the fourteen-year-old boy he was, and not like a young man at all.

"Nothing," Stieg said, and he folded the newspaper and tucked it away.

Hanne was seized by fear. Suddenly she could not breathe. Anyone on the train might know who they were.

She shot out of her seat.

"Hanne," Stieg said. "What's wrong with you? Sit down!"

KETIL WAS SLEEPING off a drunk, and Rolf was enjoying the quiet. Ketil had wanted to sit in the same car as the Nytteson, but Rolf had said no. He knew that Ketil could not resist provoking the children during the six-day journey to Montana. Rolf had had a much better idea. They were riding in the coach and baggage car, at the end of the train. Three cars back from the Berserker and his siblings. Rolf could see their fine, old trunk through the bars of the cage the luggage was stored inside. To his practiced eye, it was obvious that the trunk had been carved by a Shipwright. This was a family of Nytteson, no doubt about it.

Only the conductors and the baggage handlers had access to the luggage cage. Rolf and Ketil would simply disembark when the baggage men came and removed that trunk.

Ketil had taunted Rolf regularly about the likelihood of losing track of the Nytteson. Rolf bore the idle abuse for the first leg of the trip—New York to Chicago. But then he'd bought Ketil a bottle of whiskey at a rail-side saloon. That had been a very fine idea.

Ketil turned inward when drunk. He'd stopped flirting shamelessly with the girls and ladies passing through the cabin on their promenades. He'd stopped his continual boasting and was content to sit and stare out the window, and eventually he'd fallen asleep.

Rolf had his rune stone in his hand. He liked to roll it over in his palm. It helped him to relax. The train ride made him think of poems about ships crossing the oceans. He thought of his favorite:

The hero's hand skimmed the foam
As he pondered Ymir's skull.
The sea-steed rode the eternal waves.

The train did seem to ride the waves of prairie grass like a ship cutting through the sea.

Rolf closed his eyes for a moment, vaguely aware that the train was about to start moving, when he felt suddenly and keenly that something was wrong. It was akin to the sensation he'd had back at the immigration depot. It traveled from the stone in his hand up to his heart, like the wave of a current. Something was wrong with the Berserker. Rolf could sense the Berserker's distress, as if a line connected them.

He put his hand on Ketil's shoulder to wake him, then thought twice of it. If he was wrong, and everything was fine with Amund's children, then Ketil would mock him. If he was right, and something was happening, did he really want Ketil's interference? Rolf left him to sleep.

The train was still stopped, people disembarking, others coming aboard. A sign near a large depot read: LIVINGSTON. Rolf walked briskly up through the two compartments. He pulled open the door to the car where the young Nytteson were.

He entered the cabin, keeping his head ducked, lest one of the Nytteson pay attention to his features. But when he looked up, the elder girl was standing in the aisle, hands in fists. She turned and stared right at him, eyes keen and furious.

THE MAN WHO had entered the cabin behind them, the one with the pocked face, he was a threat. Hanne felt it with certainty.

"Get up!" she told Stieg. "We must leave."

"What?"

"We must leave, now!" she said. The train was beginning to move. "Up!"

Stieg and Knut hopped up.

"Is there a problem, dear?" the tired mother asked out of politeness. "Is everything all right?"

Hanne ignored her, grabbing Sissel and shoving her down the aisle. "Out the door! Onto the platform. All of you, go!"

"What are you doing?" Sissel cried.

Hanne pushed her siblings ahead of her toward the door that led outside to the platform. It was set in the side of the cabin, toward the front.

The train began to gather speed.

"The train's moving!" Stieg yelled.

Hanne's wide eyes sought weapons. There was a chain hanging from the window blinds. She could pull it off—But no. *No!* She wasn't going to kill him. She wouldn't.

"We can't get off now—" Sissel protested. "What about our things?"

"They don't matter," Hanne said. "We must get off this train now."

"Wait," the stranger said in Norwegian. "I'm a friend." He was stalking down the aisle toward them.

The door to the platform was locked, but Hanne grabbed it and wrenched and the handle gave. She threw it open. Gravel and dried weeds trackside flew past in a blur.

"Hanne, have you lost your mind?" Stieg shouted.

"He is a bad man! He is after us."

"We can't *jump* off the train!"

The train wasn't yet at full speed. They would be fine. She knew it.

"Yes, we can!" she shouted. Then she shoved her brother out the door onto the rushing ground. Stieg hit the ground tumbling.

Several passengers screamed, protesting.

"Knut, jump!" she said. He stood staring in the aisle, his mouth open.

The stranger approached, hands out. "Please, young miss, hear me out! I know who you are—what you are—"

The Nytte flared. Overtook her instantly. There was no greater danger than someone who knew what she was.

Hanne grabbed the man by the collar, opened the door that led to the next train car, and threw the man into the shifting space between the cars.

The old man banged on the glass panel of the door. "I'm a friend," he shouted in Norwegian.

SNAP! She kicked off the handle to the door, locking the man out. He was stuck out there between the cars, hemmed in on either side by safety cables.

BANG! The man stuck between the cars rammed on the glass with his fist.

"This is a mistake," he shouted. "Listen to me!"

A concerned conductor came up behind him.

Now the train was moving faster.

"Jump, Knut!" Hanne yelled. He squeezed his eyes shut and leaped off.

"Come, Sissel, we'll hold hands." She grabbed for Sissel's hand just as the conductor kicked the passageway door in. It hit her squarely on the back, and she fell, tumbling down the stairs.

She flew out the open door, into the wind and the dust. Her body hit gravel. She rolled away, away from the moving train in a cloud of grit and chipped stone.

"Hanne!" Sissel screamed from the gaping door of the train. Hanne looked up—Sissel was poised to leap, but was afraid.

"Jump!" Hanne screamed.

Then the scarred man had his hand on Sissel's arm, pulling her inside, as the train sped away.

"Sissel!" Hanne shrieked.

"Jump, Sissel," shouted Stieg, from somewhere behind Hanne.

"Let her go!" Hanne screamed at the man on the train.

And then there was a blur. A blur of animal, moving toward Hanne.

It was a man on a gray horse. And there was a dog, at the heels of the horse.

The man thundered past Hanne, galloped up alongside the train, and snatched Sissel off it. Simple as that.

The train roared away.

The man trotted the gray horse in a wide circle, letting the horse slow on its own. Hanne rose to her feet, her back aching from where she'd been hit with the door. Her brothers walked toward her through the weeds and dry grass. She cleared grit from her eyes, nose, and mouth. She had cuts and scrapes on her hands and legs.

Stieg grabbed her by the forearms.

"Hanne, what in the heavens possessed you?"

"That man," she panted, "was a threat to us."

"He wanted to talk to us!"

"He knew all about us, Stieg! He was Norwegian! He knew what I did!"

By then the man on the horse had circled back with their sister.

There was lather from the horse. Everyone was heaving—the

horse, the dog, the man. His face was covered in dust. He wore a blanket on his shoulders. Hanne noticed this. The blanket, too, was covered in dust.

The man bore Sissel lightly in his arms, as if she were a bunch of laundry he'd taken off a line. Sissel was weeping, pressing her face into his collarbone. Hanne could see dark spots on the dirt of his neck made by her sister's tears.

While he had the look of a ruffian, with a fading black eye and a wicked bruise along his jaw, there was an openness to his expression.

The way he sat his horse, Hanne had thought him to be fully grown, but now she saw he was not much older than Stieg. He had lines near his eyes from squinting in the sun, and stubble on his jaw. Hanne realized he was a cowboy. She had seen pictures of cowboys in the newspapers. And here was one in the flesh.

She caught herself staring at him and found he was staring at her, too. She looked away.

It was a strange spell that had been cast. Disaster had been so narrowly averted, and by such sudden heroics. No one could think of quite what to do next.

The cowboy still held Sissel in his arms. He was breathing hard and looking off at the disappearing train.

Sissel moved to be released. Knut stepped forward, and the cowboy passed Sissel into her brother's large arms.

"Thank you, sir! Many thanks!" Stieg was finally able to say.

The dog wove between their legs, barking with excitement, wagging her tail. She was a white dog with large black patches on her face, and black ears.

Sissel clung to Knut, whimpering as the dog came near. She had never gotten over her fear of dogs after the bite.

"Down, stay," the cowboy said to the dog. The dog stopped barking and lay down, just like that. The cowboy dismounted in one fluid movement.

"Where did you come from?" Hanne said in English, just as Stieg said, "Sissel, are you all right?" in Norwegian.

"I was at the depot, asking about a job, when I saw you jump from the train."

He took off his hat and scratched at his hair. It was very dark, and matted down from the hat brim.

"Round here it's custom to depart the train when it's stopped."

"The fault is mine," Hanne said. "I was afraid of a man on the train, and I said we must leave."

From the corner of her eye, she knew Stieg was staring at her. It was hardly characteristic of her to speak to a strange man, let alone speak the truth.

The cowboy nodded.

Knut had set Sissel down on her feet. She clung to her brother, pressing her face into Knut's arm.

"You're all right, little miss?" he asked.

Sissel sniffled and gave a shy shrug.

"I guess that man from the train won't be bothering you. Next stop's not until Bozeman. At least twenty-five miles away."

"If you please," Hanne said. "What is your name?"

"Owen Bennett, ma'am. Pleased to meet you."

He reached for her hand, and she extended it. His hand was warm and large, a bit sweaty from the reins. He was careful with her hand, like it was something important.

"I'm Hanne Hemstad," she said. The new surname felt odd in her mouth. Like she was playacting. "These are my brothers, Stieg and Knut. And my sister, Sissel."

Stieg and the cowboy shook hands as well.

"We cannot thank you enough," Stieg said.

"Naw. You have," Owen said. "I was just glad I was in the right place to be of help. There's a lot of crass men in this part of the country, I'm sorry to say. You were right to get away from him. Is there anything else I can do?"

"No, thank you," Stieg said. "We will walk to the depot."

"All right then. Safe journey to you.".

He turned toward his horse and was up in the saddle in a heartbeat.

"Wait!" Hanne said. "What is the name of your dog?"

"Daisy," he said. She felt his eyes on her face.

Then the cowboy whistled for his dog and set off toward the town.

As she watched him ride away, Hanne's stomach growled. She had not killed anyone, or hurt anyone, but her Nytte had been roused and now she was hungry.

OWEN FLICKED THE REINS and urged the horse into a canter. Pal needed to be cooled down. Going all out that way, all of a sudden, wasn't easy. Pal had done well in the heat of the moment, and Owen decided to get him some turnips or carrots if there were any to be had.

He couldn't ride away the strange feeling he'd drawn from that girl. Not the one he'd plucked off the train, but her sister.

She wasn't pretty like the girl on the Pears' Soap advertisement his older brother Harvey had hidden in his tack box, but she was striking to look at. She had light blond hair the color of parched straw, and it was up in braids, woven around her head like a crown. Her eyes were wide set and skeptical. He thought they'd been blue.

Anyway, it wasn't the way she looked, but something about the way she held herself. Graceful, wary. She's fallen off a moving train, then brushed herself right off without complaint. And he liked the way she'd told him about the bad man on the train. It made it easier to help someone if they just came out and told you what was wrong.

Pal plodded into town, Owen letting the horse set his own pace.

His meeting at the depot was a dead end. The stationmaster, Jerry Walsh, had not seemed happy to hear his sister's name at all. He had, in fact, cussed her, calling her a relentless busybody.

Owen's best chance, Walsh said, was to try the livery stables in Livingston. There were three of them. Owen walked his horse toward the first.

THE CONDUCTOR WAS upset about the Hemstads departing the train in such a way, but far more upset about the shattered lock and two busted doors.

"Lookit! The glass is broke and the handle ruined! I need their names." He had a red complexion, and the breakage was making his face even more inflamed.

"I don't know them, sir," Rolf stated.

"I heard you banging on the door, shouting as how you meant them no harm. What was that about?"

"It was a misunderstanding," Rolf insisted.

"Describe them to me, then. I'll be making a report to the police when we get in to Bozeman." The conductor took a small, leather-covered notebook and a pencil from his pocket. "What'd the one who broke the door look like?"

Rolf found his wallet in his pocket. He removed two ten-dollar bills. He wasn't entirely sure this was enough money; figuring out the exchange rate between kroner and dollars still gave him pause.

"Listen," Rolf said. "Perhaps we could let this go."

Rolf offered the bills up awkwardly, not sure how to hand them over.

The conductor shot a glance over Rolf's shoulder to make sure they were not being observed, then he picked the bills out of Rolf's fingers and stuffed them in an interior pocket. "I've got to interview the other people in the car and write it all up."

"You could interview them. But who's to say what goes in your report but you."

The conductor eyed Rolf's wallet. Gave a discreet nod.

"I'll need your name, at the very least," he said.

Rolf opened it and removed another ten-dollar bill. He handed it to the conductor, who took it without acknowledging the transfer in the least. The conductor's attention was focused on the notebook in his hands.

"Jake Durham," the conductor said. He recorded the name in a little notebook. "A rowdy out of Castle Rock, Colorado. That should do it."

He gave a little self-satisfied chuckle and repeated himself. "Jake Durham. It just came into my head."

Rolf nodded. The man seemed to need some validation. "Yes, a good invention."

Rolf marveled—somehow he'd found himself surrounded by vain, immoral men.

Tired and discouraged, he made his way back to his seat only to find Ketil still sleeping.

In fifteen minutes—no, less than that—everything was ruined. The Nytteson had jumped the train, and Rolf and Ketil would have to find their trail or lose them forever in the endless western frontier of the United States of America.

It was a headache upon a headache.

The train was moving too fast for Rolf and Ketil to jump off now, though for a moment, as he watched his handsome and despicable partner sleeping, Rolf considered hurtling himself off, anyway.

"*Despair and failure,*" Rolf thought. "*Same stone, gritty between the teeth/Odin disavows me.*"

Ketil opened one eye.

"What's happened?" he asked.

Ketil laughed when Rolf told him. He thought it a great joke and said he couldn't wait to tell the Baron. Rolf was aghast at Ketil's reaction. It was hardly a comical turn of events.

When they disembarked at the next station, some twenty-five long miles down the track, Rolf was able to convince the baggage men to give them the children's trunk by using the same method of persuasion he had used with the conductor. He hoped the contents might offer some clues about these Nytteson.

Rolf had decided not to tell Ketil what he'd learned, that the Berserker was a girl. Legends spoke of the great female Viking Berserkers, hair braids dipped in the blood of their enemies. He had found an account of a female Berserker archer, able to kill at great distances, with supreme precision. What might this girl be able to do?

CHAPTER THIRTEEN

Stieg wanted to purchase new tickets and set out right away for Helena. He proposed it even as they walked away from the rails and toward the town.

"I can't get on another train!" Sissel cried, her limp more pronounced than usual. "Not today!"

"But they may have put our trunk off at the next stop," Stieg reasoned. "Don't you want it back? After all, your embroidery is inside it. Think of the many hours you worked on it."

"The bad man might well wait at the next station, or in Helena," Hanne said. "We cannot take the train."

Stieg scratched the back of his head.

"Very well," he said. "We'll spend the night. I would like to think about what we should do next. We need to see how much things cost."

"I think we should have a bath," Hanne ventured. She wasn't in the best position to be making requests, and Stieg's irritated glance told her so. "We are filthy, Stieg. And we have plenty of money left over from the first coin."

"What is the purpose of bathing if we are only to put on our dirty clothes again?" Sissel complained. "We cannot even wash our clothes and change into other garments, for we have none now that our trunk is gone."

"That man knew who we were," Hanne said resolutely. "He meant us harm."

Not one of her siblings would look at her. They all trudged toward town, heads down, marching through the brown grass. Knut rubbed at his elbow. He'd hurt it when he jumped from the train. Stieg was limping, as well.

"I cannot describe to you what I felt, but I tell you, we were in danger!" Hanne repeated.

"Very well, Sister, we believe you," Stieg said, though he clearly did not. "But you must remember that we want to pass unnoticed. Jumping off a train draws attention to us. I would imagine that the people in our car will be talking about it for some time to come."

Hanne's chest was tight. Her brother was correct. Her rash actions had probably placed them in more danger. But as she felt the prick of tears in her eyes, she felt Stieg's hand on her arm.

"Easy, Sister. It has been a long journey. A hot meal and a night of rest will do us good."

Hanne nodded. She gave her brother a small smile.

The town of Livingston was bustling. It had been founded to serve as a hub for the Northern Pacific Railroad and was booming to life. The noise of hammers and of men calling to one another could be heard as the siblings drew closer. Buildings were going up at a fast pace—fine brick buildings as well as wooden houses and shops. There was already a busy main street, and another one intersecting it. The streets were hard-packed dirt, edged with wooden boardwalks so that in foul weather one might stay out of the mud. The Hemstads stepped up onto them and walked toward the center of town. Small homes made a grid around the crossed thoroughfares. Hanne counted at least five hotels and three general stores, as well as a dry goods emporium, even a haberdashery.

Hanne wanted them to keep to the shadows at the side of the walkway. As they ventured farther into town, she became conscious of the heavy clomping her wooden-soled shoes made. She worried they would stand out, as immigrants, and freshly arrived, due to how tired and dirty they looked. Knut's size meant they already drew notice. If lawmen were hunting for them, they might give themselves away by looking so road weary. But she found there was such a variety and quantity of people in the town that no one seemed to notice them one way or another. There were shopkeepers in tidy clothes and cowboys toting their saddles around on their hips. There were two well-dressed women with parasols who seemed to be aristocrats, if there were such positions in America, as well as women in plain garb, wearing work clothes and homespun wraps like their own.

"There," Sissel said. "I want to stay there."

She was pointing to a three-storied wood-shingled hotel painted bright white, with a blue door and shutters. THE REGENCY HOTEL, proclaimed the sign. A placard hung from the sign: HOT BATHS. FREE SOAP.

"It looks like an excellent hotel," Stieg said. "Only but the best for you, my small and dirty sister."

Sissel giggled, and that sound cheered Hanne somewhat.

AFTER THEY HAD been shown to their rooms, a young, petite housemaid led Hanne and Sissel to the bathing room. It was set at the back of the building. The walls were wooden, covered with sheets of canvas tacked up with brass rivets. Three hooks were nailed to the wall for a person's clothing, and two more held white flannel towels for drying off. The room had its own small wood-burning stove to heat the water, so it was warm and cozy inside.

The maid showed them in, hanging a lantern on the wall for light, as there were no windows in the room. There was already water steaming in the large metal washtub, and the maid set another full pot up onto the wood stove to warm.

"If you need more water, just call," the maid said in a voice no louder than a whisper. She handed Hanne a dish with a slimy chunk of homemade soap and several washrags. For fifteen cents per bath, the "free" soap should have been store bought, but Hanne put the thought aside. She would soon be clean.

"You can go first," Hanne said. She turned her back to give Sissel privacy. Sissel did not question this. She began to strip out of her clothing, first shedding her oversize shawl, then her apron, and then her skirt and blouse.

"Let me take your clothes outside," Hanne said. "I'll try to beat them to get some of the dust out."

"No! You can't go!" Sissel said. "What if someone comes in? Don't leave me!"

Hanne leaned on the door. "All right. Never mind. I'll guard the door for you," she said.

She was keeping her eyes on the floor out of respect for Sissel's modesty, but she glanced up and gasped. Her sister was in her shift now, and she was far too thin. Her ribs showed under the skin.

"What?" Sissel said. She had shucked the shift over her head, but held it now to cover her flat chest. She quickly stepped into the tub, only then casting aside the shift. The underdress was stained from the journey, when Sissel had been sick on the boat.

Hanne said nothing.

"Oooh," Sissel said, sitting in the steaming water. "Oh, Hanne, you cannot imagine how good this feels."

Hanne saw her sister's frail body relax. Her head lolled back, supported by the edge of the tin tub.

"Here, let me wash your hair," Hanne said.

Sissel did not protest. She dipped her head under the water, and then Hanne lathered the thick, slimy soap into foam, massaging it into Sissel's scalp. Her hair was so fine; when wet, it seemed hardly there and the outlines of Sissel's skull were in Hanne's hands.

"I am so glad we stopped," Sissel said.

"Me too." And Hanne was glad. But mostly she was glad she and Sissel were speaking again.

"Was that man on the train really bad?" Sissel asked.

"Of course!" Hanne replied. "Do you think I would make you jump from the train for nothing?"

Sissel shrugged.

"Hanne," Sissel said. And then she paused. She didn't meet Hanne's eye. Hanne's imagination began to race with all the things Sissel might be about to say, the many ways she could blame Hanne or insult her or attack. Instead, Sissel asked, "If I were to receive a Nytte, what do you think I'd be?"

When Hanne didn't reply, Sissel pressed on. "I imagine I'd be a Storm-Rend, like Stieg, for he is tall and thin, and I am thin, if not very tall. I couldn't imagine I'd be an Oar-Breaker, like Knut. That would be something, wouldn't it?"

Hanne smiled. "I should like to see you gain huge strength," she said.

"Can you imagine, me lifting up cows and horses?" Sissel laughed.

"You might be a Shipwright, like our father," Hanne said softly. Sissel's back stiffened. "It wouldn't bother me, you know. Even though it's what I wished to be. I would be happy for you—"

"I shouldn't be happy for me! To have my fingers and toes start to fall off once I reached forty? I'd rather be anything than a Shipwright!" she spat. "I'd rather be a Berserker!"

Hanne knew Sissel did not mean to give offense. She wasn't the type to purposely hurt another person, but more the type who never gave a thought to another's feelings one way or the other.

"Believe me, you would rather be a Shipwright. For if the price you pay is dear"—Hanne held up her hand when Sissel started to protest—"at least you are creating something. It is a power that builds, not destroys.

"All the gifts besides mine make something," Hanne continued.

"A Storm-Rend can make a squall or calm one. An Oar-Breaker can build many things with his massive strength. A Shipwright creates with wood. But a Berserker kills. A Berserker takes life and crushes it out," Hanne said.

Hanne rose, took up Sissel's skirts, and shook them out.

"What was it like?" Sissel said very quietly. She said it so quietly Hanne could pretend not to hear the question over the rustling fabric. "To kill a man?"

"Time to get out," Hanne said. "I'll help you dress."

"HALLO, MY SISTERS!" Stieg greeted them. He looked refreshed after his bath, as did Knut.

One of the kitchen maids rang a bell on the front porch, and suddenly doors banged open and people came streaming down the stairs. It was suppertime.

The Hemstads were swept up in the mass of diners, some families, but mostly single men, who came in from both inside and outside the hotel. There were about forty people in all, and they crowded into the dining room together, seating themselves at the five large, round tables that held eight settings each.

Before the Hemstads could gather their wits to claim four chairs together, everyone was seated, leaving only singleton seats scattered among the tables.

Stieg shrugged at his siblings. Sissel clutched at Hanne's hand, and Hanne found seats for them at a table filled with carpenters, distinguished as such by both their conversation about their project and some bits of sawdust in their hair.

Stieg sat with a large family of German immigrants, and Knut was nearby, seated with several officious-looking men in suits.

The doors to the kitchen opened, and housemaids began bringing out an array of dishes. Each table got a platter of fried brown trout and one of sliced potatoes in cream sauce, a dish of steaming boiled turnips, a basket of biscuits, and a bowl with stewed apples.

There was little conversation when the platters first arrived, but once everyone had been served, people seemed to feel more amenable and chatter sprung up.

Hanne and Sissel were saved from conversation because their table partners were discussing the laying of a roof, specifically a poorly set gable that they might need to take down and reframe.

Hanne heard Stieg making limited conversation in German, and then, as she was eating her turnips, she heard Knut's voice come through.

He was speaking in Norwegian to the gentlemen at his table.

"Yah," he told them. "I've arrived with my brother and sisters." She could not hear the voices of the men, but they must have been questioning Knut, for then she heard him answer, "From Øystese." And then, "We're going by train to visit my uncle—"

A sudden wind that rattled all the windows. Several of the women shrieked, and someone's elbow sent a water pitcher crashing to the floor.

All attention went to the windows, and conversations turned to the unpredictability of Montana weather.

Hanne glanced at her brothers. Knut was looking at Stieg, surprised and abashed, and Stieg was signaling him to stop talking. A blush spread across Knut's face. He was so without guile, he had forgotten not to speak the truth.

Knut looked down at his plate, returned to his chicken pie, and didn't say another word.

AFTER DINNER, Stieg took Knut by the elbow and marched him outside. Hanne and Sissel followed. They went down, off the front porch, and stood near the stairs, at the level of the street.

"They were nice men," Knut said in Norwegian. "I didn't think—"

"We must leave this town," Stieg answered.

A woman passing by with two children looked up abruptly as Stieg spoke. Stieg drew his siblings closer. "Does *everyone* in this town speak Norwegian?" he said with dismay.

Hanne could tell from the way Stieg was wincing that he had a headache from using his Nytte.

"They were just being friendly," Knut said. "They said they might have work for me. They're building a bank."

"They of all the people in town are most likely to receive newspapers from home. Knut, listen, I must tell you something: All of Norway is in a scandal over the . . . over what happened, and they suspect you!"

Hanne watched comprehension dawn over Knut's face. His eyebrows drew together.

"They think I did it? But, Stieg—"

"We must get out of this town and find our uncle," Stieg said.

"What will we do?" Sissel wailed.

"Shall we try for another train?" Hanne asked, even though she hated the idea of being caged up on another car—or running into the man with the pockmarked face at the station.

"Stieg—" Knut tried to cut in.

"We will buy horses and gear and a map and set out for Wolf Creek by land," Stieg said.

"Brother!" Knut cried. "Do they think I killed Papa, too?"

Hanne felt a yank in her chest, like someone jerking out her heart. She put her hands on either side of Knut's face.

"No, dear brother," she said. "They do not think that. They think you killed them to avenge his death. Like a knight."

She nodded and he nodded slowly, with her.

"I will not let anything happen to you, Knut. You know it," Hanne said.

Knut smiled.

The men in suits were walking out of the restaurant. "Come," Stieg said. "We must leave Livingston."

They hurried down the street and ducked into a stable called Erlich's Livery. There were several horses tied out front, and next door there was a blacksmith, a handy combination.

The stable was large but hastily built, with stalls housing horses, donkeys, and oxen. A boy in an unraveling sweater was currying down a slab-sided sorrel who was tethered to an iron bracket on the wall.

Voices could be heard coming from the back.

"I've already got a boy, and I can scarcely pay him."

"All I ask is room and board, sir, in exchange for the winter's work," came a younger voice in response.

"And I suppose I am to board your horse, too? And your dog?"

The men belonging to the voices walked through the open doors at the rear of the stable. It was a small, gray-haired man with a potbelly and their very own cowboy from the rails. His dog was right on his heels.

"I can find work to pay for their board," Owen said. "But you'll see the dog is good with animals. She'll earn her keep, Mr. Erlich."

The old man and Owen fell off speaking at once when they saw the Hemstads. Owen seemed as surprised to see them as they were him. His dog came over right away to lick Hanne's hand again and to sniff around them happily. Sissel drew closer to Knut, in fear of the animal.

"The answer's no, boy. Apologies." Erlich turned to the Hemstads with an oily smile. "Now, what can I do for you young folk? Seems I'm to spend my day waiting on young'uns."

"We need to purchase four horses," Stieg said stiffly.

"You have money? Not meaning to offend, but well, I don't have time to waste."

"Neither do we," Stieg said. Hanne could tell Stieg didn't like or trust this man Erlich, but she was distracted by the cowboy. He seemed terribly embarrassed and was studying the hat he held in his hands.

"We have plenty of money for livestock," Stieg said. "We are headed to the north."

"This late in the season?" Erlich croaked. "That's unwise, to say the least."

Owen put his hat on and started moving through the Hemstads, aiming for the door. His gray quarter horse was tied out front. Hanne felt she should have recognized the horse.

"Fall weather turns quick out here. Everyone digging in and holing up. Perhaps you're not used to a Montana winter, being from . . . ?"

"Finland," Stieg lied coolly.

All through her bath Hanne had thought of the things she should have said to Owen Bennett. Or could have said. But having come upon him asking for work, and being so harshly denied, she felt embarrassed. She could not bring a single phrase to mind.

"Finland!" Erlich snorted dismissively. "Them European countries don't get snow, not like we do."

"I assure you, we have plenty of it," Stieg said.

"He had the right of it, though, about the weather." The cowboy paused at the door. They all turned to look at him. He seemed shy for a moment, but continued. "It's no time to be setting out for the north. This is dangerous country. And you don't know it well. You four could die out there."

"We plan on purchasing a good map."

"A map will do little to help you if the weather turns, or if you're attacked by bears or wolves, or if your horses founder in a slough. And you've got to cross the Missouri." Stieg began to protest again, but Owen held up his hands. "I've said my piece. You'll do what you want."

He turned and walked out the open doorway. Hanne felt the air go out of her lungs when he was no longer in sight.

"If you're determined to go, I have the best horses for it," Erlich said. "I have horses that are bred to the snow. You don't have any like 'em in Finland. Look here at this gelding." Erlich turned to show Stieg a sloped-shouldered chestnut with an ugly sore on his left eyelid.

Stieg turned abruptly and wheeled out of the stable.

Hanne, Knut, and Sissel followed.

"Sir!" Stieg yelled to Owen's retreating back. "Mr. Bennett!"

The cowboy stopped and turned his horse. He edged his horse back toward the sidewalk.

"Would you please consider being our guide?" Stieg said. "We need to get to Wolf Creek, and we need to leave soon."

"Wolf Creek? It's a hundred and fifty miles straight north," Owen said.

"We can pay you handsomely," Stieg said. "For us, it's a matter of utmost importance."

"What's in Wolf Creek?" Owen asked.

Hanne felt Stieg search out her gaze. She met her brother's eyes and shrugged. Stieg exhaled.

"That's our business," Stieg said. "We can pay you very well."

"I think you should wait another day and take the train," Owen told them. "Chances are you won't meet any more rough characters. And take the first one you can get on. After the first big snow, trains don't run so often. Snow'll come any day now."

"The train is not an option for us," Stieg said. Owen began to question him, but Stieg crossed his arms. "My sister Hanne is wary of strangers. She becomes . . . afraid."

Hanne felt a searing blush flood her neck and cheeks. It was a lie, but not so far from the truth.

Now the cowboy looked at her with what seemed to be pity.

"Aren't there roads? Trails?" Stieg asked. "With a map, why couldn't we find our way?"

Owen leaned forward in his saddle, toward them.

"I don't know what it's like in Europe, but this country is big. There's no people, the way you need to go, see?" he explained. "You could ride for days and not run into anyone."

Hanne thought about this. There was open country in Norway, but you were always within a day's journey to a town or village. The country was old, had been explored and charted thousands of years ago.

"There's no one there to ask for help if you need it," Owen said. "I'm sorry."

The cowboy turned his horse and trotted away.

Stieg tried to hide his disappointment and dismay for the sake of his siblings, but Hanne could see he was deeply worried.

"It's all right," Stieg told them. "We'll find a way."

Hanne felt sorry for Stieg, all of a sudden. He had been set to go on a great adventure to create a new life for himself in America, and now he was in the middle of nowhere, trying to shepherd his strange and broken siblings to the care of an uncle they'd never met.

"Maybe we can try the train again," Hanne ventured. "If it's really as dangerous as Mr. Bennett says to go by land."

"No. Like you, I worry about being around people. We'll find another guide and go by land," Stieg said. "Come, we will provision ourselves. The sooner we are out of this town, the better."

CHAPTER FOURTEEN

Owen had drawn a crowd. School had let out for the afternoon, and he had inadvertently chosen the back field of the school-house as a training ground for Daisy.

He needed to clear his mind, and thought he'd put Daisy through her commands. Nothing cleared the mind like work.

Those Norwegians were trouble. A blind man could see they were trouble. What kind of trouble? That was the question. Because he was, himself, in trouble enough.

If he didn't find work in the next day or so, he'd have to turn tail and head north himself. The thought of returning to the ranch a failure made him sick down to his gut. Though maybe he was just hungry.

"Away to me," he yelled to Daisy. She raced away in a counter-clockwise circle.

"Go by," he yelled as she approached him, and she swerved, running to make a circle in the opposite direction.

The kids oohed all together. They ranged in age from five to somewhere near sixteen. He didn't blame them for watching. Daisy was awfully fast. Her muscles rippled under her fur. All playfulness was gone when Daisy was drilling for trail work. She was pure animal.

Better than animal, in a way, because her keen, sharp mind was being directed. She could work without double-thinking. Unlike himself. His mind kept going to the idea of taking the Hemstads to Wolf Creek, worrying the topic like a child trying to undo a wet knot of shoelaces.

"Aw, he sure is fast, mister!" a pudgy redheaded boy called. "What's his name?"

"Her name's Daisy," Owen corrected. As far as Daisy's training went, it was fine to have an audience. He'd work her through the distractions.

What if he took them? They'd pay him well, he'd insist on it. He might ask them for twenty-five dollars. And for what, a week's work? It would see him through the winter until he could get onto a new ranching team.

Owen sent Daisy far into the field and called her back fast, then he sent her out again and called her back slow. He had her "walk up," walk to him in a straight line, from seven or eight directions.

They should not risk it on their own. They might encounter animals on the way. Bears, mountain lions. There could be an avalanche. There could be a blizzard. Owen took off his hat and wiped down his brow. Maybe it was better not to imagine all the things that could go wrong.

He thought about the Hemstads. The large, muscular one, Knut, was somewhat dull in the head, but seemed the sweet type of simpleton. The only risk he posed was that he might lame a horse under his vast bulk. And the younger girl seemed fairly docile. Afraid of dogs, but Daisy might well cure her of that.

He sent Daisy far, at top speed.

Owen rather liked the older boy, Stieg. He was smart—Owen could get that from his command of English—and he was playful, too. He was probably just around Owen's age, couldn't have been more than twenty.

Owen called Daisy back at a walk.

If he took them, he could winter in Wolf Creek. It was a small, rough town. There was gold nearby, or rumors of gold, and some failed forty-niners had set up there. Even if work was scarce, he could use his twenty-five-dollar stake to rent a room in a boardinghouse and sit out the winter.

Owen called to Daisy to lie down, and she did, dropping neatly on her belly, her tongue lolling. It had been a long day, and she was getting tired. He let her rest for a moment as his mind turned to the very thing he'd been trying not to think about—the girl Hanne.

Girls had been in short supply on the ranch. But Owen's father had bought a pretty little surrey for the use of his sons, once they began turning eighteen in rapid order. The surrey was lacquered wood with red leather seats, and built snugly for two. The Bennett brothers called it, laughingly, the "courting carriage" and fought about who got to use it, and when.

Once Harvey and Matthew had fallen to blows over a girl named Lizzie Volpe. She had bright green eyes, a lilting laugh, and a tiny waist, maybe the width of a man's hand from pinky to thumb. She fainted frequently at the barn dances that were held from time to time. What was special about being so frail you couldn't handle a jig or two?

Owen hadn't understood why his brothers vied for Lizzie Volpe's attention. They fought over her even when she wasn't around. It was an attraction that Owen hadn't grasped. Well, he was beginning to grasp it now.

Hanne was dirty and tired. She didn't smell too good. None of them did. But he couldn't stop thinking about her. He kept seeing her face. The wisps of her hair that had come free from their braids and the way they'd played around her face in the breeze. How hopeful she looked when Stieg had asked Owen to be their guide, and how crestfallen she looked when he had turned them down.

What had really happened on the train? What could have happened to cause them to take the risk of traveling over land instead of by rail?

Someone on the train had frightened her enough for her to make her whole family jump off. Maybe some rough man; that could be. But he wondered if maybe it was someone they knew. They might have relations who didn't want them to connect with their uncle. Could that be? Maybe someone wanted to break the four of them up and they were determined to stick together. So they were going to their uncle for help.

Owen rubbed his eyes. These Hemstads were a dilemma.

The thing about them was that although they were in trouble for sure, they seemed like good people. Good people who needed some help.

How could he refuse to help them, especially when it was in his benefit to do so? He wasn't scared of a blizzard. Or a bear, for that matter.

There was a cough from behind him and Owen realized the children were still watching, and Daisy was out in the field, waiting for a command.

"Come fast!" he called, and Daisy was up and racing in a quarter heartbeat.

Going full out, she almost seemed to fly.

"To me!" Owen shouted, and Daisy did her spectacular leap landing, coming to skid in the dirt at his feet.

A cheer went up from the kids. Owen had made up his mind.

THE HEMSTADS ENTERED the dry goods emporium in a glum mood. The store was cheerful enough, with shelves full of bolts of cloth and glass counters displaying all manner of yarn, ribbon, and buttons, as well as knitting and sewing materials. Best of all, at the back of the store, near a curtained-off area for trying clothes on, were ready-made garments for men and ladies both.

That was a relief. With all that faced them, Hanne had been dreading what she should do if they could not purchase clothes ready-made.

The proprietress was a squat, pleasant woman who held a few pins in the corner of her mouth as she showed the girls her wares. There were white cotton blouses in several different sizes, all cut voluminously, as seemed to be the fashion, with dainty buttons at the necks and wrists. There were also fine full skirts of wool gabardine. In a small room off behind the counter, a girl Hanne's age with nut-colored hair and a pretty blue calico dress was hemming a skirt on a sewing machine. Hanne examined the fine, even stitching on the skirts as Stieg spoke to the proprietress.

"I wonder," Stieg said. "Might you know any men who would be willing to act as our guide? We need to head north."

"North?" she asked, her eyebrows expressing her opinion before she gave voice to it. "No time to travel now. It's blizzard season."

The bell at the door jangled as several new customers entered.

"Yes, yes," Stieg said, sighing as he thumbed through the limited selection of winter coats. "So we hear."

"You might try at the saloon if you're looking for a guide," said the proprietress. "Though I'd hardly call the men at the saloon the best sort."

It was then that Hanne saw Owen Bennett. He was standing near Stieg, having come in unnoticed by them all.

"A good horse is going to cost nigh on forty dollars," the cowboy said. Stieg spun around to face him. "Then there's saddles. Bridles. Grub and bedrolls. Do you have enough money to get good gear? I mean really good gear?"

A grin broke over Stieg's face.

"Yes," Stieg said. "We have good money. We can buy whatever you think we will need."

The proprietress shook her head and went to tend to the other customers.

"What would be your fee?" Stieg asked. "How about fifty American dollars?"

The cowboy's face broke into a grin as big as the one Stieg wore. "I'd settle for forty."

"Let's make it fifty, and you make sure we all arrive in one piece."

"I can't guarantee it, but I'll do my best." Owen shook Stieg's hand.

"Mr. Bennett, thank you," Hanne said. She reached out and touched him on the arm. She'd not been able to stop herself from doing it.

Owen looked away and thought for a moment.

"I liked the look of the stock down at McCallister's Livery better than the ones at Erlich's. We'll take tomorrow to gear up—"

"No, no, Mr. Bennett," Stieg said.

"Please, call me Owen—"

"We need to leave as soon as we can. Tonight, if possible," Stieg said.

Owen thought about this for a moment.

"Look," he said. "If I'm gonna take you, you're going to have to do as I say. There can only be one trail boss."

Stieg began to speak, but Owen held up his hand.

"Get a good night's sleep tonight. In the morning, we'll meet at the Loveland General Stores.

"In the meantime, you can see to your personal effects. You'll all need good, thick coats. Mittens. Thick mufflers. Wool under . . . undergarments." He colored a bit mentioning the unmentionables. "I'll go look at horses now, and we'll be off by midday tomorrow."

Stieg drew close to Owen, and lowered his voice.

"We would ask that you keep the news of this hire to yourself," Stieg said.

"I don't know a soul in this town besides my dog and my horse," Owen said. "But you have my word."

"Very good," Stieg said. He looked profoundly relieved.

Hanne herself couldn't help but smile.

Owen seemed suddenly hesitant. He cleared his throat. "Before we part ways for the evening, I'll need a deposit of ten dollars. If it's not an inconvenience."

Stieg agreed happily. He retrieved his wallet from his vest pocket and counted out ten one-dollar bills.

"See you bright and early," Owen said to them, and he tipped his hat in farewell.

"I like him," Sissel said once he'd gone. "I like the way he talks, and I like the way he looks."

Hanne had to admit she agreed.

HANNE AND SISSEL each came away with a long, sweeping gray wool skirt, two white blouses, a cotton shift, and a set of long woolen underwear. The proprietress had wanted to sell Hanne a boned corset, but Hanne had declined. She bought some soft white wool material of a similar weight to the type she used at home to bind her chest and waist. That was the type of "corset" they wore at home, and it would do well enough in America.

The seamstress also offered them a good, used women's coat made of a wool blanket. The coat was rose colored and had cream stripes near the wrists. Sissel declared at once that she did not want a used coat, but Hanne liked it and it fit her perfectly. Sissel chose instead a plain gray wool coat, very thick. They both selected sturdy knitted socks, mufflers for their heads, and mittens.

The proprietress was using the information she had—that they were headed north—to her advantage in making sales.

"If you meet a blizzard, you'll be glad to have these beaver fur mittens!" she told Stieg. And, "Little girl like her, she needs two pairs of woolens!"

Stieg allowed her to add another set of woolens for each Hanne and Sissel to their growing pile of goods. And he got the fur mittens for Sissel. The fur faced inward, leather on the outside. But he had protested when the seamstress showed Hanne and Sissel two pairs of fine American-style button-up boots.

"Your own shoes are good enough," he'd told his sisters, "and probably warmer!" He seemed slightly alarmed at the expenditures they were already making, and there were certainly more costs to come, so Hanne did not press further, though she did admire the boots. So light compared with her own.

For himself, Stieg bought two blue shirts, wool underwear, a dark brown jacket, and a pair of brown trousers with "suspenders." He bought a thick wool coat, as well as mittens, a neck scarf, and socks.

There was nothing in the store that would fit Knut but long underwear and some socks and gloves, but the proprietress said her seamstress could take measurements and have pants and a shirt ready by the next morning. That was plenty fast and would have to do. Hanne glanced into the back room at the young seamstress, happily sewing away, unaware that her employer had just committed her to a long night's work.

The skirt they had purchased for Sissel was too large at the waist, but the seamstress nipped in the waistband while the Hemstads waited. Then, after Knut had been measured, and their purchases wrapped, the Hemstads returned to their rooms at the hotel, arms full.

TEN DOLLARS AGAINST forty more! Owen felt like doing a jig. It was a stroke of good luck—wonderful good luck. And he'd even offered to lower the price, so he didn't need to feel as if he were taking advantage of the Norwegians.

Owen ducked into the closest general store. They had corned beef sandwiches for sale. Each was wrapped in brown paper and tied with a string. His mouth started watering just looking at the spots of grease on the paper.

Owen bought three sandwiches, two pickled cucumbers from a barrel, a paper twist of oyster crackers, a jar of canned peaches, and a small bag of horehound drops.

He was awful hungry.

He would sleep in a hotel room tonight, he decided, as he stepped out into the crisp air. And have a nice, hot dinner. He might just get that shave he'd missed in Helena, too.

Then Owen turned and went back into the store and bought a fourth sandwich, the last one they had made up. He decided Daisy should have her own.

KETIL HAD POPPED the lock of the Nytteson's lovely, old trunk with his pocketknife, and now he rifled through the contents carelessly.

"Ah, look at these," he said, withdrawing the sisters' finely embroidered national costumes from the trunk. "Mmm, I love a girl in traditional clothes, don't you?"

To Rolf's horror, Ketil brought what must have been the Berserker's skirt up to his face, pressed it over his nose, and inhaled it.

Rolf snatched it away.

"Be an adult, for heaven's sake!" he chastised the younger man.

Ketil laughed. "You're such a nanny goat, Rolf."

Rolf was glad he had concealed the Berserker's identity from Ketil. It was impossible to know how he would take the news that they were tracking a female Berserker.

Ketil pawed through the rest of the items in the trunk, handing them out to Rolf. There were books—two books by Charles Dickens, a volume of romantic poetry in English, but most important, a family Bible. This was invaluable to Rolf.

He opened the worn pages carefully. There, written in various hands, was a list of ancestors. Such a record, containing the names and dates of a chain of potential Nytteson, was treasure for their cause.

How he wished he could retreat to the library at Gamlehaugen to pore over the names, cross-referencing them with his lists. This type of information was precious and rare.

Ketil nudged Rolf with his elbow, jarring him from the pages.

"What's the plan now?" Ketil said. "Shall we sit here and study while the Berserker gets away? It's your decision, boss."

His smile held impatience and disdain.

Rolf closed the book.

"Pack up the trunk, please. I will go and inquire of a coach or livery to take us back to Livingston."

"We should get our own horses and ride ourselves," Ketil said. "We can follow the tracks."

"Ride into the evening, in a country we do not know? I don't think that wise. You wait here, and I will return once I make arrangements."

"I'll wait over there." Ketil nodded toward a large, two-story saloon painted a flaking canary yellow. There was a pair of ladies' bloomers run halfway up the flagpole outside the establishment.

Rolf sighed. He did not care to argue with this young hothead.

"I will return within a half hour," Rolf said. "Be sure to pack the trunk before you go. And ask the baggage men to store it for us."

Ketil nodded, barely hearing, as he shoveled the precious belongings of the Nytteson family back into their beautiful trunk.

Rolf slipped the Bible into his valise. He would not be parted with it for anything.

He hoped he would be able to find a coach willing to travel into the night. He felt all at once too old for this kind of adventure.

CHAPTER FIFTEEN

The sheets weren't entirely clean, and a few strands of horsehair pushed through the limp mattress, but Hanne and Sissel slept deeply on the hotel bed and woke refreshed.

Sissel grabbed her wrapped parcels from the dry goods emporium and tore open the paper.

"Oh, Hanne! Can you imagine? Real American clothes, made on a machine!"

She had slept in her new shift. Now she pulled on her new wool stockings.

"Oooh, these are heavenly!" Sissel cried. "Hanne, wait until you feel them!"

Hanne opened her packages more carefully, setting aside the brown paper for some future use.

She shook out her new skirt with pleasure and ran her fingertips over the machine-sewed seams. They were so flat and even.

There was a looking glass in the main hall. After the girls had dressed, they went downstairs to the mirror. They could not help but gawk at themselves. Hanne had plaited Sissel's hair, and Sissel had returned the favor. Their old hairstyles were the only thing about them that looked familiar.

Hanne glanced at herself in the voluminous white shirt, buttoned up to the throat, and the tight-waisted skirt. If she glanced at her image from a distance, she might have mistaken herself for an American.

Sissel marveled at her reflection. "Isn't it terribly odd, to be without an apron!" she said.

In Norway they wore them every day—work aprons or dress aprons with elaborate embroidery. The ones they'd lost in their trunk had been worked on over several long winters.

"Look at us," Sissel said. "We're Americans! The only thing we're missing are boots and bonnets."

Hanne looked again at her reflection in the wavy mirror. Her forehead looked too large, and her eyes enormous and too solemn. She looked serious and plain.

How odd it was, she thought, that she could feel such strong emotion inside, but look so sedate and benign? She was the most dangerous person in the hotel, but no one would give her a second glance.

"Do you like the way we look? I like the way we look," Sissel said.

Hanne turned this way and that, making her heavy skirt sway. She thought of Owen. What would he make of their transformation? What was such a small thing for some, merely a change of clothes, was for Hanne and Sissel a grand, sweeping change. They had never worn clothes made by a stranger's hand. Never worn fabric not spun and woven within ten miles of their home. Would the cowboy even notice the difference?

"So?" Sissel pressed.

"I like it well enough," Hanne said.

It was foolishness to think he would notice the way she looked, and foolishness that she should care if he did.

THERE WAS NO ONE in the lobby of the hotel, though they could hear the workers making breakfast in the kitchen at the back of the hotel.

Stieg and Knut were waiting for them.

"You look so pretty," Knut told them.

Hanne waved the compliment away. "Let's get out of here before anyone comes down."

The Loveland General Stores wasn't open, but there was a man moving about near the back shelves, and when they rapped on the glass he let them in.

It was a cluttered, wonderful store. Every inch of the walls was stacked with tins or loaded with tools. Large barrels on the floor held wheat flour and graham, oats and barley. Smaller tins of light brown sugar and sparkling white "visiting" sugar stood on shelves. There were harnesses, too, and some farm tools. Hanne tried not to gaze longingly at the boots.

"Oh, look at the treasure boxes, Hanne!" Sissel said. There was a display case with beautiful porcelain jewel boxes inside. There were silver brooches as well, and even a silver-backed brush and mirror set.

"Can you imagine?" Sissel said, with desire rich in her voice. "Oh, I want a set like that someday!"

Hanne looked down into the glass case. Her first instinct was to chide Sissel for wanting such lavish, costly things, but she could not bear to puncture the elevated mood.

Hanne sighed. She had been right about the clothes; they had returned her sister to her chatty self. Hanne wondered if she might miss the sullen Sissel, who was somewhat more quiet than this one.

The door opened, and Owen came in with a cold gust of wind. He wore his hat and had his rifle slung over his poncho.

Owen touched the brim of his hat at her. Hanne rested her fingers on the top of the glass cabinet and nodded back. She found her chest tight when he drew near.

If he noticed their new clothing, he did not indicate it.

Stieg and Knut were looking at coats, to see if one might fit Knut. They had already picked up Knut's new clothes from the seamstress. His new pants and jacket were fitted closer than Hanne had made his other clothes. He cut a fine figure, muscular and broad shouldered.

Owen spoke to Stieg. "I picked out horses," he said. "If you and I can step over to the livery, I'll let you settle up for them."

"Good morning," Loveland, the shopkeeper, greeted Owen. "More sandwiches?" He winked.

Owen ducked his head, with a small, bashful shake no.

"Truth be told, we're gearing up for a bit of a ride," he told the shopkeeper. "We need two weeks' worth of victuals. Beans, flour, salt pork, coffee."

"Victuals!" Stieg said. "I like that word."

Owen turned to Hanne.

"Can you get started here with the foodstuff while we settle at the livery?"

"Yes," she said.

"Good." He paused and scratched his ear. "Are you . . . um, how do I put this . . . miss, can you cook?"

"Yes. Of course. I can do everything." She felt her face flush. Those words hadn't come out the way she'd wanted. She meant to say, she knew how to clean game, and roast it, as well as bake.

Owen nodded. He didn't seem to know what to say, either, so he turned on his heel and crossed back over to Stieg.

The three men left, and Hanne and Sissel selected goods. Loveland had a fair hand. Hanne watched him with his scales. He sold them the supplies Owen had mentioned, as well as hard-tack, which faintly resembled their own *flatbrød*, but was much harder and less crispy. Loveland said it would keep for up to two months.

He sold them a cast-iron spider—a pot with a long handle and three legs that you could sit directly in a campfire. He also recommended a dutch oven, and explained how she could fill it with beans and set it into the fire, then heap coals on top of it.

The shopkeeper provided small sacks of flour, cornmeal, and beans. The beans were different from the dried beans they had at home—bigger and light brown, instead of white, but Hanne assumed beans were beans.

The coffee beans were put through a grinder, and the dark, heavenly smell filled the store.

Hanne also bought a pound of light brown sugar and a small bag of dried apples. She even purchased a small loaf of butter. It was cold enough that it would keep if they packed it away from the heat of the horse's body.

When the men came back, Owen nodded with approval at the items Hanne had selected. She tsked at herself inwardly that his praise should please her.

It was a large pile, and when Hanne wondered how on earth they would get it all onto their horses, Stieg mentioned they'd bought a pack mule for that very reason.

"Oh, wait until you see the horses," Stieg said. "Sure enough, Mr. Bennett has bought us the finest mounts to be had in town."

"Please, I'm Owen."

"Very well," Stieg said. He clapped his hands. "What else do we need, Owen?"

"How're you set for bedrolls?" Loveland asked. "I've got some good wool blankets, and down pillows."

Hanne looked at Owen. Pillows? That seemed an unnecessary luxury, but she didn't want to speak against him.

Owen shook his head. "We won't be lugging pillows around. And as for bedrolls, I bought some secondhand at the livery."

"All righty," Loveland said amiably. He could hardly be upset with their business; they were buying such an awful lot at once.

Owen gave their outer gear a look-over. He was satisfied with the coats Hanne and Sissel had selected. Stieg had purchased a good, stiff coat as well. But they were at a loss as for what to do for Knut. None of the coats fit his large frame.

Owen selected two thick blankets for Knut and had Loveland cut a slit in the center with his good, sharp shears. These were improvised ponchos, second-class cousins to the one he wore himself. He made Knut wear both the blankets at once.

Owen added two canvas tents to the large pile on the counter.

Then he bought himself a sturdy oilskin coat, the type cowboys seemed to favor. He patted it with a look of private satisfaction.

"Do you and your brother need rifles?" Owen asked Stieg.

Stieg, Hanne was interested to see, grew flustered.

"We don't . . . I don't know how to shoot," he confessed.

"Really?" Owen asked. He seemed genuinely nonplussed. "Aren't there dangers in Norway?"

"The dangers come mostly from men," Stieg said. "And better not to go about shooting men, I suppose."

Owen shrugged. "Guess not," he said.

"What about hunting?"

"Mostly we fish," Stieg said.

"I see."

Owen had his own rifle in hand. Hanne supposed he hadn't wanted to leave it outside, where it might get stolen. How odd that a man should become accustomed to carrying a rifle with him everywhere he went.

OUTSIDE, THE TOWN was coming to life. Hanne could hear carpenters banging on a new building down the main street, and the breakfast bell was ringing at the nearest hotel.

Near the blacksmith's shop, a young farmer bringing an old swayback horse to be shod passed by. He eyed Hanne, and her heart froze for a moment, thinking he might mean them harm, but then he doffed his hat. Hanne realized he might have been paying her a compliment. It was an odd feeling. She nodded to him shyly, feeling silly.

"We should be off," Stieg said.

"Yup," Owen said, making last adjustments to the saddlebags. He straightened up his back and turned to face them all. "I just wanted to say, before we go, we're a smart group, and as long as everyone does what I tell them, we should make it to Wolf Creek within a week."

Hanne watched him intently, her head tilted to the side. He was making a speech. It was endearing, to her, that he felt they might require such a formality.

"We'll rotate the horses, so don't get too attached to your steed. This way, they'll each get a chance to rest."

His eyes flickered toward Knut's bulky frame.

"All right. That's enough of a speech, I guess. Who needs a hand up on their horse?" Only Sissel took him up on his offer.

And then they were on their way out of Livingston, and Hanne was glad for it.

THEY HEADED NORTH, following a road for a few miles. When the road branched in two directions, they took the narrower one, which led up into the foothills of a mountain range. The tufts of spiky prairie grass were dead and brown; that didn't stop the gelding Hanne was riding from swiping at mouthfuls as they passed. The horse was dun colored, actually the same color as the grass, and had the improbable name of Joyful. It was sullen and stubborn, and seemed about as far from joyful as an animal could be.

Owen rode at the head, and because there was enough space on the road, Sissel rode right next to him. Hanne came next, and Knut and Stieg rode side by side behind her. Daisy ranged ahead and fell back, always staying within eyesight, and keeping well out of the way of the horses' hooves.

Sissel remained fearful of Owen's black-and-white dog. This seemed silly to Hanne. There wasn't a more pleasant or gentle dog than Daisy. She took obvious delight in the trip, frisking around like a puppy.

Hanne looked behind them every so often, worried the man from the train might be coming after them. Once, Stieg caught her turning and shook his head subtly. He nodded for her to keep her eyes on the road ahead. Hanne supposed that Stieg didn't want Owen clued in that being trailed was a concern.

Was it right to keep the danger from Owen Bennett? Maybe not, but how could they possibly explain their predicament to him? No, best to mention nothing.

From time to time they met other travelers headed to town. There were several wagons loaded with goods to sell. And they overtook one man carrying a bleating yearling lamb on his shoulders, apparently heading home with his prize. He was whistling a jaunty tune and looked very pleased with his new charge.

As they rode, Sissel pestered the cowboy with chatter nonstop. Her sister kept up a steady stream of questions in halting English, and he kept answering, to be polite.

So far, Sissel had pried out of him that he was born and raised in Montana. He had three brothers, no sisters. He had raised Daisy from a pup.

"Is it good to be a cowboy?" she asked him now. "You like to cowboy?"

"Yep," Owen said. "It's always changing—that's something I like about it. In the spring, you're rounding up the horses, branding the colts. There's horse breaking to do then. Once the ranch boss decides how many head of cattle he wants to send to market in the fall, then there's rounding up and driving to market."

Sissel nodded and said, "yes," and "I see," as if she could understand his cowboy English. Hanne was certain she could not.

"Your brothers are cowboys?"

"Two of them are. One's still too young. He's in school. We all had to go to school till we were sixteen. Then my father made us each give two years to the ranch. But once we reach eighteen, we're free to go and that's what I did."

"And your brothers? They leave with you?"

The cowboy shook his head.

"No."

"No?" Sissel repeated.

"No. My brothers, well, they all want the ranch so they have to stay on and try to outdo each other. Me, it was better for me to head out."

"Goodness, Sissel," Hanne said in Norwegian. "Don't be a busybody!"

"My sister says I ask too much," Sissel told Owen.

"Well, maybe you can tell me something about you all," he said. "How did you all come to be in America?"

Now Sissel fell silent.

"We came to start a new life," Hanne offered. "Our brother Stieg—"

"Our father died," Sissel interrupted her. "He was killed, so we came away."

Hanne sat back, as if stung. It was the truth, but the way her sister said it was so frank.

Joyful gave a snort.

Owen glanced over his shoulder at Hanne. She looked down to the reins balled in her fist.

"I'm sorry to hear that," Owen said. "Must have been real rough."

"Yes," Sissel said. "It was frightful. And now we are going to find our uncle Håkon. We will live with him now."

"What can you tell me about these meadow grasses, Owen?" Stieg called up from the rear. "Do they make good feed for horses?"

Hanne wasn't sure if Stieg was trying to cut off Sissel's conversation, or if he was just jealous that Sissel was getting such a good chance to practice her English, but she was glad he broke in. Hanne was so irritated with her sister she half wished Sissel's horse would spook and gallop off into the wilderness.

* * *

THEY HAD FOLLOWED the wagon-wheel road through the low rocky hills for most of the morning, stopping at a small stream to water the horses at noon and to eat their own lunch—some sandwiches that Loveland had thrown in for free when it came time to settle their bill.

Stieg had made small talk about the weather and the vegetation during lunch. Owen answered politely enough, asking questions in return about the climate of Norway.

Hanne was shy of speaking in front of the cowboy now. It was not a pleasure trip—they were not there to tour the sights of Montana. She wished everyone would just stop talking and eat.

Owen made time at lunch to try to get Sissel used to Daisy. After the meal was over, he asked Sissel if she'd like to give Daisy her meal. He had saved a half a sandwich for the dog. Sissel refused, eyeing the dog from behind Hanne.

Owen then set Daisy through some drills and tricks. He finished by having Daisy jump up and take the sandwich from his own mouth.

Sissel laughed and clapped at that.

Hanne smiled at Owen, trying to make her gratitude known. He ducked his head and called out it was time to start up again.

The road became more and more rutted and bumpy the farther they got from town. Slowly, they were climbing up, into the low mountains. Above them, there was more and more snow, banked in drifts against the hillside.

Hanne's afternoon steed was a black mare who seemed indifferent to the journey. She neither tried to sneak grass, nor did she show any interest in Hanne, nor the scents in the air, but kept her head down and walked patiently after Pal.

Hanne was looking down at the rose color of her coat and thinking of not much at all, when Daisy barked ahead frantically and Owen urged his horse into a sudden gallop. He reached for his rifle and had it out of the scabbard in seconds.

There was a voice. She heard it now, coming from over the next rise in the road. "Oh dear Lord! Help!" came a man's voice.

Owen's horse, Pal, galloped ahead as Hanne and her siblings tried to get their horses to speed up. The horses responded with no more than a lazy canter, but after a moment they came up and over the hilltop. At the bottom of the valley below, they saw an overturned wagon. An ox stood some distance off, uninjured.

A man was trying to lift the wagon—another man was trapped underneath! Owen jumped off Pal and ran over to the wagon. He got his hands under it and strained, trying to budge it.

"Can you help us?" Owen shouted to Knut and Stieg as they rode up and dismounted.

"Stand back!" Stieg shouted as Knut bent and lifted the wagon clear off the ground. Beneath the layers of clothing, Knut's vast muscles strained and pulled.

Owen exclaimed with surprise, but Stieg tugged him forward. Stieg and Owen ducked under the wagon and pulled the injured man free. He screamed with pain, then passed out.

Instead of setting the wagon down, as they all expected him to do, Knut shifted its weight in his hands, lifting it and turning it in the air, so that it fell back to earth righted.

The wagon jounced on its iron springs, the metal jangling as it came to rest.

The man who'd been calling for help stared up at Knut, his mouth agape.

"Lord Almighty," he said. "Is you part giant?"

Knut was staring at his hands with an odd expression of wonder on his face. He looked up and beamed at them all.

"My brother is uncommonly strong," Stieg said. Then, trying to distract them, "Is your friend well?"

Now all attention turned to the wounded man. He lay on the frozen ground, his skin gray and clammy.

Blood soaked through the leg of his pants, and the bone, snapped cleanly, was jutting through the fabric.

"Aw jeez," the other man moaned. "Hal! Oh Lord. Look at that leg! Oh God, what am I going to do?" He pulled at his hair, looking down at his fallen partner. "Lookit the blood! Oh Lord! That's bone!"

"It's all right. Calm down," Owen said. "If we can set the leg, he'll be all right."

"He's my younger cousin, and I promised his mother no harm would befall him! Oh Lord, what am I gonna do?" He paused to vomit into some scrub.

"Do you know how to do this kind of thing?" Owen asked Stieg. "I've seen it done, but I've never done it."

Stieg looked a bit pale, and so did Owen, truth be told. Hanne stepped forward.

"Knut, come," she directed. "You hold his shoulders, and I'll set the bone."

"You?" Owen asked.

"Yes. Me." She shrugged. "I'm not afraid of blood."

She wanted to explain that she and Knut butchered livestock back home, but at the same time, she did not want him to know about her expertise in this area, it was so unladylike. But she did not have time to waste on such niceties—the man was passed out, and she should set his leg before he woke up.

Knut sat behind the injured man, and shifted back and forth on his haunches until he drew up right behind him. He wrapped his arms around the man's torso, pinning his arms to his sides. Hanne knelt down beside them.

"He may wake up, so hold him well," Hanne told Knut. She put her hands on the man's lower leg, feeling around until she was satisfied with the grip.

"I'll hold tight," Knut said.

"On three," she said. Then she counted it out and pulled.

The man's eyes flew open. He screamed and thrashed. He kicked at her, landing a good blow to her upper arm. Her Nytte flared to life, but faintly.

Owen darted forward and grabbed the man's good leg so he would not kick her again.

She pulled hard and gently rotated the leg. There was an audible click as the pieces of bone lined up. The man shrieked.

Hanne released the leg, and the man fainted away again.

She exhaled and sat back. Owen was next to her, his thigh pressed into hers. She was breathing hard, sweat prickling her brow.

She glanced up and found Owen studying her face. He quickly looked away, down to the man sprawled on the ground.

"We ought to splint the leg," Owen said.

Hanne nodded. She pushed back from the man and stood up, shaky on her feet. Her new skirt was dirty with mud and dead grass. Never mind, she told herself, it had to get soiled eventually.

Stieg cut some strips of canvas out of a sack that had been in the wagon. They bound the leg, loosely, to a plank that had broken off in the accident. Sissel remained on her horse the whole time. Hanne wasn't sure if it was because she was afraid to dismount without help or was still shy of the dog.

The wounded man's partner had recovered his wits enough to be thankful for the help that Providence had brought him. He kept up a steady stream of thanks, to them and mostly to the Lord. Knut loaded up the goods that had fallen from the wagon while Owen jerry-rigged the broken harness and got the ox hooked up. When the wagon was ready again, Hanne held the wounded man's leg steady as Knut carefully lifted him into the wagon bed.

The men would reach Livingston by evening, and they could see the doctor there. Hanne wondered what tales the men might tell. Would they speak of a great Norse boy who could lift a wagon by himself? Might one of their countrymen overhear and become interested? Or the man from the train?

Hanne was impatient to be on the way again. Soon enough, they returned to the road.

Owen became silent and pensive as they rode, pulling out ahead a bit. Hanne turned her mind from the men who might be following them to the one leading them.

Surely he must be glad they were able to be helpful. That man would have died had they not come along. Or was he wondering about Knut's strength and Hanne's ability to set a limb so easily?

She could not tell what he was thinking by his posture, and she could not summon the courage to ride up, so she simply watched his back sway in the saddle and wondered.

CHAPTER SIXTEEN

Mr. Erlich was not amused by his visitors.

"It's dark and I'm tired. I already told you what I know. Time for you to git!"

The old man had finished checking the doors on the paddocks of his livery stable and was shutting down for the night. The horses were quiet, munching on hay inside the stalls. The only light came from a smoky oil lantern that he held in his hand.

Rolf stood near him, Ketil at the door.

"Are you sure they didn't mention the name of the town?" Rolf asked again.

"They offered a young cowboy with a busted-up face some money to take them up north. That's all I know."

"Was it one of the Norwegians who hurt the cowboy?" Ketil asked. "Did you see it happen?"

"I don't know who busted him up! He was already busted up when I met him!"

He hung the lantern ring over a nail and tugged on one of the stall doors to make sure it was closed firmly.

From the shopkeeper at one of the general stores they had learned that the Nytteson were now outfitted for a major trip. They might have learned more if Ketil had not frightened the shopkeeper's thirteen-year-old girl by trying to flirt with her. After that, the shopkeeper, who seemed a decent man, had all but escorted them to the door.

"It's time for you all to go on, now!" Erlich said.

Ketil grabbed his arm and squeezed.

"I told you what I know!" the old man whined.

"Has anyone else been asking for them?" Rolf asked.

"No! They're just a bunch of kids, for God's sake. Why are *you* two looking for them, anyway?"

"Never you mind that," Ketil said, releasing the man.

Rolf walked toward the door and Ketil followed him.

Behind them, a gob of brown tobacco-juice spit smacked the planks and splashed onto the back of Ketil's trouser leg.

"Good riddance," Erlich said.

Ketil was across the room in two strides.

"No!" Rolf shouted, but Ketil kicked up a shovel and caught it neatly.

He hit a glancing blow to the old man's head. A measured blow, just enough to fell him. Then he chopped with the blade of the shovel, and with one fast, savage slash, he severed the man's head.

For a moment, no blood erupted.

"See!" Ketil called. "I've been working on this. It's a crimping blow."

Then the flesh parted, and the blood gushed out onto the floorboards.

"It doesn't last long, but it's getting there." Ketil looked very pleased. The blood seeped into the sawdust. "And to think it even works with a dull old shovel!"

Ketil turned back to Rolf, his eyes shining.

"He was no risk to us!" Rolf exclaimed.

"He could have told someone we'd been here, asking for the Nytteson. And he could have told someone else what he knew about them. With that article in *Morgenbladet*, Norwegians will be searching them out."

"It was an unnecessary death!" Rolf protested. He felt sick to his stomach. The blood was gushing all over the floor.

"He was an old, ugly man. And I needed the practice. This is boring work."

Ketil looked like a child, a petulant pout twisting his mustache. Inside the stalls, the horses made sounds of distress. They smelled the blood.

Rolf tried to swallow his anger, but his weariness and frustration got the better of him.

"The last thing we need is a posse on our trail! Do you not think?" He slammed his palm onto a post. "Why in the name of Odin All-Father did I allow the Baron to saddle me with a Berserker?"

Ketil went deadly still.

"Come now, Rolfy. You don't mean to insult me, do you?" Ketil said.

Ketil stared at him across the dim stable, menace glimmering in his eyes.

Rolf lowered his gaze. He could not afford to antagonize this young man. "It's just that . . . you can control your gift. I know you can. And you must. You must work at it."

"Yes, yes. You've told me before all about your ideas of how I should control the Nytte. Use it to honor the Gods. Surrender to the Gods. But your ideas amount to very little, since you, Rolf Tjossem, are not a Nytteson," Ketil said.

Rolf rubbed the back of his neck. He moved toward the front window and looked outside. "What do we do about the body? Do you think the local authorities will not care about a murder in their town?"

"Relax. There are hogs out back. They'll dispose of the body for us."

Rolf looked across the dimly lit barn at his partner. Ketil was studying the corpse, pleased with the kill. He looked up, grinning. "It was an awfully dull shovel."

Rolf gritted his teeth in irritation.

"You have to admit it was a pretty blow," Ketil said, trying for a bit of praise, perhaps.

Someone pounded on the front door. Ketil reached for the shovel. Rolf held his arm.

"Erlich, you in there, you old, deaf bastard?"

The voice outside sounded weak and drunk. After a moment, shuffling steps retreated outside the door.

"We've got to get out of here, and quietly," Rolf said.

"What about the body?" Ketil asked.

"Leave it. We cannot hide the blood. It was dark when we came in. We will have to hope no one saw us enter."

They had not been able to find a coach or stage the evening before, so had spent the night in Bozeman. After the long ride in the morning and a day of questioning the storekeepers in town, and now this pointless murder, Rolf was exhausted and disheartened. Barely able to keep his eyes open.

"My friend, you look worn out," Ketil said. He sighed theatrically. "I look forward to a hot meal and a soft bed. And maybe a soft lady, too. If they keep some in stock here."

"Keep your wits about you," Rolf snapped. "This is no time to be womanizing."

They exited the stable's back doors and walked quietly down the alley behind. Seeing the shabby backsides of the false fronts of the buildings added to Rolf's dark mood. They made him think of the way men sometimes combed their hair to cover thin spots. They fooled no one. Livingston was a small town, full of small buildings. And now it was poorer by one man.

"In the morning we will inquire of a few more businesses, then we will depart," Rolf said. "The law will not connect us to this man's death unless we flee as if we're guilty."

"Ah, well, why don't you go knocking while I have a bit of a lie-in?"

Rolf glared at his companion. Ketil smiled back.

"The Baron will be so disappointed to hear we've lost the

Nytteson," Ketil said. "But as long as I'm getting up early, I might as well telegraph him and let him know."

"I see no need to trouble him," Rolf said. "We can telegraph him once we've found them."

Ketil slapped Rolf on the back. He was grinning in a way Rolf did not like.

"You sleep in tomorrow," Rolf said. "In fact, why don't you wait for me here in Livingston and I'll go find them myself?"

Ketil shook his head.

"I have my orders, Tjossem. To keep an eye on you and make sure you don't screw this up."

Rolf stopped in his tracks.

"You have it wrong, Ketil. The Baron Fjelstad made it very clear. You are here to learn how to reach out to the Nytteson, to offer them hope and protection," Rolf said.

Ketil swung around and stood right up against Rolf's body. He was half a head taller and spoke down at him.

"So he told *you*. But I think perhaps you do not know the Baron as well as you think you do," Ketil said. Then he laughed and slugged Rolf on the shoulder. "Come on," he said. "I'm terribly hungry. My Nytte demands a steak."

CHAPTER SEVENTEEN

O h, how they ached when they at last fell out of their saddles at the end of the day.

Owen had found them a flat campsite near a clear gurgling stream, with snow on the banks. The aspen trees that bordered it had tall white trunks. Their yellow leaves still clung to the branches and fluttered in the air, though there was only a hint of a breeze.

"How many miles would you say we covered today?" Stieg asked, stretching.

"Round about fifteen, I should think. Given our late start. Tomorrow we'll aim for twenty," Owen answered. He deftly unloaded the mule. First came the tents, then the bedrolls. Owen carried his own bedroll on Pal and did not use a tent.

Knut rubbed his sore bottom unabashedly.

"Knut and Stieg, if you can scare up some kindling and wood, I'll get a fire going."

Hanne walked over to Owen. After the day's long ride, her legs had forgotten the feel of earth underfoot. She took the sack of beans from him. He handed her a slab of salt pork, wrapped in a piece of brown paper. And then the cornmeal.

Hanne thought about what she could make. Beans would take too long, but she could soak them for the next morning's meal.

They had a bucket. A shiny new tin bucket and a coffeepot just as nice. Hanne took them to the stream. The water was clear and fresh looking. It reminded her of the glacial streams back home.

Returning to the campsite, she saw Owen had cleared a small depression in the earth and was arranging kindling for their fire.

Owen looked up at her and nodded. "I'll have it ready soon," he told her.

Hanne put the coffeepot near the fire and set the bucket down. She scooped some water into a pie tin and began to stir in cornmeal, a handful at a time, with a fork. She added a pinch of salt. She would try her hand at some *pannekaker*. She wished they had some milk, but water would have to do. The batter seemed awfully coarse, so she added some of their flour, and sweetened the batter with some brown sugar.

The cowboy had not mentioned anything about Knut's heroics during the accident. Hanne hoped that he had simply attributed Knut's strength to his large size, and did not suspect them of anything unnatural.

He had enough to be suspicious of them already—he knew they had jumped off a train and were determined to stay away from people.

The fire was burning now, so she put a precious pat of their butter into the spider. Once it melted, she spooned it out and into the batter, stirring it well.

The camp was busy, Owen showing Knut how to set out the bedrolls and Stieg puttering over the coffeepot.

Out of the corner of her eye, Hanne saw Sissel pet Daisy. This was progress. Hanne didn't turn quickly, didn't want to spook the child or the animal, but she was happy to see her sister engaging with the dog.

As she tried to turn the cakes in the spider with only a fork, Hanne longed for her long wooden spatula from home. Nevertheless, she managed to flip them. Hanne wished she had purchased molasses. How could she have forgotten molasses? She sprinkled a bit of sugar on the cakes and gave each a small pat of butter. The group ate from the remaining pie tins she had collected, and there were no complaints. Even Daisy, who only got the burned pieces, seemed content.

As they drank their coffee, Stieg asked Owen if he knew the story of the pancake. Owen did not, and so Stieg told the old folktale, recounting the rolling pancake and his clever escapes from Manny Panny, Henny Penny, Goosey Poosey, and the rest.

Hanne watched Owen's face. In the glimmering firelight, some of the age and experience seemed to fall away. He looked much younger, and was rapt with attention at Stieg's silly story. He laughed when Piggy Wiggy gobbled up the runaway pancake at the end of the story. Sissel and Knut laughed along with him.

Hanne observed that her sister's eyes were lit up with admiration for Owen.

She felt a stab of possessiveness. The idea that she herself wanted to make a claim on the cowboy startled her so much she stood up abruptly. She turned and clumsily sought out the tin bucket among the kitchen items, her skirts knocking her pie tin off the rock where it had been sitting.

"Hanne?" Stieg asked.

"Nothing. I must fetch water to soak the beans, that's all."

"Beans for breakfast and pancakes for dinner," Knut said in Norwegian. "Our food is backward!"

Stieg translated for Owen. Hanne heard their laughter as she set off toward the stream in the dark.

She slowed her pace as she approached the stream. She did not want to make a further fool of herself by falling in the cold water.

The moon was only a sliver. The sky was so black it seemed clean and fresh, and the stars were bright. Was the sky so big at home? It must have been, for it was the same sky.

"Pretty dark out here." She jumped at Owen's voice behind her. "I brought a lantern. Wouldn't do to lose you our first night on the trail."

"Yes," she answered. "It is dark."

Hanne felt nervous and reluctant. It wasn't proper for her to be alone with this strange boy. They ought to have a chaperone. Only that was how they did it in Norway, and they were no longer there. Maybe in America it was acceptable for a young woman to be alone with a young man.

Anyway, she was not in any danger. That was certain.

"I can get the water if you like," Owen offered.

"I can do it," she said. But she didn't want to send him away. "Can you hold the lantern toward the stream?"

"Sure," he answered.

He held the lantern forward, and together they picked their way across the slippery rocks at the edge of the stream.

Hanne settled the bucket into the icy water.

"I wanted to say something. I wanted to thank you for taking the job of being our guide," Hanne said.

Owen made a dismissive noise.

"It's my pleasure," he replied.

Hanne stood up with the bucket, now streaming water. Owen put his hand on the handle, next to hers. A warm current traveled up Hanne's arm, and she realized their fingers were touching.

"Let me carry it for you," he said. When she withdrew her hand, the bucket was transferred to Owen's firm grip.

"Yes," she said. "Very well."

"And, Miss Hanne, you don't have to thank me."

Hanne glanced at his face. In the dark, his bruises didn't show so much. The light from the lantern fell on his strong jawline and the shape of his lips.

He was a handsome young man, it could not be denied. She wondered what it would be like to kiss him.

It was dark, but did she see his eyes flickering toward her own lips? Was he leaning in to her, ever so slightly?

"I'm glad . . . that is to say . . ." He paused here, and the pause made her heart rise up in her rib cage. He regained speech. "I'm grateful for the work," he said.

He looked to the bucket.

The work. Of course he was grateful for the work. Nothing but the work.

"And, uh, Miss Hanne, just so you know. There's mountain lions up here," Owen said. Hanne realized now that he had his long rifle tucked under his arm. "So if you're going to go out in the dark, it's best to have company."

"Very well," she said stiffly.

Of course he would think her a defenseless girl who would need his help to stay safe. A part of her wished it were so.

Hanne took the lantern and led the way back to the campsite.

CHAPTER EIGHTEEN

Owen had wondered if they'd complain or give him trouble, but the Norwegians were the easiest company he'd ever known. They exclaimed over the cleverness of every little thing. The protective coil on the handle of the cast-iron spider was ingenious. The tents, which came with a canvas bottom to keep mud out. And the bedrolls—made of a large rectangle of canvas that lay flat, with blankets layered inside—what a marvel! Even the tin bucket was fussed over. Sissel had admired how shiny it was. For all their stake money, these were people who weren't accustomed to new things.

Owen worried about the weather, which was turning colder each day. In the morning, the water in the bucket had two fingers of ice on it. If it got any colder, he'd have to ask the boys if he could bunk with them in their tent, though he preferred to sleep out in the air with Daisy at his feet.

Owen kept an eye out for blizzards, watching for any change of color, but the sky was big and blue. By the third morning of clear weather, Stieg teased him about fretting like a mother hen.

The Hemstads were a genial and hardy bunch. The few Swedes and Norwegians he'd met had been quiet and serious. But maybe they'd just not had a knack for the tongue. Stieg's English put his own to shame. He kept them all amused on the trail, and Owen found himself learning, too. He'd never known that cloud formations had names. Stieg pointed them out. Stieg's favorite clouds were the great, fluffy cumulus clouds. Sissel liked nimbus just for the name. Hanne said she liked the wavy cirrocumulus clouds. She said they reminded her of sea foam. Owen hadn't ever thought to pick a favorite, but he chose cirrocumulus. He'd never seen sea foam, but he liked the way Hanne made it sound.

Owen could not help but admire her. Hanne worked harder than either of her brothers. She was the first up in the morning, was the first down from the saddle, the first to haul water. She did all the cooking and washed the dishes. Sissel was pleasant enough, but she was a lazy girl. She only helped when nagged, and Hanne had clearly stopped nagging some time ago. Sissel reminded Owen of his younger brother, Paul. Perhaps all youngest children were spoiled.

Unfortunately Hanne would not meet Owen's eye. She avoided him, even on the trail, and kept her horse toward the back.

Owen knew it had to do with how he'd behaved on the first night, at the stream. He'd offended her somehow, but he didn't have any idea how. Likely she could sense his interest in her and was simply letting him know she didn't return the sentiment.

And why should she think of him, he reminded himself. He was broke—anyone could see that. His prospects were lean. She had the sense to steer clear of him, so that should have made it easy, but it didn't.

Hanne looked awfully pretty in her pink coat. Against the drab tree trunks, the black rocks, and the dingy, dust-blown snowbanks, that coat offered a welcome burst of color. The color reminded Owen of one of the songbirds that used to riot over dried corncobs the cook would set on a nail outside the kitchen window back on the ranch.

He wished he knew their story, wished he could ask more about what type of work Knut did back in Norway that would make him so strong—or how Hanne came to know how to set a bone so well, but he could not bring himself to ask. Owen told himself he was respecting their privacy—for obviously there was something weighing heavily on the Norwegians. There was trouble riding with the Hemstads, and he meant to keep level with it, but he didn't want to disturb the easy camaraderie they were enjoying. It had been a long time since he'd felt a part of a group in this way, if ever.

THEY WERE COMING down the north side of the Horseshoe Mountain lowlands when Owen called an early finish for the day. He didn't like to travel downhill in the twilight. Too easy for a tired horse to place a foot wrong.

Also, he'd seen some rabbit tracks and he thought everyone would like a little fresh meat. It would be nice to walk into camp with a couple of big jackrabbits.

He stopped near a big drift of snow, which they could use for water, so they wouldn't have to go down to the stream. It was a nice protected spot, with a slate shoulder on one side to break the wind.

"This'll do for camp," Owen said.

"Yes? We are stopping early today?" asked Stieg.

Owen nodded.

"When will we be to Wolf Creek?" Sissel asked.

Owen removed his hat and scratched his head. He was aware that his hair was matted down and greasy, but that could hardly be helped.

"I'd say we're three days out, if the weather holds," Owen told them. "Maybe less."

"Come, Sissel," Hanne said. She had sprung from her horse and was helping her sister down.

"I wonder if Uncle Håkon will be excited to see us," Sissel said.

Hanne began to unpack the provisions for their evening meal. She asked something in Norwegian, and Knut set off into the brush. She'd asked him to get firewood, Owen figured.

"I'm going to see after some meat for dinner," Owen said. Then he called Daisy, "To me!"

Daisy was at his heel in an instant, tail wagging though it had been a long day's journey.

"I'll see if I can't scare up some rabbit," Owen said.

"Take Hanne with you," Stieg said. "She's good at hunting, too."

Hanne looked at her brother, a flash of surprise playing on her features. She said something in Norwegian. It was clear to Owen that she didn't want to go.

"It's all right, Miss Hanne," Owen said. He felt a blush threatening at his neck. "You don't need to come. Me and Daisy will be right back."

"WHY WOULD YOU press me to go?" Hanne said, rounding on Stieg when Owen was out of hearing. "It's not proper he and I should be alone!"

"Pah, you are safe from him and from any man," Stieg said. "I thought it would do you some good to stretch your legs."

"I have enough to do with supper to get," she said.

"Why don't you like him?" Stieg asked. "He's trustworthy. He's a good fellow."

"You don't like Owen?" Sissel said. "I think he's lovely. I think he's very brave."

"I never said I don't like him!"

"You act as though he's beneath your notice," Stieg said. "You hardly say two words to him in a day's time."

"That's not so."

"It is, too. Stieg's right," Sissel said. "Owen must think you hate him."

Hanne stared at her sister and brother. Stieg was digging out a fire pit a few feet away from the snowbank at the stone wall.

"Do you really think so, Stieg?" she asked him. She felt bad if it was true. "Or are you teasing me?"

Stieg looked up, attention drawn by the serious tone of her voice.

Knut came back with an armload of fallen branches.

"Do you think Owen feels I dislike him?" she asked Knut.

Knut dropped the wood. "Why would he? You like him, don't you?"

"It's not a problem, I don't think," Stieg interrupted. "He's never seen you happy. He probably thinks you're like this all the time. It doesn't matter. I wouldn't worry about it."

Hanne felt herself get hot in the chest.

It did matter, to her.

"I have more important things to worry about," she said crossly. "That man from the train—"

"Is nowhere to be seen, Hanne," said Stieg. "Your own body will sound an alarm if we are in any danger. Why don't you relax? It is possible we have left the danger behind."

He could be optimistic, she brooded. *He* was not weighed down with sin.

Hanne began to unpack the supplies from the mule, whom they had eventually named "Muley Wuley" after Stieg's story.

Her hands fell on the small sack of dried apples. She would make an apple cake in the Dutch oven—a nice cake to go with the meat, if Owen should be successful in his hunting. She could be amiable and gracious. She would show them.

It pained her to use the last of the butter, but a cake wouldn't be any good without it. They could do without butter for the next three days, certainly.

OWEN AND DAISY returned with two skinned creatures so long Hanne could scarcely believe they were rabbits. Owen said he'd seen lots of tracks down at the river and set some traps, so there would likely be more in the morning.

Hanne spit-roasted the hares over the fire. And her cake smelled wonderful as it cooled in the dutch oven. She made a point to be pleasant to everyone, especially Owen.

Around them, night fell. The light from the fire was shining off their faces as they drew close to the campfire. Grease from the rabbit meat made their faces shinier still. Hanne hazarded a smile across the fire at Owen. He seemed surprised, but answered it with a grin.

But then it was time to serve the apple cake, and it was stuck in the Dutch oven. It would not come out except in soggy, crumbly chunks.

She was mortified, but Knut chopped out a portion of the lumpy mess, plopped it onto his plate, and smiled so broadly at the smell of the steaming mush that they all broke into laughter.

Hanne saw Stieg watching her laugh. She saw he was glad for her. It multiplied her happiness, somehow. Their spat was forgotten.

"To Hanne!" Stieg said, toasting with his tin mug of coffee. "And the worst apple cake in Montana."

Her siblings laughed, but Owen held up his hands. "I protest!" he said. "This is good eats!"

"It is supposed to be a cake. Not just a mush of apples," Hanne said.

"It's a delicious mush, though," Owen went on. "If you'd ever eaten on a roundup, you'd know bad cooking. Our last cook's biscuits were so hard Daisy nearly chipped a tooth on them."

"That's what Hanne's were like when she first started cooking after our mother left," Sissel said. She kept on talking, not realizing she had revealed a piece of their history Owen had not possessed before. Stieg's eyes met Hanne's for a moment.

"Well, she's a very good cook now," Owen said amiably. "I can't believe how good everything tastes, considering we've got only a spider and a kettle to cook with! She's a top hand. I'd hire her on in a heartbeat."

Hanne could not help but smile. Owen was looking at her with an easy, open admiration. But her smile faltered as her eyes caught her sister's expression. Sissel was staring at her jealously, thin arms crossed over her narrow chest.

THAT NIGHT THE HEMSTADS had declared they wanted to sleep like cowboys and forgo their tents, which further solidified Owen's good opinion of them. He wanted them to enjoy it, too. There was nothing like sleeping under the open sky.

But during the night, clouds rolled in. It started to snow, and in the morning there were two inches of snow on their bedrolls.

"Oh no!" Stieg joked. "It's that blizzard you've been expecting!"

Owen smiled. "I suppose we may well make it to Wolf Creek without seeing one. Hold still now, I'll sweep you all out."

Owen got up and brushed off each bedroll with a pine bough. Steam rose when Knut shifted his massive body inside his bedroll. It was astounding how warm one could stay with the canvas, wool blankets, and two inches of snow as insulation, especially when sleeping fully clothed.

While the Hemstads rose and shook out their bedding, Owen checked on the horses. He'd tethered them to a young, stout juniper pine. The horses had kicked up grass under the snow and seemed content. Owen patted Pal's side.

When Hanne smiled at him across the fire last night, whatever resolve Owen had to keep away from her had melted. Then he'd given her a modest compliment, and she beamed. He'd seen it. No, he'd *felt* it. He'd felt her happiness from across the campfire. It had settled something for him.

They would be on the trail for at least two or three more days. Owen would try to gain Hanne's affection.

"I'll go see about the traps I laid last night," he said. "Miss Hanne, would you like to come with me?"

"Good idea," Stieg said. "Maybe you could teach her how to set a snare. I'm useless with knots, and Knut is too tenderhearted to hunt."

"We can make johnnycakes and coffee," Knut told Hanne. He scooped fresh snow into the coffeepot and set it to the side so he could build a fire. "See?"

"Very well," Hanne said. She seemed to be avoiding Stieg's eyes. "But we need to make the sugar last a few days more. Don't use it in the batter."

"Yes, my lady," Stieg said, bowing and grinning.

"Fry them in the grease from the pork. We've no butter."

"Yes, my lady," Stieg repeated.

Hanne gathered her mittens from inside her bedroll.

"I will come also," Sissel volunteered in English.

"Don't be silly," Stieg rebuked her in their native tongue. "Your leg will ache too much. And you know I'll burn the breakfast!"

Sissel pulled a face at this.

Owen felt a little bit bad for her. Sometimes the youngest Hemstad seemed to be sweet on him. Sissel couldn't think anything would come of it, though. She was just a child, and he a man grown.

"I'll leave Daisy with you, Sissel," he offered. "She'd be grateful for a brush-out."

Owen rummaged through his saddlebag to find Daisy's curry brush. He put Daisy in a down stay and handed the brush to Sissel, who sighed. Sissel had lost her fear of Daisy, but it was clear she was disappointed to be left behind. For that matter, so was Daisy. The dog watched with her head on her paws, resigned to a heavy brushing, as Owen led Hanne down the hill, his rifle slung over his shoulder.

NOW THAT OWEN had her to himself, he was stuck for topics of conversation.

"Was it a hard journey, coming to Montana?" Owen asked.

Hanne thought for a moment as she picked her way down the snowy incline.

"I did not like the Great Plains. So flat. Very dull to look at. In Norway we have big mountains and great fjords cut by the sea. Do you know the fjords?"

"I can't say I do."

Why they both should smile at each other over that, it wasn't clear to Owen. But they did.

"Do you like it here? In Montana."

"Yes. This I like better. I like there to be some rocks and shrubbery."

"I've always appreciated the shrubbery," he said, teasing just a little.

"Is that the word?" she asked.

"Yep," he said. "Though mostly we call them bushes."

"Bushes, I see. And I like these trees." She patted an aspen. "We have them at home, too."

"I like the way their leaves flutter," Owen agreed. "We call them aspens."

"And we have another one; looks similar to this, with bark like paper."

"Sure. Birch trees."

"We call them *bjørketre*."

"*Bjørketre*," Owen said.

Hanne laughed at his pronunciation.

"*Bjørketre*," he said again. She rewarded him with another giggle.

By then they'd reached the water.

There were some thin rafts of ice on the river, in the still places.

"It's getting colder," she commented.

"That it is," he answered. Then he saw the figure of a rabbit, hanging from the spring snare trap he'd devised.

"Look!" he said.

The animal was twitching, held aloft by the strong, young sapling he had tied the noose to. The animal was alive, but he quickly dispatched it by breaking its neck.

He showed Hanne how he'd set the leather thong on a stick that rested between two other notched sticks. He had bent a sapling over and then tied it to the stick, effectively loading the trap. The hare had passed through the loop, triggered the snare, and been snatched up into the air.

He'd not had so much luck with two other snares he'd set, but Hanne seemed pleased about their one catch. She admired the cleverness of the snare, and Owen felt proud of it, though he could take no credit for its design. Owen retrieved the carefully notched sticks and the leather cords of the snares while Hanne cleaned and gutted the animal. She was fast at it, and neat. Neater than he would have been.

As they walked back up the hill, there was a companionable, comfortable silence between them. Big flakes of snow had started falling. The sky was flat gray, evenly bright, and hard to read.

"Why'd you leave Norway, anyhow?" he asked carelessly. It had been on his mind to ask so many times that it slipped out.

Hanne stiffened.

"You don't have to say," he quickly amended.

She kept her face turned down, toward the ground. Her whole posture had changed. He hadn't even realized that she had been walking straight, with her head held up, until he saw her reassume her old stance. Her shoulders were rounded now, as if she were protecting her rib cage, ashamed.

"I'm sorry," he said. "I'm a fool. Forget I asked."

"It's all right," she said feebly.

He'd spooked her for sure.

"Is your uncle a nice man?" he asked, trying to change the subject. "The one we're headed for in Wolf Creek?"

"We've not met him," Hanne said.

The rest of the climb was silent. Owen was so mad at himself he wanted to kick a rock.

He saw that the snow was sticking now. Hanne's wooden-soled shoes left deep prints. They needed to get rolling. They'd have to save the rabbit for supper.

They huffed up the hill, and then they were close to camp, but

Daisy did not come to greet him. Owen could smell burned flapjacks. Stieg and Knut were sitting near the fire, hunched over the spider.

"Where's Daisy?" Owen asked, just as Hanne asked, "Where's Sissel?" in Norwegian.

Stieg stood up.

"She's not with you?" he said.

"SISSEL!" THE HEMSTADS and Owen yelled at once.

Owen cried, "Daisy, to me!" He whistled twice, then repeated the calls.

There was no sound from the brush.

"They must be far away, if Daisy's not coming," Owen said.

"She wanted to go with you. We sent Daisy with her. They left not five minutes after you did," Stieg said.

"We never saw them," Hanne said.

Owen quickly made a plan. Knut would stay at camp, with the fire, feeding it constantly with the most damp wood he could find. It would send up black smoke, easily visible against the light snow, which might help guide Sissel back to them.

Hanne, Owen, and Stieg would search. Owen showed them how he wanted them to do it—each taking a third of the area in front. Hanne in the center, Owen on the left, and Stieg on the right. They would zigzag back and forth, working their way down the slope. This way they should stay within shouting distance of one another.

Stieg nodded; he was listening to Owen, but Hanne was staring off into space. She seemed to be listening for some distant sound, her whole body tensed for it.

"Do you hear me, Miss Hanne?" Owen said. He put a hand on her arm, and she jumped. "It won't do for us to go getting lost searching for her. Did you understand my directions?"

"Yes," she said. "Stay in this area." She made her arms in a V, showing the area Owen wanted her to cover.

"Yes, good. We need to be able to hear each other if we can't see each other. Okay?"

They both nodded.

"Let's go."

The three of them set out, working their way in tandem across the land.

"Daisy!" Owen kept yelling. He whistled and whistled.

It was terrible his dog wasn't coming. It meant she was either more than a half mile away or hurt or worse.

He whistled again and again.

Owen could hear Hanne moving in the brush to his right. They were all working their way downhill.

"Sissel!" she called. Falling snow dampened the cry. Her voice sounded panicked. "Sissel, where are you?"

Owen tried to think. If they didn't find her in a half hour, they'd go back to the campsite. If she wasn't there, he'd tell the Hemstads to stay at the fire and he'd go out on horseback. With the snow coming down heavy now, the risk of the searchers getting separated was too great.

Suddenly everything around him was still. The silence made him aware of how closely he'd been tracking Hanne.

Then there was an explosion of movement to his right. He caught sight of Hanne, racing down the hillside. She was pumping her arms, half galloping, half falling down the incline of the hill.

"Hanne! What is it?" he called.

She didn't seem to hear.

Owen crashed through the brush after her.

He heard it then. He didn't stop running, but over the sound of the branches snapping as he hurtled through the bushes, and over the sound of his own gasping breaths, he heard Daisy barking.

"Daisy!" he shouted.

There was a scream. An enraged half-human shriek of fury and anger. Owen knew the sound—the fighting cry of a mountain lion.

Ahead, Owen made out the dark, whirling slash of the riverbed cutting through the white of the snow. On the other side of the river, he saw Sissel, fallen, with Daisy standing in front of her, barking. A great, tan cat stalked around them.

"Sissel!" Owen heard Stieg cry. He was coming from upstream, scurrying around the boulders and mossy rocks of the riverbed.

Owen raised his gun to fire just as the cat leaped onto Daisy, slashing forward so fast it was but a golden blur of motion.

The sounds of the fight were terrible. Owen cussed. He couldn't make the shot. Not clean. He'd hit his dog. Or worse, the girl! He was too far away.

He ran. He'd . . . He'd . . . He'd hit the beast with the barrel of the gun.

The lion had its teeth sunk into Daisy's neck.

"No!" Owen cried.

And then the cat yowled. It drew back, releasing Daisy. It had been struck by a rock, Owen realized.

It was Hanne, another rock launched by now. She was scooping them up and running without missing a step, her skirts whipping as she raced toward the fight. She crossed the river, running on the icy rock tops as easily as if on a hard-packed road.

Owen had never seen anyone move so fast, beast or man. He stumbled to a stop, shocked, as Hanne gathered her muscles and leaped at the lion, nearly flying parallel to the ground.

The mountain lion screamed again and reared up with bared claws slashing the air, but the girl was faster than the cat. She was in its arms before it could strike, and as their two bodies hit the ground, Hanne bashed the cat's head against a boulder.

Stunned but not felled, the great cat writhed, trying to get away. It hissed and growled, scrambling, but Hanne had a jagged rock in her fist. As the cat turned with flattened ears to bite her, Hanne finished it with a final blow, a heavy, pulpy *thump*.

The beast flopped down, the lithe tension gone out of it all at once. Its tail gave one final undulation.

Owen was brought out of his daze by the sound of Sissel's sobbing. He stumbled forward, made his feet move. He crossed the river to where Sissel sat on the riverbank. She was clutching her arm. She must have been slashed during the fight. The sleeve of her coat was in tatters.

Stieg came to kneel at Sissel's side, asking her questions in Norwegian and seeing to her wound. Owen went on to his dog.

Daisy was lying on the ground, licking her left flank, which had been torn open. She whimpered as Owen came near. "Stay," he told her. "Good girl."

He petted Daisy's head, keeping his eye on Hanne, who was on all fours, disentangling herself from the body of the dead great cat.

He'd need to bind Daisy's wounds and carry her, but first . . . But first, Hanne.

Hanne had killed a mountain lion with nothing but a rock.

She was staring at the paw of the cat, which looked harmless now. With its claws retracted it looked like the oversize paw of a tawny kitten. Tears were leaking from the corners of her eyes.

"Miss Hanne," he said. "Are you hurt?"

She looked up at him, her pupils wide and black. Her eyes burned with an almost unnatural light. She shook her head. Her stomach growled, and she clutched at it. She mumbled something.

"What?" he asked.

"Don't look at me," she said low. "Please, don't look at me so."

He had been staring, he realized, and his mouth was agape.

Owen turned back to his dog, began to check her gently, to see where she'd been injured.

There were punctures at the back of her neck where the cat had sunk in its teeth. They would need salve. The wound at her upper thigh was the worst. The muscles connecting the hip to the leg had been raked deeply. She needed stitches.

He could hear Stieg getting Sissel to her feet. He was questioning her about how she'd gotten lost and what had happened. Owen didn't need to speak Norwegian to follow the story. She'd gotten lost, and Daisy had protected her.

To his left, Hanne was getting to her feet as well, breathing hard. Dazed. She brushed rocks and snow off her skirts.

Owen took off his poncho and wrapped Daisy tightly in it. She was such a good dog, letting him lift her body though she was clearly in pain.

He wanted to get them back to camp, all together, get their wounds tended to.

He wanted to know *what* had just happened.

How did a Norwegian farm girl come to such training? He glanced at her askance. Her silhouette was so slender and shapely. So feminine. Yet she was stronger than any cowboy he'd ever seen. Faster, too.

What had he just seen? It wasn't natural.

That thought hit him hard. The way she'd killed that mountain lion wasn't natural.

Owen realized suddenly that the light was poor. It had gotten dark, as if twilight were falling on the quiet, bloody scene by the riverbanks.

He looked into the sky, darkening rapidly in the north.

Stieg was looking in the same direction. "I think a storm is coming," Stieg said. He shivered. "A big one."

"Yes, we're in for some weather," Owen said. "We need to get back to camp. Right away."

"Come, Sissel," Stieg said. "We must do as Owen says. Quickly."

Owen shouldered his gun and held Daisy tight to his chest, crashing back across the icy river. The Hemstads followed.

Was there a cave? He thought desperately back to the terrain they had passed. Of course there were no haystacks they could burrow into—there were no farms or ranches. They'd have to make do with their tents. At least the camp was protected from the wind by the rock wall at its back.

If they could make it up the hill.

The sky was growing darker with every moment. The snow was

gusting about them now, as if playing a game of tag, whipping the girls' skirts this way and that.

"We've got to hurry," Owen said, slowing so he could speak to them. "The blizzard will hit in full soon. We've got to get back to the horses!"

Hanne staggered to her siblings and came to stand at Sissel's other side, supporting her. The snow whirled around them, flakes coming faster now, but not so thick they couldn't see.

They hurried up the hill, following the remains of the tracks Owen had made in his rapid descent.

Daisy whined. She reached her head up to lick Owen's neck.

He felt wetness on his upper leg, which meant the dog was bleeding and the blood had flowed down his oilskin coat. It was snowing too hard to see if there was blood on the trail behind them.

They weren't moving fast enough. He pressed up behind Stieg, Hanne, and Sissel, urging them to hurry, but Sissel was walking clumsily, still wailing. Stieg was looking around, dazed and shivering. He seemed to be listening intently to the distant but rising shrieks of the gusting blizzard winds. Only Hanne was moving quickly enough.

A more granular snow was falling now. It began to whirl faster, gritting against their exposed faces like blowing sand.

Sissel stumbled again.

"Hold up," Owen shouted. "Here, take my dog."

He meant to place Daisy in Stieg's arms, but Stieg was staring up at the sky, his mouth open in awe or terror. Instead Owen shifted Daisy into Hanne's arms.

"Thank you," he said. Then he moved his gun so that it was slung over his chest, uncomfortable but necessary if he was to carry the girl. He bent down in front of Sissel, putting one hand on the ground to steady himself.

"Sissel, get on!"

It took her a moment to understand what he wanted to do. She leaned her weight over him, and he hoisted her up, looping his arms under her legs. She clung to his neck with her good arm.

They must go faster.

Up, up, they moved.

"Hold on to my coat, if you must," Owen shouted over his shoulder. And then the blizzard hit them. The snow slammed into them. It was like running into a barn wall.

The snow abraded their faces, streaming up and into their noses and mouths and clothes.

"Don't let go," he tried to shout.

Owen could not see three feet ahead of him. Only due to the incline of the earth under his feet could he tell that he was still traveling in the right direction.

If they didn't reach the horses and their supplies, they would die. And it'd be his fault, because he had been stupid enough to lead them into the wild during early blizzard season.

He cursed himself, driving on. He fought against fatigue and weakness, though his thighs burned and his arms were beginning to cramp from the weight of the girl. It was terribly cold. A killing cold. They would not be able to walk much farther. And where was Hanne? Had she stumbled in the snow somewhere behind him?

The wind hacked at him, slicing into any exposed skin. Without his poncho, he could not last long in these conditions.

Then it seemed to him that the trail in front of him became clearer. Sissel shifted on his back, and he shrugged her up to get a better hold.

It couldn't be true, but his hands began to feel warm. They were clutching Sissel's ankles. He thought he must be losing sensation in them. Maybe he was freezing to death. Then he realized he could see. The air around him was clearing up, though three feet ahead the blizzard muted out the world.

Owen turned his upper body and saw Stieg, walking behind, taking great breaths and blowing forward, his mouth a great O shape.

Hanne was stumbling next to Stieg, holding Daisy close to her chest.

Owen stopped, the storm raging around his lower legs, but hardly touching his face. Stieg trudged onward, past Owen. Stieg was somehow blowing the storm away from them.

"Come, Owen," Hanne said. He stumbled after them, dumbfounded, his head and shoulders in the warm pocket of air Stieg was creating.

Soon they stumbled right into Pal. Knut was there, hunched near Pal's side. Knut had tied the livestock together.

Knut looked up as the warm air pocket Stieg was creating enveloped him. He grinned at his brother in amazement, saying something in Norwegian that could only be an exclamation of delight.

The warm air swayed and shifted over them, like a veil blowing in the wind.

Owen felt dizzy, his mind reeling. It was as if the blizzard were inside his own head—inside his understanding of the way the world worked.

Hanne was looking at Owen with great, horror-struck eyes. Daisy whimpered and licked Hanne's hands.

Owen shook himself. He did not have time to be incapacitated by the strangeness of what was happening. They must have shelter, or perish.

"I'll go for the tents," he told them as he let Sissel down.

Stieg stopped to draw a breath, and the storm came rushing in. The moisture on Owen's face froze instantly. Snow blanked out his vision as Stieg leaned toward him, melted snow running from his face.

"I need a large pile of snow!" Stieg shouted, over the howling wind. "I will make us a cave in the snow."

"Stay here!" Owen shouted to the other siblings.

Owen grabbed Stieg's arm and dragged him toward the stone wall at the back of their camp. There had already been a sizable drift—if they were lucky, it would have collected more snow by now.

Owen pulled Stieg toward it. Stieg seemed weak, was saving his breath for whatever miracle he would next perform, so Owen got his arm under Stieg's shoulder and half dragged him to the drift.

Stieg stuck his head into the snowdrift and began to exhale forcefully.

After a few moments, Stieg pulled his head out from the snow. His face was, for a moment, moist, red, and entirely clear of snow, then the flakes stuck again.

A hole was forming. A hole with crisp, glassy edges. Warm air was coming out of the hole, and the hole was growing, within the snowbank, as if Stieg were blowing a bubble inside it.

Stieg sought better footing and drew a big breath and put his head back in the hole. Steam issued from around his neck.

Owen came up behind him and looked in. Hot air steamed past his face. Stieg drew in another deep breath and then exhaled into the hole.

He was making an ice cave.

The snow scoured against the back side of Owen's body, while his face and front began to get sticky with the warm, moist air coming out of the hole Stieg was making.

Who were these people?

The hole was large enough, and Stieg stepped through it, and then sank down to his knees. He had made a small space within, maybe two feet around.

Behind him, the gray surface of the stone cliff wall showed through in one dry circle surrounded with ice, then snow. A trickle of blood was falling from each of Stieg's nostrils. He wiped them away with the back of his hand.

Stieg took in Owen's shocked, blanched face.

"Get the others," he said. "We will explain. I promise."

"Good," Owen said.

"Wait," Stieg said. "Will the horses survive out there?"

"They don't need a cave. They'll make it, if it doesn't blow too long," Owen said.

Stieg nodded, took another breath, and began to blow again.

The gritty snow scoured Owen's face again, and he was grateful for the whiteout of it. The shocking, numbing cold.

Owen felt betrayed. Yet another secret. He felt left out. Again. Always left out. Always different. It was stupid, he knew it was. But feelings didn't seem to care if they made sense. He had felt like one of the Hemstads for a few days, and now he knew that they were different from him. Not only different, but *superior.*

It was an ugly feeling he had in his gut, ugly and familiar. Owen struggled in the direction of the horses, fighting against the biting snow and the slamming, howling wind.

Owen found the flank of one of the horses; then, by feeling along, he found the siblings. Hanne was facing Knut. The two of them bowed together, protecting Sissel from the worst of the snow.

Owen pulled Knut's arm.

"This way!" he shouted. The wind snatched his voice out of the air. He grabbed them and pulled them toward the ice cavern their brother was carving from a snowdrift with nothing but his breath.

CHAPTER NINETEEN

Hanne gnawed on a piece of hardtack. It was meant to be soaked in coffee or fried in grease, but the hunger in her gut could wait no longer.

Owen was trying to build a fire near the rock wall of their ice cave, though the wood was wet. He had poked two vent holes in the icy dome of the ceiling to let smoke out and fresh air in. One was near the rock wall, the other near their entrance hole.

Owen was not asking any questions. That was a blessing, Hanne supposed. He would leave them when it was safe enough to do so. That seemed a certainty.

He had been working with a steady efficiency for the last hour. He had unloaded the mule and unfolded and spread out the canvas cover sheet from his bedroll on the floor of the cave.

Sissel insisted that Owen tend to the dog before he examined the wound on her arm, explaining that the dog had surely saved her life.

The arm of Sissel's coat and the new shirt beneath had been ripped to shreds. Hanne's muffler was wrapped around her arm.

Hanne had been proud of her sister at that moment, and also while Sissel held the lantern as Owen sewed up Daisy's wound. Knut held the dog down, his fist clamped around her muzzle, in case the pain overcame the dog's training and she tried to bite. She hadn't, though. She'd borne the surgery well, only struggling when Owen tied off the stitches at the very end.

Now she was sleeping again, after having licked the wound thoroughly.

The walls in the shelter had frozen, slick with melted water. What a strange, dark cave it was.

Under Stieg's direction, Knut had used scoops of snow from outside to form a wall, bit by bit shutting the hole they had come through. Once Stieg thought it had thickened enough from the snow piling against it outside, he had blown on it softly, melting it into place.

Now the air was warm, moist, and close, despite the whistling vent in the ceiling. The snow on their clothes was melting, which meant everything was damp, and the canvas "floor" Owen had laid out was muddy. The cave bore the smell of too many bodies in a tight space.

Stieg sat with his head cradled in his hands. Coffee might help the crushing headache that accompanied his using his Nytte.

Hanne wanted to make her brother some coffee, but in this state of hunger, she could help no one but herself. She had kept herself out of their small supply of sugar only by feeling how great the shame would be if she gave in. She would not have Owen see her eat up the sugar straight from the bag. She would not! The hardtack would have to hold her.

Owen cussed under his breath. The wood seemed too wet to light.

"Owen, are you frightened of us?" Stieg said softly. His voice had a raspiness to it. He sounded old.

Hanne stopped chewing. All was silent in the ice hut, except for the intermittent whistling of wind down the chimney hole. Sissel was sitting curled in a ball, against Knut.

"No," Owen said. "I don't see as you'd hurt me."

The two young men met eyes across the small space. There was blood clotted around Stieg's nostrils.

"Would you?" Owen asked.

"No!" Hanne cried. "We would never hurt you."

Sissel scoffed. "*You* might," she said.

"Sissel!" Stieg reprimanded her. A new trickle of blood came flowing down his lip, and he brushed it away.

Sissel made a sour face and then dropped her head on her drawn-up knees.

"I would like to tell you about the way we are, if I may," Stieg said.

Owen shrugged assent, but then made no sign of listening. Hanne was not even certain he was paying attention. He was still trying to light the damp wood.

"We are from an ancient bloodline. A Viking bloodline. This gift was given to our forefathers, three Norse kings, to create successful war parties. We call it the Nytte. If two people with the Nytte have children, their offspring frequently, but not always, will be Nytteson—children of the gift.

"Of the many children a father might sire, one might be gifted with immense strength, another with an ability to protect members of the group, another with the ability to create winds to power the ships. That is what I have. I am a Storm-Rend.

"Knut is an Oar-Breaker—he possesses great strength—and Hanne is a Berserker. You've seen her gift, a drive to protect those she loves.

"There are other types of Nytte as well, which aren't represented among us. Our father was a Shipwright. Our mother had no Nytte. Sissel hasn't found her gift yet, as she is still a child."

"I'm not so much a child," Sissel said. "I'm just not getting a Nytte. It's skipped me over. Aunty Aud said so."

Owen did not speak, only kept trying to start the fire.

Stieg let out a long breath. He was in pain, Hanne could see it.

She worried about him using so much power. One day, he would "blow himself blind." That was how Aud had described it.

"Do you have any questions?" Stieg asked Owen.

Owen said nothing.

"I must rest," Stieg snapped. "My head is splitting open. But I want to answer your questions, if you have them."

Owen still did not meet his eye, but kept knapping at his flint stone, sending sparks onto the wet wood.

With irritation, Stieg leaned forward and blew on the wood. Hot air issued from his mouth, drying the wood as if it were in a kiln. Owen's next spark caught the tinder easily.

Smoke went up and milled around them. It bloused out, for a moment, then was sucked, as if by a straw, through the hole at the top of the cave.

"I got a lot of questions," Owen finally said. "Only I need to think awhile on which order I want to put them."

He looked up at Stieg and met his eye.

"That's the truth of it."

Stieg sat back.

"Very well. Wake me when you wish to speak."

Owen nodded. Stieg settled down onto the ground. Everyone relaxed a bit.

"Knut," Hanne said. "Could you break me off some ice so I can make some coffee?"

While Hanne heated water on the growing fire, Sissel sat next to Daisy, peering anxiously at the sleeping dog.

"Good dog," she said, petting the dog's soft black-and-white fur.

"Let her rest," Hanne said.

Sissel rolled her eyes and snuggled down next to Knut, who watched the fire with drowsy eyes.

Hanne made strong coffee and then some weak oat porridge. She woke Stieg and forced him to choke down some coffee. He would not eat and went back to sleep right away.

Hanne knew Owen was studiously avoiding her gaze. She tried not to look at him, lest they meet eyes, but it was a small space and he sat opposite the fire from her, leaning against the stone wall.

Whispering in Norwegian, Knut asked Hanne to ask Owen if he was worried about the horses.

"My brother wishes to know if you think the animals will die," Hanne said.

"If the horses stay together, and likely they will, they should be all right." Hanne translated this for Knut. "We get blizzards like this, and the livestock manage. Biggest danger is they'll smother in their own breath. It frosts up around their faces. But I'll clear the ice tomorrow morning, if it hasn't stopped blowing by then."

Owen looked at the thick ice walls, likely wondering how he'd get through.

Knut patted the walls and told Owen in Norwegian that he'd help him to get out.

Owen nodded his understanding.

With Stieg asleep, Hanne realized how often he had spoken for them. It was somber without him, and very quiet.

Hanne did not know what to do with herself. The dishes could not be washed, nor scrubbed out. They were in a stack, inside the cast-iron spider. Soon the fire would go out. They'd only had a few sticks of wood to start with, and now that the food had been cooked, they didn't need it. The little ice cave was, in fact, overly warm. The air moist and close.

Soon Knut's breathing grew heavier and rumbled into steady snores. Owen cleared his throat.

"Will Stieg be all right?" Owen asked her softly.

She met his gaze across the coals of the dying fire. Owen's eyes glimmered with warmth, it seemed to Hanne.

"Yes," she said. "I think so."

Owen poked the fire with a stick and sparks flew, dancing up to flare out against the ice cavern's sloped ceiling.

Hanne did not want them to fall into silence again, so she offered more information. "Each Nytte has a . . . a punishment?" She did not know the word in English for *penalty*. And penalty wasn't quite the right word either. "Storm-Rend suffer from headaches, and eventually the headaches take their vision away. But this headache should fade in a day or perhaps two."

"And Knut, what's his punishment?"

"It is horrible, what happens to Oar-Breakers. Their hearts stop. They get too big, and their hearts give out. You see, it's not such a good thing, the Nytte. Stieg calls it a gift, but it doesn't feel like a gift."

Owen said nothing. His hand was petting Daisy's fur rhythmically. The dog looked weak and weary, but her breathing was steady.

Hanne knew he was too polite to ask her—and you? And what happens to you? So she told him, "And Berserkers like me are possessed with hunger. If I don't eat after I kill, I will become sick and die from it. Though Berserkers are usually killed before that can happen."

"Why's that?" Owen asked.

Hanne looked at him. Her voice came out strangled. "Because we are killers. And killers get killed. Which is good and right."

"No," Owen said softly. "Don't say that."

She shrugged.

"You must be an excellent hunter," Owen ventured. "With your . . . how do you say it? Knit?"

"Nytte—like, um, *knit-eh*."

"*Knit-eh.*"

"That's it. But no, I cannot use the Nytte that way. I only have the power when someone I love is in danger, or there is danger to myself."

"And you keep them safe, then. That's good, isn't it?"

"No. It is not good."

Owen stared into the fading fire.

"I've been thinking about it," he said. "And it's magic. That's what it is. And though I've never seen magic before, I don't know why I should think it doesn't exist."

Rising in her chest was a feeling of hope married to despair. Oh, that he should be so good as to forgive them their cursed inhuman abilities. It was frightening. She could not bear for him to be so kind.

The anguish rose so strong and with such urgency she didn't know how she could keep it in. The feeling was violently, urgently seeking escape.

"What is it?" Owen asked.

Hanne shook her head.

Tears, damn tears, spilled over the rims of her eyes. Hanne rubbed at them with the back of her hand.

"Can't you tell me?" Owen said.

She shook her head again.

"Please. Let me alone," she managed to say. She turned away from him, hiding her face. "You don't understand. You can't!"

Owen's face was stricken. He had been reaching toward her, but drew back now, stung.

Hanne curled away from him, putting her back to the fire. She knew he could see she was crying, but she tried to make no sound. Eventually she slept.

SHE WAS AWAKENED by a tug on her arm. The fire was entirely out, and it was very dark and still in the cave.

"Hanne!" It was her sister, whispering urgently. "Wake up."

"What is it?" Hanne mumbled.

"My arm hurts, and I have to go."

"What?"

"You know, I need to go," Sissel whispered again.

Hanne sat up. Her mouth tasted stale, and she was thirsty. She felt disoriented and shaky, but could feel the same need to relieve herself.

"What do we do?" Sissel said, her voice near tears.

"Are you awake, girls?" came Owen's voice. "I'm thinking I'd better go and check on the livestock."

"We will come, too," Hanne said. He had likely heard them and parsed out the issue in question. She burned with embarrassment, especially when she thought of their exchange the night before.

Owen struck his flint and lit one of their candles. Then he set it into the lantern.

"Oh," Stieg said, moaning from near the rock wall of their cavern.

"I saved the rest of the coffee for you," Hanne said. "It's cold, though."

"Thank you," he replied in Norwegian.

"Is it very bad?" Hanne asked.

"Yes."

"Well, my arm hurts, too," Sissel said. "It hurts terribly bad!"

"Oh, be quiet!" Knut said. "It's because of you we got in this whole mess!"

"It is not!" Sissel protested. "Is it my fault I got attacked by a mountain cat?"

"If you had just stayed with us, like Stieg said, it never would have happened!" Knut answered.

"Quiet!" Stieg said, in a voice stricken with pain. In the candlelight, his cheeks looked sunken and there were dark circles under his eyes.

"Sorry," they both muttered at once.

KNUT USED A rock to shatter the ice behind where he sat. The snow beyond it was hard-packed for only a couple of inches, so when Knut pushed it away, his head and shoulders went clear through.

Anyone outside would have thought it a funny sight, suddenly the arms, head, and shoulders of a tall, blond boy poking up out of a snowdrift.

Inside, a cascade of snow all over the floor.

"It's clear!" he said in Norwegian. "Clear and still. The sun is coming up. It's pretty."

"Do you see the animals?" Owen asked, but Knut was stepping out, wading into the deep snow.

Owen was next out of the cave. He went right toward the livestock. They were tied together, near the old fir tree. The horses were glad to see their riders, but did not seem too much aggrieved. They'd not been saddled when the storm hit, so the snow had slid off their backs.

The world was all white and shining. As they stood near the horses, Stieg had to shield his eyes from the bright blue sky.

Owen turned to Hanne. She felt a sinking in her gut. He had offered her understanding and kindness, and she had pushed him away. Surely this would be the moment when he told them he was leaving—they were safe, the storm was over, and he knew who they were. What they were.

Hanne set her shoulders, readying herself to receive the information. She did not want her face to reveal her mixed emotions.

"If I can scrounge up some firewood, are you up to cooking breakfast?" he asked her.

Hanne's face must have conveyed her deep surprise.

"What?" he asked.

"I thought . . . I thought you would surely—"

"Would surely what?"

"Leave us."

Owen was taken aback. An emotion twisted his mouth. Hanne hadn't seen it on him before: anger. His brown eyes sparked fury, and his lips pressed into a line.

He looked at her, then around at the faces of her siblings.

"Do you really think so little of me?" he said.

Hanne was astonished. Then she scrambled to make amends. "I am happy to make breakfast," she offered.

He shook his head.

"I may not have royal blood, like you all, or magic powers I can use to shape the world to my liking—"

"Wait, Owen, I'm sorry—" Hanne protested.

"But I'm a man of my word!"

Hanne felt miserable, felt heartsick that she'd given him offense, but before she could protest, Sissel let out a wail and sat down in the snow abruptly. Knut had been trying to help her over a mound of snow and had touched her injured arm. She cradled it to her chest.

"My arm!" she cried. "Oh, it hurts!"

"Shut up," Hanne snapped.

Stieg rebuked her as well. "This is not the time to complain about your arm!"

But Owen waded over to her through the snow.

"Let's have a see," he said.

"No. I'm fine!" she said. Hanne came over and tried to examine it. "Don't touch it."

"Sissel, for shame!" Hanne chastised her. "Show us the wound so we can see if you're faking or not!"

Pouting, Sissel unwrapped the muffler. She took such a long time, Hanne wanted to rip it off. But when Hanne saw the makeshift bandage they had applied, her breath caught in her throat. The cloth was stained with dried blood, and yellow pus seeped through. It clung to the wound, and Sissel cried as they removed it.

The marks from the lion's claws were each swollen and festering.

"She needs a doctor," Owen said.

Stieg came over. "Yes, she does."

"No!" Sissel said. "No doctor!"

"Hush!" Stieg said. "A wound like that could cost you your arm!" He turned to Owen, who was scratching his head. "What do we do?"

"We ride for Townsend," Owen said.

"Is it out of the way?" Hanne asked.

Owen nodded.

CHAPTER TWENTY

Their outer garments were not warm enough. They did not have mittens. They did not have a good pan to cook on. They did not have enough food to cook. Nor did either of them have, for that matter, any knowledge of *how* to cook!

Rolf had assumed there would be roadhouses or inns along the way. Places where travelers could stop for a night and count on a warm bed and a hot breakfast. There was nothing. The area was wild and desolate.

And worst of all, far worse, they had lost the trail of the Nytteson.

Rolf sat on the floor of the crude, abandoned shack they'd chanced upon. They had passed it on the trail, the squat building so overgrown with brush it was barely recognizable as a structure. It blended in with the hill behind it, except for the rusted metal roof and the square window staring empty at them from the front of the shack.

Then, as the sky had turned a sick, dark green in the north, they doubled back, searching for any shelter from the gathering storm. They had galloped their worn-out horses and stumbled into the shack just as the blizzard hit.

There was no furniture, only a long, narrow table that was attached to the walls and supported by legs. It likely served its owner as both table and bedstead. Ketil reclined upon it now, while Rolf sat next to the wood-burning cookstove, warming his hands.

Rolf had dug kindling and logs out of the woodpile he found buried in the snow outside. With luck and prayers to the Gods, he managed to start a fire. He had started some porridge for them, mixing snow and oats in their kettle.

The glass in the window was long gone, either taken, stolen, or broken, so Rolf had shoved saddlebags into the hole to keep out the driving snow.

Rolf was wearing every piece of clothing he had brought, and he had the blanket from his bedroll wrapped around his shoulders, but still he shivered. He grasped the handle of the kettle, using his blanket so he wouldn't burn his hand, and peered inside. It didn't look promising. Their kettle was scorched on the bottom, and it made everything taste burned. Rolf poured half the watery porridge into one of their two tin cups and handed it to Ketil.

"Blech," Ketil said, sniffing at the oats. "Is there no bacon? I cannot stomach this gruel for much longer."

"We'll stomach it or starve," Rolf said.

Ketil sighed, then dropped the tin cup. The oats slopped out onto the floor.

"I would have eaten that!" Rolf said.

Ketil turned on his side and gazed down at Rolf.

"Are you feeling terribly sad, Tjossem, about how you've botched this operation?"

Rolf did not reply. He was being baited, the Berserker trolling for a fight.

"Do you think the Baron will keep you in his employ once we return, empty-handed? I doubt it, my friend.

"No. I think your time has come. The Baron knows what he wants now. Strong men, proper Nytteson, to lead the way. Superior men."

Rolf rolled his eyes.

"You know he means to breed us," Ketil said.

Rolf's attention was snagged. "That's not true."

"Oh yes. Why do you think he's so intent on finding Nyttes-dotters?" Ketil continued. "I think he wants to breed an army of Berserkers. Just like in the olden days. Can you imagine? We'd be unstoppable."

"The Baron brings you together to keep you safe. He doesn't want the Nytte to die out," Rolf protested. "He is not a violent man, Ketil. I've known him for many years."

Ketil shrugged. "He gathers us together. He keeps us close. We'll intermarry, of course, and breed more Nytteson. That's what he wants. You saw how happy he was when Martin married that Helga cow."

Rolf had recruited Helga, a Shipwright, and she married Martin Larsson, who was an Oar-Breaker. The Baron had thrown them a lovely wedding, and there was a feeling of accomplishment at the party. The Baron had, indeed, seemed very pleased.

"I think he wants an army. War's coming, they say, what with Germany making alliances everywhere. It's time for Norway to stand strong."

"That's absurd," Rolf said. He jerked open the rusted door to the stove and stuck another piece of wood into the fire. With snow building up around the walls of the shack, the air inside was finally beginning to warm. He knew he should try to sleep.

"I'll tell you a secret, Tjossem," Ketil said. He dangled an arm over the side of the table and mussed Rolf's hair. "The Baron promised me a Nyttesdotter bride. A nice young one."

Goose bumps ran along Rolf's arms.

"I'm going to sleep now," Rolf snapped. "Don't let the fire go out. We're almost out of matches."

Rolf lay down on the floor and arranged the canvas outer layer of his bedroll so that it enveloped him, then he curled as close to the stove as he could get.

His mind was racing with the thoughts Ketil had planted there.

Rolf remembered little Emma Stenehjem, the orphaned Storm-Rend he had located in Flåm. She'd been working in the kitchens of a grand estate. She was a sad girl, only thirteen years old, shy because her front teeth bucked out, but she'd brightened when Rolf had persuaded her to go with him to Gamlehaugen.

The Baron had clapped his hands when Rolf presented Emma to him. He embraced timid, little Emma and told her she was to be his new ward.

Rolf had enjoyed seeing the girl bloom with the care she received. The Baron dressed her in lace and silk. She had a governess and was taught to write and read. She was an ungainly girl, but happiness made her lovely.

Rolf developed the habit of bringing her bits of ceramics from his travels. Little button boxes or figurines. Her favorite had been a little black swan. She was chatty and playful around him, coming out of her shell. She even began to call him "uncle."

And then one day she would not see him. Her maid said she had a terrible headache. The maid added to Rolf, in a scared whisper, that Emma had not left her room in several days. Rolf had been terribly concerned; he'd spoken to Fjelstad about it. How often did these headaches occur? Was the child eating well?

If they had not been such old friends, Fjelstad might have discharged him, for Rolf spoke with uncharacteristic force and emotion.

But the Baron understood Rolf's agitation. Together, they consulted with the governess, who told them the girl was having difficulties in her lessons. The governess found Emma mulish and recalcitrant. That didn't sound right to Rolf, either.

But the child would not speak to him and by the next time Rolf visited, Emma had run away, taking none of her lace dresses or fine hair ribbons or china figurines with her. Not even the little black swan. Fjelstad seemed just as brokenhearted as Rolf had been.

But now Rolf wondered—what had really happened to Emma Stenehjem?

WHEN HE WOKE, the fire was dying down and Ketil was snoring, oblivious. Rolf stoked the fire and sat watching the flames through the grate. Rolf prayed to the old Gods. What did they want him to do? He wished for a full set of divination rune stones, that he might throw them and try to find some wisdom.

They had lost the trail of the Berserker. He had failed on this mission. They would find the road back to Livingston and take the train from there. He would wire ahead, and the Baron's disappointment would have time to settle before he and Ketil arrived home.

Then he would, he must, speak to the Baron about the Nytteson he was recruiting. The rights of the Nyttesdotters must be safeguarded, at all costs. Moreover, Ketil should not be encouraged to have children who might have the Nytte. Rolf knew the Baron would bristle if Rolf brought it up, but Ketil was unfit to be a father to a normal child, much less one with a gift that could be destructive if not properly guided.

Though they had lost the Nytteson, Rolf still had the children's Bible to study—there might be a lead in there to other relatives in Europe. He must get back to Gamlehaugen.

By the time the blizzard blew itself out, Rolf was ready to face the tasks ahead.

He woke Ketil, handed him his mug, scraped clean, wiped out, and now filled with hot coffee.

"I've decided we should turn back," Rolf told him. "We've lost the trail. We should return home."

Ketil snorted. "You're going to pay hell—"

"I know. I know. But the Baron is an old friend, and I hope he will forgive me."

"I hope he won't," Ketil said.

"Yes, I know. You'd like to see me ruined."

They began to pack up. Rolf fingered the rune stone in his pocket.

The arrow flew false,
The horse fell lame,
The waterskin punctured,
The deer shied away,
The trail dwindled to nothing.

Thus in small treacheries
Did the warrior learn himself
Deserted by the Gods.

Ketil shoved open the door, pushing out the snow that had accumulated. The sky was crisp and blue. The earth was covered in a thick blanket of white. A slight depression indicated the road they had taken—the road they must now follow to retrace their steps.

Their horses stood in the brush, the snow around them packed and melted by their heat. Ketil swore, stomping through the snow toward them.

Rolf closed his eyes and prayed, *Please, Odin, if this is a mistake, please show me the way.*

"Let's go, Rolfy. It's cold!"

Rolf slogged through the snow, raised up his arm to throw his saddlebag over the bare back of his horse, when he froze.

There, on the branch above the head of his horse, sat a fat black raven. Its glossy, beady eye was fixed on Rolf.

The hairs on the back of Rolf's neck stood up.

"*CAW!*" the bird called to him.

A raven, Odin's escort, sitting right there, as if waiting to guide them.

"What's wrong with you?" Ketil asked, coming close.

The raven gave a loud, coarse cry and flew off to another bush, ten feet away.

"Odin has sent us a guide," Rolf said. "Quickly, mount up!"

* * *

AS MUCH OFFENSE as Owen had taken when Hanne had suggested he might leave, now he was considering doing just that. He'd get them to Townsend. From Townsend, they could find someone else to get them to Wolf Creek.

She thought he might abandon them? And after he'd tried to make peace, to tell her he wasn't scared of their witchy abilities? It galled him.

She thought he was a man of no honor. A man who would leave them stranded out-country.

They had packed up camp without having a proper meal. Owen's stomach growled as the horses plodded through the snow. He looked down to check on Daisy. He'd loaded his dog into his saddlebag. She fit snugly inside, and didn't whine or complain. If he reached back, he could pat her on the head.

But even that couldn't break his stormy mood.

Skipping breakfast had been a poor decision, but he wanted to get to Townsend as quickly as possible. Sissel was so thin and sickly already, he wasn't sure how quickly the infection on her arm would spread.

He ought to have tended the girl's arm before taking care of his dog back in the cave.

It was one poor decision after another with him, he told himself. They'd be better off without him.

"Hey!" came a call behind him.

Owen twisted in his saddle.

The Hemstads were strung out behind him. Stieg was stooped in the saddle, and shading his eyes with his hand. The girls rode in the middle, and last was Knut, the horse plodding on valiantly under his weight. It was Knut who had shouted.

Owen looked where Knut was pointing and saw it. A lazy plume of smoke drifting up from a stand of pine about half a mile down-valley.

A homestead.

"Good eyes!" he called to the boy.

Knut grinned.

Owen pointed his horse in the direction of the chimney smoke.

AS THEY APPROACHED the farm, a broad-shouldered, ruddy-faced woman came hustling out of the house. At her heels was an old but handsome black dog.

Daisy perked up somewhat in the saddlebag. She gave a little whine to be let down.

After sizing them up, the woman spoke at them in a foreign language without pausing for breath. Owen placed it as German. She came right up to their horses, patting Pal's neck and nose, clearly giving them all directions, though none of them could understand.

Stieg, weary as he was, had a smile for the woman. "Is she a friend of yours?" he asked Owen.

"Never laid eyes on her in my life," Owen responded, nodding and smiling to the woman as she made motions to usher them inside. "*Kommt essen!*" she said loudly, while she mimed eating. Owen nodded.

"Yes, please," he said.

She put out her hand, tapping her palm, signaling he would pay her. Owen told her he would pay whatever she asked.

She thumped her chest. "*Ich heiße Frau Gerlinger.*"

"*Ich heiße* Stieg Hemstad," Stieg said, then turned to Owen, "but that's the last of my German, I'm afraid."

Frau Gerlinger called to someone within the house. A short, bald man came out to squint at them. He looked distinctly displeased to see them.

Owen helped Sissel dismount, careful not to jolt her injured arm. She was even paler than usual, and she kept her arm cradled into her body. Her eyes looked glassy. Finding this homestead had been providential.

Frau Gerlinger took one look at Sissel's pale face, torn sleeve, and makeshift bandage and put her arm around the girl protectively.

She scolded Owen, asking him questions in rapid German. Owen shrugged. He mimed the action of a great cat clawing.

Frau Gerlinger tutted as she led her new charge toward the house. She barked some instructions at the short man, who had to be her husband. Hanne and Stieg followed the woman, after Owen indicated he and Knut would get the horses stabled.

There was work to be done, and Owen was grateful for it.

The horses needed to be fed, watered, and curried. He wanted to check their hooves for stones and their legs and ears for any signs of frostbite. He was glad he'd be away from Hanne for a while. Chores would help him set his mind in order.

Knut began unloading the mule.

The husband led the way to the stable. His old black dog

accompanied them at the man's heel, eyes on his master. The dog had been trained well.

It was one of the largest and cleanest barns Owen had ever seen, even with the flock of brown bantams and fat barred Plymouth hens clucking about underfoot.

The floor was hard-packed dirt, and might have been swept clean, it was so tidy. Brushes and tack hung on nails from the log walls of the barn, and a handsome trough ran the length of the back wall. Nesting boxes were set in the wall at hip height for easy collecting of the eggs, with roosting perches set below.

There were two doe-eyed milch cows chewing their cud in the first of six large stalls. A fat sorrel mare stood in the next enclosure. The rest of the stalls were empty. The husband did not explain where his livestock had gone to, just pitchforked some hay down from the loft above onto the center of the floor, while Owen led the horses in.

The German man watched, hands on hips, while Owen eased Daisy from the saddlebag. He made a sniff of approval when he saw Owen's neat, tidy stitches on Daisy's leg. Owen set her down. She tried a few steps, but sat down, whining.

Owen patted her head. "Good girl," he told her.

The black dog came near. Owen straightened up and ignored the two dogs, hoping for peace, but knowing better than to interfere. They sniffed each other, then came easily to the agreement that they'd be friends. Tails began to wag.

The old dog walked over to what seemed to be his bed, in a corner of the barn, a wooden frame heaped with straw. He climbed in and sat up, wagging his stumpy tail. Daisy limped over and sniffed at the straw, then heaved herself over the edge of the bed. Both dogs curled up, as if they'd been littermates.

If only humans could get along so easily, Owen thought.

The German man grunted with equal appreciation of the sight. Then he showed Owen where there were buckets and pointed to a stone well out in the center of the yard. Owen nodded that he understood. The slight little man grumped back toward the house.

After the horses had drunk of the clear water he put in the trough, Owen removed their blankets and saddles, one by one, as they crunched the fresh straw. He curried each of them with a brush he found hanging on the wall.

Knut entered the barn, carrying the mule packs. It would have taken Owen two trips to carry the heavy packs, but Knut could've handled twice the load.

Their work with the horses took over an hour. By that time Owen's stomach was rumbling with hunger, but he was pleased to have this unexpected chance to care for their mounts. Once they started again, they'd make good time. He'd get the Hemstads delivered. Get paid. Find a place to hole up for the winter.

He would move on from these eerie people.

Maybe he would try out for Great Falls and see if he couldn't find Hoakes. Hoakes had been a good friend to him, Owen saw that now.

He knocked at the door of the farmhouse. No one came. He knocked again, and then, with a shrug to Knut, he finally pushed the door open.

From inside came a clamoring of pots and pans and the Frau Gerlinger's animated chatter. No wonder they hadn't heard the knock.

"Howdy," Owen said. "May we enter?"

"*Ja! Komme rein,*" came Frau Gerlinger's voice.

The log home was cheerful and bigger than most. The husband sat grim faced in a rocking chair near a tidy stone hearth. Stieg sat across from him, still cradling his head in his hands.

Three doors led off the main room. There were two bedrooms, and there was a door near the kitchen area that Owen supposed led to a lean-to of some kind. This house had been built for more than two people, just like the barn had been built to accommodate more livestock.

Sissel was nowhere to be seen, probably having a rest in the bedroom. Hanne was helping Frau Gerlinger in the kitchen, and they were cooking up a feast.

Knut made his way directly to the table and sat on the most sturdy-looking seat. He took up the fork and knife in anticipation.

Owen crossed the room to Hanne. She was beating egg whites under the German woman's direction.

"*Shneller! Schneller!*" the woman told Hanne.

Hanne whipped faster.

When she was satisfied, Frau Gerlinger took the bowl from Hanne and emptied a pitcher of creamy milk into the beaten whites. She stirred in sugar. Owen smiled, realizing they were making eggnog.

Hanne shook out her arm, her muscles stiff from beating the eggs.

"Is Sissel all right?" Owen asked.

"The lady bathed the wound and applied a paste of some kind. Then tied new cloths on it," Hanne reported.

"I thought I would ride into town and see about a doctor after we eat," Owen said stiffly.

Hanne nodded. "It would be a good idea. And a doctor might have headache powder for Stieg."

The German woman shooed Owen to the table. The husband rose to come, too, but the wife scolded him back into his chair.

She commenced to lay out food. Each of them got a plate with a nice chunk of bacon. In the center of the table, she set a platter heaped with fried eggs. She placed a loaf of bread on the table, along with a china dish overflowing with chokecherry preserves and another with good, homemade butter. She proudly brought the pitcher of eggnog to the table and poured them each a cup full. Owen could see specks of nutmeg floating on top. Frau Gerlinger also set a cutting board on the table with a round of white cheese and sliced them each a good hunk.

She exhorted them to eat, eat!

Owen had not seen a spread like this for some time. He wondered how much money it would cost, but she didn't seem the type to cheat anyone. She seemed simply like the type of woman who couldn't get enough of mothering, and liked to see young people eat.

Owen knew that homesteading could make people lonely. Mrs. Bennett had often complained of the lack of society at the farm. She had even tried to befriend Lucy, the cook. Owen remembered Mrs. Bennett once asking Lucy if she'd like to take a cup of tea, and Lucy asking, "Take it where?"

Frau Gerlinger ushered Hanne into the final seat. She hovered over the table and made Hanne a plate. Stieg still looked pale and weak, but he tried his best to keep a pleasant expression on his face. As for Knut, hunger was shining in his eyes.

"*Greist zu!*" Frau Gerlinger said.

Owen forked two eggs onto his plate. He helped himself to bread and spread it with butter and preserves. Delicious.

The husband grumbled something from the fireplace. The wife shut him up with a barrage of harsh-sounding German.

Never had Owen been in the presence of such a strong maternal force. This woman might well mother one to death.

"This looks real good," Owen said, but she shushed him and motioned for him to eat. Owen watched Knut sample his eggnog and enjoyed the rapturous face he made.

Knut was humming with happiness. The woman ruffled Knut's hair and chattered on. Though they didn't understand her words, it was clear that she was talking about how healthy and able-bodied Knut was.

From her gestures and expressions, it was also clear she was complaining about her husband, who was glowering at the hearth. She brought a framed tintype down from the mantelpiece. It showed three sturdy, stone-faced farm boys, dressed in their Sunday best, against a linen backdrop. Frau Gerlinger kept pointing at the photo, then at her husband. She kept saying *Herr Gerlinger* this and *Herr Gerlinger* that. Owen decided she must be telling them that their own sons had left the farm after some kind of fight with her husband.

This explained both the large house and the empty stalls in the barn.

After a while, she set the tintype back on the mantel. Then she bustled back to the kitchen area, poured a cup of eggnog, and took it off to Sissel in the bedroom. On her way out of the room, she gave

Herr Gerlinger permission to get up and make himself a plate. He did not look happy about it, but refused a seat at the table when Owen, Stieg, and Knut each offered up his own.

"I've never eaten so well," Stieg said. He had some color back in his face and seemed to be recovering. Then, his eyes flashing to Hanne, "Sorry, Sister. I did not mean to insult your cooking. I meant to say, I've not eaten so well *since* we left home."

"No," Hanne said. "You've never eaten so well, because *I've* never eaten this well, either."

"I've never eaten this well," Owen said. "And I never met either of you before last Thursday."

He wasn't trying to be funny, but this struck all three of them as hilarious. Knut was surprised by their laughter, and hadn't followed the exchange, but that didn't keep him from joining in.

Owen couldn't deny it felt good to laugh.

Herr Gerlinger harrumphed and stormed out of the house, taking his plate. This struck them as extra funny, and the four of them started laughing anew.

"*Gut!*" said the woman, hustling out of the bedroom. "*Lachen ist gut!*" She made a motion for them to continue laughing, which helped them to do just that.

Hanne was giggling. She had to wipe tears from her eyes. She smiled at Owen, and they laughed together.

Owen felt his anger at her dissolve. How could he hold what she'd said against her when the circumstances were so utterly bewildering? If their positions had been reversed, he would likely have expected her to leave him.

Owen let out a breath he hadn't known he was holding. He told Stieg of his plan to go for the doctor, and Stieg approved. He gave Owen five dollars to buy medicine and provisions for the rest of the journey. Hanne specified butter and sugar. Owen tucked the bills carefully into his vest pocket.

Stieg leaned his chin on his hand. Sleep seemed to be overtaking him. When his head bobbed and he jerked awake with a startled gasp, Frau Gerlinger shooed him in the direction of her own bedroom, to have a rest on the bed.

She made it clear that she wanted Owen, Knut, and Hanne to rest as well. For whatever reason, she seemed to have taken their wellness as a private mission. Anyway, Owen wasn't about to look a gift horse in the mouth. They were all wiped out and needed to recover.

Frau Gerlinger ushered Hanne into the back bedroom where Sissel was resting. Then she took Owen and Knut outside, to the barn. She pointed up to the hayloft; she meant for them to sleep up there.

Owen told her he was going to town to fetch the doctor, but she shook her head.

"*Wir brauchen keinen Doktor*," she said, thumping herself on the chest.

"No," Owen insisted. He began to saddle Pal. The girl needed a real doctor, and the Hemstads had the money for it. And of course, there was Daisy to be considered—the doctor might take a look at her stitches.

After some fussing, Frau Gerlinger relented. He asked her the directions to town; she pointed the way.

Knut asked if he could come. Owen didn't see why not. It wasn't far, and the boy seemed eager for some adventure. He didn't see the need to tell Stieg or Hanne. They were resting and he was the trail boss, after all.

IT WASN'T HARD to find the road to town. Owen could make out the wagon wheel furrows even though the road was buried in snow.

With a full belly and the knowledge that his charges were safe and resting, and his dog was on the mend, Owen felt relieved.

Townsend was a small town, hardly more than a train stop. It had only one main street, though another street was shaping up behind the first one. The snow was being pounded into the muddy street by the teams of horses.

"Look," Knut said. This was one of his most frequently used English words. He was pointing to a pair of beautifully matched draft horses, lifting their feathered forelegs in a way that was almost showy, as if they well knew their worth.

"Good horses!" Knut said. "Pretty." He grinned affably.

"Very nice," Owen agreed.

Passersby looked and then looked again at the giant boy wearing a horse blanket as a poncho, who gaped so unselfconsciously at the pretty horses.

While Knut waited outside, taking in the sights of the town, Owen inquired at the livery and was told the doctor's office was located above the Barstow Saloon, down at the train station end of town.

Owen and Knut walked their horses down toward the train

tracks. The mud outside the saloon stank of whiskey and vomit, and the planks that made up the clapboard building were stained from the ground up. The sound of rough voices inside carried out the poorly hung door.

"You stay here," Owen told Knut. The boy nodded, his eyes big. "We don't want trouble."

A thick-waisted man with one eye crushed in came crashing out the door. He cussed over his shoulder at a short, dark man behind him.

"Lord!" the big one exclaimed as he got a look at Knut. "Look at this great big bruiser. Was your mother a bear, kid?"

Knut's face flushed, and he looked down at his feet.

Owen cleared his throat. "We're just looking for the doctor."

"You're not going inside, are you?" The big man ignored Owen, just talking to Knut. "'Cause if you ride our whores, you'll wear 'em out!" He roared with laughter at his joke.

"Aw, leave him be, Kelvin. He's just a dumb kid," the short fellow said. His voice was whiny, like a pleading child.

Knut edged away from the men.

The big man came clomping down the steps, with the heavy feet of a drunk. He seemed to be looking for a fight.

Owen stepped in front of him.

"He's a kid," Owen said. "And we're just here for the doctor."

The man's breath was foul, smelling of whiskey and tooth decay, but Owen held his ground.

"We mean no trouble and we want none," Owen said.

The big man pushed him backward, hard.

"We mean no trouble and we want none," he parroted, taunting. "What a couple of Nancys!"

"Come on, Kelvin. I want pie," the smaller man said. He grabbed his partner and led him away from Owen and Knut.

After they'd gone, Knut offered Owen a shaky smile. Owen shrugged. "I thought it was a pretty good line, myself," he said.

CHAPTER TWENTY-ONE

When Hanne awoke, the cozy log room was painted gold by the midday sunshine coming through the window. She'd slept for an hour or more. She was lying on one of the two narrow beds, fully clothed, atop the quilt. She could not remember the last time she had rested in a bed during the daytime.

Hanne marveled at their good fortune of coming across the Gerlinger homestead. Now that she was inside stout log walls and resting on a real bed, she appreciated how much she had missed such comforts.

Sissel was asleep on the other bed. Her color had improved. Hanne leaned over and laid her hand on Sissel's forehead. Her fever had lowered.

Sissel opened her eyes.

"Do you think there's more of that milk punch?" she asked.

"That was good," Hanne said.

"Heavenly good. Did you see how she made it?"

"It was eggs and cream and sugar, with milk, too. I'll watch if she makes it again."

"I'd like to learn it, too," Sissel said.

Hanne bit back a comment—Sissel could pick and choose what she wanted to learn, because it was assumed that Hanne would make everything else.

When Hanne went out into the main room, Frau Gerlinger strode over and clapped her on the back.

"*Gut!*" Frau Gerlinger said, grinning. She made muscles and said something that must have meant *strong girl.*

Hanne smiled.

Frau Gerlinger put on her wraps and opened the door out into the snowy yard. She grabbed a bucket and headed outside. There was another bucket near the door, so Hanne put on her coat, took up the bucket, and followed her.

Frau Gerlinger turned, saw Hanne behind her, and grinned again. "*Du bist ein gutes Mädchen.*"

Outside, Hanne held both the buckets while Frau Gerlinger pulled aside the heavy wooden cover for the well. Once lifted, it slid to the side on the snow.

It was a good well, made of stone, the edge just lower than waist level with a metal crank to raise the bucket on its rope.

At the sound of the winch, Herr Gerlinger came out of the barn. He came over to the well and apparently asked for a drink. Frau Gerlinger rolled her eyes and began to criticize him even as she pulled up the bucket and handed it to him to drink.

Herr Gerlinger bore the abuse stoically. Hanne did not know

what to make of their relationship. To her, it seemed that man and wife created their own new world in marriage, and the world of the Gerlingers seemed to include a lot of scolding. When the argument was over and the buckets filled, Hanne followed Frau Gerlinger back into the house to make supper.

As the water boiled, Frau Gerlinger went outside and killed two cockerels. After scalding them, she and Hanne sat outside in the cold sunshine, plucking the feathers and adding them to a big bag of feathers Frau Gerlinger had already collected.

Frau Gerlinger talked, and though she couldn't understand the words, Hanne felt sure she was saying that Hanne and her siblings should stay with her. She kept saying, "*Gut!*" and pointing to Hanne and then pointing to the house and saying, "*Gutes Haus.*"

Could they stay? It was a strange idea. But if the woman was willing to feed them all, they could stay and work. It was a big farm. Knut's size and strength would be a great help to them, and once Stieg recovered he, too, would prove himself useful.

It might work. It was an isolated homestead, and the woman's loneliness made her suspect they had few visitors.

Hanne let herself imagine it. Staying on the big farm in the log house that was so cheerful and bright. Eating eggs and butter every day. Not being in charge of the cooking or the washing. Simply following directions.

She found herself humming as she worked. Smiling.

With Frau Gerlinger's encouragement, Hanne gutted the chickens. The woman nodded, happy with Hanne's work.

There was a bowl for the organs, and Hanne thought she meant to save them for chicken stock, but the woman gestured to the black dog who'd come out to watch them.

Hanne gave the old-timer half of the entrails and brought the rest to Daisy in the barn. Daisy seemed to be much recovered, and even rose from the dog bed to hobble over and sniff at the offerings.

It was only then that Hanne realized Knut was not resting in the barn. Her heart lurched. Pal was gone and so was the stoutest of their trail horses. Knut had gone with Owen!

Hanne's heartbeat blocked up her throat. He was in town! He was in town with Owen, and Owen didn't know Knut was a wanted man.

She pressed the heels of her hands into her eye sockets. She must take a horse. She must go into town. All the calm contentment she'd felt was shattered.

She strode out of the barn to tell Sissel where she was going when Owen and Knut rode in.

They were laughing about something.

They were fine.

Hanne turned away from them, her hands in fists. She was shaking with fear, and, now, anger flushed through her limbs.

"Hanne!" Knut cried. "Owen bought me candy!"

Knut saw Hanne's expression and stopped. "Don't be mad, Sister. He bought some for you, too."

"Knut! You should know not to go off without telling us!" she said in Norwegian.

"I told him he could come along," Owen said. He was wearing a new wool poncho to replace the one ruined by Daisy's blood.

Hanne bit the inside of her cheek. She nodded. She was tired suddenly, very tired of keeping secrets from Owen Bennett.

"I just got scared for a moment."

"He was fine," Owen said. "He was with me. We went to fetch the doctor. He wasn't there, but we left a message for him at the store. They said I ought to come back tomorrow morning."

"Ah," she said. "Good. Fine." She smoothed her sweaty palms on her skirts. "I will go back to helping Frau Gerlinger."

Owen nodded at her. She felt awkward and stupid.

AS UPSET AS she had been, Hanne's distress melted away at supper. It was such a lovely table Frau Gerlinger had set, complete with a pretty cloth embroidered with flowers.

She had had her husband roll in two sawn-off logs from outside, so there were seats enough for them all. Knut took the largest one.

There was chicken stew and a platter of buttermilk biscuits, steaming hot. A bowl of pickled beets was offered, gleaming in a pool of pink vinegar.

Stieg entered from the main bedroom, where he'd slept away the afternoon.

"Brother, you look well," Hanne said. She brushed a feather from his hair.

"As do you!" he answered. "You are smiling, Hanne. Your face was in a smile, all by itself, just then. That's a nice thing to see. It has been a long while."

He turned to the table, laden with food. "Ah, what a beautiful sight," he said to Frau Gerlinger.

To his surprise, Frau Gerlinger swept Stieg into a hug, and then put him at an arm's length so she could look him over. She prodded at his belly and felt his limbs, then shook her head. She clearly felt he was too thin.

She ushered Stieg and Hanne both toward the room Sissel was resting in. Then she pointed toward a basin and a piece of store-bought soap, sitting in a porcelain dish. There was also a towel made from a coffee sack. She wanted them to wash up.

Sissel was sitting up in bed, looking through a German picture book for young children. She looked abashed when her siblings came in, and slid the book under the covers.

"Frau Gerlinger pointed me to stay here. I think I am to stay abed," Sissel said, her voice a bit guilty.

"Rest you should," Stieg said. "This place is a godsend. How's your arm?"

"It hurts," Sissel said.

Hanne pressed her hand lightly over the bandage.

"But it's not so hot."

"The ointment smells terrible," Sissel complained.

"Good," Hanne said. "Then you know it's working! You know, Stieg, I wonder if Frau Gerlinger doesn't want us to stay on."

"Really?" her brother asked. "How do you mean?"

"I can't know for sure, but the way she was speaking, it seemed to me she was talking about how we might help her on the farm."

Stieg puzzled over this as he washed.

"Then Owen wouldn't have to take us to Wolf Creek," Hanne said.

"Yes," Stieg said slowly. "He seems . . . he seems ready to be free of us."

Hanne's breath caught in her chest.

"Yes," she said. She could not keep sadness from her voice. "I think so, too."

HERR GERLINGER DID not speak a word through the meal. In fact, none of them spoke much, the food was too good, and Frau Gerlinger dominated the conversation anyhow. It seemed clear now, to all of them, that she was laying out plans for them to stay on through the winter.

After raisin streusel and coffee, and once the young travelers were so stuffed they had to push back from the table, Frau Gerlinger began to speak to her husband, softly this time. She coaxed and nudged him with her elbow. Much to Hanne's surprise, a sly smile began to twist at the corners of his mouth. She cajoled him further, and he stood and walked off into the bedroom.

Hanne and Owen exchanged a questioning look.

There was an atonal wheezing from the back room. Stieg looked at Hanne with a quizzical expression of alarm—then Herr Gerlinger came out with an accordion! He even played a gallant "ta-da!"

Amazement was spread over the faces of Owen, Stieg, and Knut. Hanne laughed and clapped.

Herr Gerlinger began to play a jolly melody. Sissel came, mouth agog, to stand in the doorway of the bedroom wearing her shift, all modesty forgotten.

Frau Gerlinger was so pleased with their reaction! She pulled Owen to his feet and tried to make him dance with her. He begged off, laughing.

"I can't!" he said. "I don't know how to dance!"

"Step aside, then," Stieg said, rising to his feet. He commenced to jig. He was a wonderful dancer, despite his height and gangly frame. Clearly his headache was gone. He lifted his feet high, dancing furiously. Frau Gerlinger, not to be outdone, began to dance just as fast.

Knut began clapping. His sisters joined in. Sissel came skipping across the floor. She'd thrown her wrap over her shoulders.

"Dance with me!" she said to Knut. "Come on, Brother!"

"Here! Let's move the table back!" Stieg called.

With the table and chairs pushed against the wall, there was more room.

Knut was no great dancer, but the boisterous, joyful music was difficult to resist. He was up and took his sister's good hand gently. They began to dance carefully, giggling all the while.

That left Hanne and Owen seated.

Hanne's feet were tapping to the beat, and she was clapping, too.

She could not expect him to ask her to dance. He had just said he didn't know how. And she had insulted him by thinking he might leave them.

But then he held out his hand to her.

"There's not room," she said over the music, trying to save him from this courtesy.

"They'll make room," he answered. And she ventured a look in his eyes. It was hard to read what she saw there, but the eyes crinkled at the corners, and his smile seemed genuine enough. "Come dance if you dare, Hanne Hemstad. I'll step on your feet for sure."

She put her hand in his, and it felt wonderful. He drew her up, and took her other hand in his. Their arms made a circuit that lit her heart on fire.

Herr Gerlinger quickened the pace of the song. Owen grinned at her and began clomping side to side. He truly was an awful dancer, but it hardly mattered.

Stieg began to show off, doing high kicks from a squat. Frau Gerlinger encouraged him, shouting, "*Ja! Ja! Ja!*" Hanne and Owen looked at each other and laughed.

Owen spun her around and around. What joy it gave her to see his smiling face in the center of the whirling room!

Knut bumped into Hanne, and she lost her footing. Owen caught her around her waist.

Now his face was but inches from hers. His breath was hot on her neck. His cheeks were flushed with exertion and happiness. His eyes flashed to her lips, and her eyes went to his. How she wanted to press her lips to his mouth and kiss him. The heat of his body was melting her from the inside out.

And then, abruptly, Frau Gerlinger was cutting in between them. She took Owen's hands and began instructing him how to jig.

Hanne's face was red hot. She was glad when Stieg suggested cracking the door open to let some cool air inside.

CHAPTER TWENTY-TWO

Owen could think of little besides the dance as he made his way to Townsend. He'd thought of it all night long, tossing in the straw up in the hayloft while Stieg and Knut snored. He could not shake off the feeling of dancing with her, the whirling, jagged happiness of holding her hands in his and twirling her around the room.

What was he to do now? His resolve to treat Hanne as his patron and deposit her in Wolf Creek was gone. But could he really stay on with her and her siblings? Would they want him to remain connected at all once he'd delivered them to their destination? It was an odd situation.

Owen found the doctor in his office above the saloon. He was a stout, bug-eyed man, bald except for around the ears. Several patients were waiting in his office. When Owen promised they would pay for a house call, the doctor told Owen he knew where the Gerlinger farm was located and would stop by later in the day.

Owen stepped out onto the damp wooden sidewalk. The snow still hadn't been shoveled off entirely, so there was a narrow path to walk on. It caused some inconvenience, as one had to step aside to let others pass.

He was making his way toward Wheeler and Company Mercantile and Supply, for Frau Gerlinger had given him fifty cents to buy sugar and flour. She was charging them merely twenty-five cents apiece a day for room and board. A bargain at twice that, with the generous meals she provided. Owen intended to purchase the goods with his own money and return her Liberty half-dollar coin to her.

Perhaps he would find a gift for Hanne in the store. Something small. The thought of shopping for her brought a smile.

A lady passed with three young children in tow. To give them room, Owen pressed himself sideways up to the announcement board outside the sheriff's office.

That's when he saw the poster.

His face pressed right up against a sketch that had to be of Knut Hemstad, only they had the eyes wrong.

WANTED, the notice read. For a triple murder committed in the country of NORWAY.

Under the drawing was the name KNUT AMUNDSSON.

The poster said the Norwegian government would reward anyone for his capture, dead or alive.

Owen walked away from the poster, as quickly as he could.

He went into the general store and paced around, not able to focus on anything.

"Can I help you, son?" the shopkeeper said. He was an old man wearing two pairs of glasses, one on his eyes and one atop his head.

Owen noted this, but otherwise paid him no mind. He kept pacing.

How could it be? *Knut?* His real name was Knut Amundsson?

Knut, a killer? It made no sense.

And then it made terrible sense. All of it fell into place. Hanne's downcast eyes. Her tears of shame.

Owen felt a punch of shock to his chest. Full understanding hit him hard. Hanne was a killer.

"I say, can I help you, young fellow?" the shopkeeper repeated.

"No, sir," Owen answered.

He went out into the bright, cold sunshine.

Then he shook his head. He reprimanded himself—he needed to act natural and calm. He went back into the store.

"Begging your pardon, sir. I need twenty-five cents' worth of flour and the same of brown sugar." The shopkeeper began to measure out the goods. "I couldn't remember what I'd been sent for, for a moment there."

The shopkeeper nodded. "Happens to folks all the time. I got one fellow comes two, three times a day. Though I suspect he comes for the checkers as much as for the groceries."

Owen made himself smile, paid, and took the package under his arm. He exited the store.

Passing by the noticeboard, he pulled off the poster with as casual a manner as he could fake.

He folded it and shoved it under his poncho, into his vest.

The school bell rang down the street. A pretty lady passing by gave him a smile. Townsend seemed a good little town.

He would not be staying.

BACK AT THE GERLINGERS, Owen found everyone in a cheerful mood. Sissel was up and helping Frau Gerlinger and Hanne to do the wash. The day was cold but crisp, the laundry freezing dry on the line.

He could not meet Hanne's bright smile, but rode Pal straight into the barn, only dismounting once inside.

Stieg was there, currying the horses.

"Owen, I'm glad to see you," he said. "The Gerlingers have made us an official proposition, and I want to hear your thoughts. They would like us all to stay here for the rest of the winter. We would help with the chores and cover grocery expenses. In return, we would receive a place to stay. That's what I understand, at least. I wish I had more German. And I know it's an odd situation, but she did mean, I believe, for the arrangement to include all of us if you wanted to stay on—"

"Stieg," Owen tried to interrupt. "We need to talk."

"Though, I suppose, she can't know you are not our family."

"Listen, Stieg—"

"No, you're right, she can tell you're not our brother. But I do believe the invitation extends to us all. And though it would be strange, we could continue our expedition in the spring."

Owen had given up speaking, waiting for Stieg to talk himself out. He stood with his hands on his hips, facing the snowy yard. Pal's steamy breath rose beside him.

Stieg finally took in Owen's reluctance and paused.

"What is it?"

"You could have told me," Owen said.

He handed over the folded wanted notice.

Stieg unfolded it, his lips pressed thin.

"You could have told me," Owen repeated, his voice dark with anger.

Stieg's expression went cold.

"You would have left us," Stieg said. "You'll leave us now, see if you don't."

"Don't you put it on me. It's wrong what you did!"

"Surely you understood we were in trouble. Think of how you found us!"

"I didn't know it was this kind of trouble!"

"I didn't know of this bounty here in America," Stieg said. "This is the first I've known."

"You tricked me!" Heat flushed Owen's neck.

Stieg's blue eyes flashed with anger.

"I did nothing of the sort. We had no obligation to tell you of our troubles at home."

Knut had heard their raised voices and came to the door of the barn. His large bulk blocked most of the sunlight.

"I took Knut to town yesterday, because I didn't know!" Owen said bitterly. "People might have recognized him. He might have been hurt! Shot!"

"As I said, I did not know there was a bounty for him here in America!"

Knut asked something in Norwegian, and Stieg handed him the

poster. Knut stared at his own face, creased by the folds of the paper. His eyes went wide. The paper began to tremble in his hands.

"You lied to me," Owen said. "You all treated me like a friend, and all the while you were lying to me."

"You knew we were in trouble, because you saw us jump from the train."

"I thought—I don't know what I thought. Maybe you had family after you. Someone who wanted to take Sissel away and break your family up."

"You took our money. You knew that fifty dollars was too much to pay, but you did it anyway. You are guilty, too."

Owen shook his head. Stieg was smarter and would run circles around him in an argument.

"All I'm saying is, you could have told me!" he shouted. "Why tell me about the Nytte and then hold back on the thing that puts us all in danger?"

Owen saw that Hanne was at the door. Her eyes were wide, her expression distraught.

"We might have told you, in time," Stieg said.

"Well, you didn't."

Hanne crossed and took the wanted poster from Knut's hands.

"Now you know," Hanne said. "Now you understand why we are running."

Owen looked away, too angry, too upset. It was hard to be so close to her.

"What is it your uncle has that's so important?" Owen said. "Will you tell me the truth about that, at least?"

"He is a Berserker, like me," Hanne said. Her eyes were big with some plea that Owen could not, would not, grant. "He can teach me how to control the Nytte, so I will never . . ." She drew herself up. "Do. What I did. Again."

Owen looked at her, standing there so straight. Goddamn, he felt tricked. Tricked and angry and left out.

He walked away from them, to the hooks where he'd hung up their saddles and bridles. He busied himself gathering up his tack.

"So you want to be done with us? All of us?" Stieg said. "Do I understand correctly?"

Devil take him, he was asking about Hanne. And she was right there. Owen counted to ten before he spoke.

"If you want me to take you to your uncle in Wolf Creek, we leave today. If you want to stay here, that's your choice." His voice sounded low and dead now, even to his own ears. "But you'll need to pay me either way."

CHAPTER TWENTY-THREE

Frau Gerlinger wept when she finally understood they meant to leave. She kept gesturing to things in the house, trying to tell Hanne about all the things they would do together, if only Hanne could persuade her siblings to stay. She showed Hanne a cake pan, a set of wooden skis. She even dragged out the accordion in its leather case, pleading, "*Gehe nicht*," all the while.

"I'm sorry, so sorry," Hanne repeated. Hanne's own sadness made her feel numb, so it was easy to be firm in the face of Frau Gerlinger's upset feelings.

Sissel began to cry, too. Frau Gerlinger clutched at the thin girl, clearly making the argument that Sissel, if none of the others, could stay with her.

"Sissel, do you want to stay here?" Hanne asked her. "They are very kind. And we could come for you, in the spring or summer."

"No. I won't stay alone!" Sissel said. "But . . . can't we rest another day or two? My arm still hurts. I'm so tired of running."

"There is a bounty on our brother's head," Hanne said. "If he stays here, it brings great risk on the Gerlingers. We cannot repay their kindness with such danger."

Sissel sat on the bed, her eyes and nose streaming.

"You ruin everything!" she cried. "This is the nicest place we've ever been and we could have a life here—"

"*You* may if you like!" Hanne shouted. "You have lots of choices. Just say the word and you can stay and we will be rid of you!"

Frau Gerlinger bustled between them, trying to soothe their feelings, not knowing what they were saying, yet understanding them quite well.

"You just want him all to yourself," Sissel hissed.

"What?" Hanne said, wheeling to face her sister.

"You knew I liked him, and so you set your cap for him just to spite me."

"That's silly," Hanne said.

"Is it? You can't stand for any boy to have an interest in me. What about those railroad boys at the station?"

Hanne scoffed before she could stop herself.

"You don't see that I am growing up into a woman," Sissel said.

"You're right. I don't," Hanne said. "You don't act like a woman. You act like a child. And none of that matters. He wants nothing to do with me."

"I won't be left behind," Sissel said.

"Then pack. We leave as soon as we can." Then Hanne turned and said over her shoulder, "Maybe you'll win his heart between here and Wolf Creek."

It was an unkind thing to say, but she felt unkind and more.

Sissel began to gather her things, pouting.

Frau Gerlinger sat on the bed to stare out the window for a moment. Hanne felt sorry for the woman. She went to the desk in the living room and used their pen and ink to write a note for Frau Gerlinger.

She blew on the scrap of paper until the ink dried. When Hanne pressed it into the older woman's hand, Frau Gerlinger swept her into an embrace.

THEY WERE A grim party, setting out, though well fed and rested. Frau Gerlinger had packed them food for the trip, and in the end, refused their money. Sissel had kept her eyes looking over her shoulder at the farm as they rode away, but Hanne kept her eyes forward.

Owen allowed Daisy to walk for a few hours. He showed kindness to his dog, but to Hanne and her siblings, he remained cool and aloof.

The afternoon sky was brilliantly blue and cloudless but had no cheering effect on the travelers. The companionable chatter they had known before had given way to a morose silence. All day long there was only the muted *clip-clop* of the horses' hooves on the snowy path. They were climbing, the horses scrambling up the rocky, pitted switchbacks.

In the early afternoon it began snowing. Fat, lazy snowflakes drifted down, taking their time. The contrast of the snow in the air made the dark colors of green pine and stone gray stand out all the more.

Daisy tired, and Owen stopped them so he could place her again in the saddlebags.

Hanne tried not to look at him too much.

As they crested the mountain, they were met with an expansive view. Montana went on and on before them. Craggy mountains and valleys overlaid with snow. There was a large, flat, dark ribbon snaking through the underbrush at the bottom of the valley that lay before them.

"What's that?" Stieg asked.

"The Missouri," Owen told them. And then, "It's a river. And we need to cross it."

EVERY TIME OWEN looked at Hanne, he felt an insatiable restlessness. Like his body wanted to run a mile or lift something heavy. He knew now that she'd never be his, and he wanted the whole thing to be over.

Owen examined the flowing water. There were stretches along the Missouri that were wide and placid. This was not one of them. The banks were narrow here, and the water was flowing quick. Snow was falling hard. Each flake was whisked away as soon as it hit the river. Flats of snow-covered ice sat on the surface of the water near the riverbank. They were thin—the water was moving too quickly for much ice to form.

Owen considered the depth. He'd warrant the river was three feet high in the center. The horses would be wet up to the flank. The water would be freezing, but if they kept the horses moving, they'd warm up.

The problem was that it was entirely possible the Hemstads—rather, the Amundssons—would get wet, at least their feet. Wet feet with temperatures below zero could lead to frostbite quickly.

He started to lead the party north, even though it was counter to their course.

"We won't cross here?" Stieg called.

"I'd rather find a more shallow spot," Owen said. "I don't want us to get wet."

"We're not afraid of a little cold water," Stieg said. "In Norway we bathe in glacial springs, in the winter and summer alike!"

"Nevertheless, I'd rather be safe than sorry—"

"It's your decision," Stieg said. "But we are behind schedule, due to our stay with the Gerlingers. I think we would be fine to cross here. Of course, the authority is yours."

Owen sighed. Heading upriver would cost them a day or two.

"Let's give it a try, then," he decided. "I'll lead the pack mule."

"Very well," Stieg said. He kicked his horse forward.

Stieg held his feet out to the side as the horse waded deeper and deeper into the water. The water rushed over the horse's flanks, and the animal had to brace itself against the strong current.

"I'm fine!" Stieg called. "Come along!"

Sissel went next. At least her feet weren't in danger of being wet. She was shorter than Owen, and the horse she rode was tall and sure-footed.

Knut followed next, his horse plodding heavily out into the water. A piece of ice came floating down the river and tapped against the horse's legs. She whinnied, but went forward. Knut did not care to keep his feet high, and so they got wet. He'd regret that. Owen tried not to care.

Hanne went next. The horse she was riding, Joyful, was ill-tempered, though obedient enough.

Hanne looked small atop a horse. Owen wondered, for a moment, at how much power could be contained by such a slight form.

Joyful picked his way across the rocky river, and Hanne held her feet out of the water.

Now it was Owen's turn. He led the pack mule, who was as uncomplaining a mule as Owen had ever met. Owen lifted his boots well out of the way of the splashing river, and checked to see that Daisy was secure in the saddlebag.

Suddenly there was a wicked crack, and his hand, holding the mule's lead, was wrenched backward.

The mule brayed loudly with pain. It seemed that the mule had set down a leg into a hole and was stuck. He struggled and bucked. Owen pulled against the rope, but the mule had him off balance, and before he could reset his weight, the mule dragged him off his horse into the water.

Owen gasped with the icy shock of it. He could barely breathe. He pushed to his feet, the current wanting to take him downriver.

The mule had its ears laid against the side of its head and was thrashing in the water, trying to free its hoof. Owen saw blood in the river spray. He cussed again.

"Are you all right?" Hanne called from the far bank.

What did she care? Owen was furious with himself. How could he make such a stupid mistake?

Now he looked a dolt, icy and wet. They'd have to stop and build a fire!

The mule was screaming with pain, and Owen could see it had broken its leg. He drew his knife from its leather holder and began to saw at the lines of the saddlebags.

"Do you need help?" Stieg called from the shore.

Owen wished he didn't, but he did.

"Yeah," he called to Stieg, and Stieg wheeled his horse back into the snowy, icy waters.

Owen could not feel his feet now, and numbness was creeping up his legs.

He got the mule packs free and handed them to Stieg when he came close enough.

Owen waded back to Pal, who stood, such a good horse, waiting for him.

He slid his Winchester out of the scabbard on his saddle.

The mule fell to its knees. The river water coursed over its back. The animal's eyes were rolling with fear. Its braying became a terrible, hacking whine. Owen put the barrels to the mule's head and pulled the trigger. From the distant shore, Sissel cried out.

The mule fell, and the water flowed over its body.

Owen's teeth were beginning to chatter. He staggered to Pal and found he couldn't get his foot in the stirrup.

He set his jaw and looked to the shore. He would walk it.

Stieg was onshore already, dropping the mule's wet saddlebags on the snow.

Hanne was watching Owen. When she saw that he meant to walk to shore, she came riding out toward him in the river.

"I'll help you onto your horse," she said, moving to swing her leg over and drop into the water.

"Don't!" he yelled. His teeth clattered. "I don't want you to!"

She stayed on her horse, taken aback.

Ten more steps and he was onshore.

Knut was already laying the foundations for a fire, Stieg would dry the wood with his magic, and Hanne would make him coffee to warm him. Owen hated them all, both because they had seen him slip up and because now they were going to help him.

He wished he'd never taken that drink, back in Helena. If he hadn't, he'd likely have a job as a stable boy right now. He'd be mucking out stalls and spending his nights dreaming about starting his own business, instead of spending his nights dreaming about a girl who was intoxicating and lovely and dangerous. A girl who didn't trust him as far as she could spit and who should not be trusted herself.

CHAPTER TWENTY-FOUR

Rolf had endured hours of Ketil's taunting. They were following a raven, now? Following a bird off into the wilderness? Was Rolf mad?

Rolf told him all about Odin and the ravens he sent as guides and messengers to his believers, but Ketil scoffed. For every poem Rolf recounted, Ketil offered up a bawdy improvisation. When Rolf recited, *"Fog bound, fog blind, | The raven's cry was their only light."*

Ketil answered, *"Whore bound, whore blind, | The lady's cry was my own delight."*

He laughed about that one for a good long time. Meanwhile the raven flew ahead, over the snowy meadows, leading them over a hill, then through a small stream, perching on rocks and barren tree limbs when they trailed too far behind. Did it not seem a marvel to Ketil that the raven stopped and waited for them? Apparently it did not.

So it was with immense satisfaction when, after they crossed the stream and climbed up another hill, the raven led them to what could only be a campsite.

The snow was trampled down. There were signs of horses in the brush. The raven was perched on an odd rounded shape against a cliff face. It was dark silver gray but also let light bounce off. As Rolf came closer he realized that was wrong—it was transmitting light. Its surface was odd, lumpy but different from a rock. It was not rock but ice! It was an ice shelter.

"Ketil, look!" Rolf had cried. "They were here! They were! *Ásáheill!*" he cried in Old Norse, giving thanks to all the Gods of Æsir. "And one of them is a Storm-Rend."

The cave was a marvel.

The young Storm-Rend was of considerable talent. Stepping inside the structure, Rolf had to bend his head. The ground was bare of ice and the snow flattened, as if they'd laid down a cloth.

Ketil came to peer into the structure and sniff.

"You can't say it's not them," Rolf cut him off. "No one but a Storm-Rend, and a very powerful one, could make a shelter like this one."

Ketil shrugged, his eyes cold.

"Not that powerful," he said. "He bled from the nose." He pointed to a smear of blood, frozen bright red on the wall of the cave. "He keeps it up, he'll go blind."

THEY FOLLOWED the trail to the tidy farm. Unfortunately, it also seemed that the trail led away from the house. The marks of many hooves led off into the woods to the northwest of the house.

"Let me do the talking, will you?" Rolf said. "I'm sure I can get it out of them."

"Ach, you're a grandmother," Ketil said. "I'm sick of doing things your way. Your way has drawn us across this cold, rocky country. We could have been home by now!"

The door to the log house was shut, with lazy curls of smoke rising from the chimney.

A dog lay on the ground by the door. It must have been old, because it didn't catch sight nor scent of the two men watching the farm from the rise above.

"We don't want to attract notice," Rolf said. "Why not just let me handle things?"

As they drew closer, it was clear why their arrival had gone unnoticed by the farmers. Music was coming from the house. Accordion music.

It was a sad, haunting song. It was a classical German song, as best as one could be played on such a boisterous instrument.

"Oh, how touching," Ketil said, putting his hand on his heart. "They're playing their own funeral dirge."

"Listen, Ketil, killing them makes it worse for us," Rolf protested. "We were lucky we weren't caught in Livingston."

Ketil was dismounting. He pretended not to hear.

"It makes it harder for us to recruit the Nytteson, if we have the law on our trail!"

"The kid is already wanted!" Ketil snorted. "What difference does it make?"

"Ketil! These Nytteson are my responsibility. You've said so many times! Please don't make my job harder—"

Ketil was already at the door. He knocked firmly. The door was thrown open by a woman whose face was full of joy. But her face fell when she saw it was Ketil.

"Who were you expecting, my lady?" Ketil asked her.

She drew up her shoulders, immediately sensing something was wrong with her visitor. Maybe she saw the dog, dead at the side of the door, its neck snapped.

The woman turned and warned her husband in German, but too late. Ketil pushed her back into the house. She fell hard on her rear end.

Rolf stepped in and shut the door behind him. He spoke in German, "Are there children here? A big one?" He indicated Knut's height and girth with his hands.

"No, no," she said. "I do not know of whom you speak."

"What's she saying?" Ketil asked in Norwegian.

"She says she knows nothing."

Ketil walked into the kitchen. He picked up a dull knife from where it soaked in a pot of water on the counter.

The player of the accordion, the woman's husband, was a small man. He'd frozen in his rocking chair, the accordion opened out and ready to make sound.

"We saw the tracks outside," Rolf said in German. "We know they were here."

Ketil stalked toward the little man, a smile on his face.

"I wonder how hard it will be to kill him with this small, dull knife," Ketil said to Rolf. "I'm sure I can. Only it will be *nasty*."

"Please tell me," Rolf pleaded. "The man I'm with is crazy. He will bring pain—"

But the woman set her mouth in a line. She turned her back on Rolf, turning to face toward the wall.

"Hilde," her husband said. "I think we should tell—"

Ketil was advancing on him.

The accordion gave a desperate, unmusical wheeze.

"Be quiet!" she scolded him. "We cannot tell them what we do not know!"

"Just tell us, when did they leave, which way did they go?" Rolf pleaded.

The man screamed. Ketil had put one hand on the back of his head and stuck the knife in the little man's right ear.

Hilde pushed past Rolf and tried to reach the shotgun Rolf now saw was mounted above the door.

Rolf grabbed her skirts and pulled her from the gun.

Ketil made a fist and pounded the knife into the little man's ear, as one would a nail into a knot of wood.

The woman was scrambling to get the door open. She had her fingers around the edge of the door, was scraping at the floor with her legs, trying to find purchase, but Rolf was in the way.

The little man screamed and screamed, and Rolf suddenly couldn't stand it. He couldn't bear for the woman to die.

Rolf threw the door open. "Go!" he shouted to the woman. Then she was running, racing toward the barn.

"What's wrong with you?" Ketil asked Rolf, with a little laugh. "Why are you such a fool?"

Ketil threw the body of the German down and crossed to the door.

"You're too soft for this work, old man," Ketil said to Rolf.

The German man's feet were twitching. Rolf staggered outside to see the woman turn to face Ketil. She stood near the barn doors, an ax in her hands.

Ketil crossed the yard, muscular energy vivid in his stance.

Ketil spun in the air and kicked the ax out of the woman's hands. He snatched the ax from the air.

"Don't!" Rolf cried. "Please!"

But Ketil brought the ax down, and then there was silence. The weapon hung from his hand as he strode back toward Rolf.

"That's enough from you," Ketil said. His head was lowered, like a bull. Rolf could see the irises of his eyes were full black. A Berserker enraged.

Rolf held up his hands.

"Slow down there, Ketil. You and I are on the same side of this."

"Do you know they laugh at you? The Baron and his noble friends? They laugh at you with your old ideas. Your precious studies."

Rolf backed away. "I've been working with Baron Fjelstad for twenty years—"

"You have these ideas about the Baron, about what he does and why he does it. You think he does it for the love of the Nytte, or for the old Gods. But that's not it at all."

Ketil threw the bloody ax aside.

"He isn't just protecting us. He is training us to fight, to kill," Ketil continued. "We do raids on the Greenlanders. Me and the other Berserkers. Did you know that? Did you know we practice slaying them, and no one finds out?"

There was a killing gleam shining in the Berserker's eyes. The pupils were huge, taking in all the light, Rolf's posture, the shadows, the fallow wheat field beyond. Rolf knew Ketil's senses were heightened. He knew the young man was reviewing all the ways he could take Rolf's life.

Rolf had to do something, or he would be the Berserker's next kill. He stepped forward and slapped Ketil across the face.

"Ketil Nilsen, do you think me a fool?"

Ketil's eyes were wide, surprised out of his blood-rage.

"I know all about the Baron's plans," Rolf bluffed. "Who do you think has helped him all these years? I know about Greenland. I encouraged him to send you!

"I am in command of this expedition. You are here to help me. Do not forget it!"

Ketil's neck was flushing. He looked away. Rolf had won his life, at least for the day.

"Now," Rolf continued. "Let us search the house. Perhaps our young Nytteson left us some clues. And there is probably bread to eat."

Ketil backed away from Rolf, and toward the house. His hands were shaking, Rolf noticed.

The house was tidy and charming, except for the body of the farmer, which lay faceup on the hearth. One boot was too close to the fire and was smoking. Rolf kicked it out. The house could burn, but not until they left.

Ketil went to the kitchen and opened the cupboard. He found leftover cornbread and fried ham from breakfast. He devoured it eagerly, not offering a bite to Rolf. But Rolf did not mind.

Rolf's attention was drawn to a slip of paper on the table, under a tin mug of coffee.

It read, "Håkon Thorson, Wolf Creek," in a schoolgirl's careful, looping handwriting.

"What's that?" Ketil asked. He was standing in the doorway to a back room. He held a bottle of schnapps by the neck.

"The name and address of their uncle," Rolf said. "He's in a town called Wolf Creek."

Rolf handed him the scrap of paper.

"We will ride all night," Rolf said with authority.

Ketil nodded soberly.

Rolf was pleased. He realized now he ought to have taken a firm hand with Ketil much earlier. The young man was a Berserker. Of course, he would respond better to stern discipline than camaraderie.

Rolf found another loaf of bread, a quart-size jar of pickled eggs, and some smaller jars of preserves, which he gave Ketil to carry.

The two men exited the house into the calm, cold sun of the midday. The chickens were scraping on the ground. A fat hen was standing on the corpse of the farm woman. The rooster chased her off and took the spot, standing on the hump of the woman's rear end. Its voice was garish and ugly when it crowed. Rolf suppressed the urge to wring the bird's neck.

"We should water the horses," Rolf said.

"Yes," Ketil answered. He went to the well and lifted off the heavy wooden lid. Ketil stood looking down into the depths of the well for a moment.

"Is there a bucket?" Rolf asked.

Ketil didn't answer, only came stalking over to Rolf.

Too late, too late, Rolf saw Ketil's eyes were dark again.

Ketil grabbed him by the collar of his coat and dragged him toward the well.

"Stop! Stop it. Ketil, in the name of the Gods, stop!"

Rolf's feet dragged great ruts through the snowy, muddy ground.

"Great All-Father, hear me!" Rolf shouted. He reached for the stone in his pocket, as if it could help him now. "*Heilir Æsir!*"

"Let's see if the Gods can hear you from down below," Ketil said.

And he threw Rolf headlong down the well.

CHAPTER TWENTY-FIVE

By the time they stopped for the night, Hanne's fingers felt frozen to the pommel, even though she wore her mittens. The day had become bitterly cold.

They made a near-silent camp. Owen seemed upset they'd had to stop at all.

Earlier in the day, after he'd fallen into the Missouri, he sat glowering by the small fire Knut had made. Hanne forced Owen to drink mug after mug of hot coffee. He changed into the creased and dirty spare clothes from his saddlebags. His boots gave off steam by the fire, as had his new poncho.

Owen had looked utterly miserable sitting there. Hanne longed to speak some words of comfort to him, but she knew she had lost that right. They had caused him real grief, she could see that now.

The ride after that had been dull and grim. Owen set a fast, unforgiving pace. He didn't call for them to make camp for the night until the sky began to darken.

Then as soon as he had asked Stieg to make the campfire, he took his rifle and stalked off in search of game for supper. Daisy whined as he walked away, but Owen didn't seem to hear.

Much of the provisions that poor Muley Wuley had been carrying were soaked and ruined. With every parcel Hanne opened, her heart sank. All the good chicken Frau Gerlinger had packed was frozen now, slimy and coated with icy sludge. The cornbread had dissolved into lumpy mush. Worse still, the beans and flour must have fallen from the bags into the river and were lost. There was hardtack, which was wet but had retained its shape. Its taste had neither improved nor worsened with a dousing in the Missouri.

The Hemstads sat around a big fire that seemed to give off little warmth, waiting for the coffeepot to boil. Hanne stirred the makeshift porridge she'd made by adding snow to the ruined cornbread. It smelled good enough to travelers with hungry bellies.

"I wish we were back at Frau Gerlinger's," Sissel complained.

"Yes, yes, we know," Stieg snapped.

"I'm cold and hungry," she continued.

"We know!"

"Why is Owen so cross with us?" Sissel said, though he might return at any moment. "What did you do to him?" she asked Hanne.

"I did nothing!" Hanne said hotly.

"Well, why is he so cross?" she persisted.

"It's complicated," Stieg said.

"You always say that when you don't want me to know something," Sissel said.

Stieg sighed and scrubbed his hand over his face.

"We found out that the law is after Knut, here in America."

"They think he was the one who committed my crimes," Hanne said.

Sissel's mouth twisted in anger.

"No wonder he's angry! The sheriff is after us? You should have told him," she said. "You should have told me!"

"We did not know about the bounty until today," Stieg protested.

"He is our friend," Sissel said.

"He only became our friend on the trail," Stieg said. "We did not know we could trust him before. We still don't know very much about him."

"That's a stupid thing to say," Knut broke in. They all looked up with surprise. "He's a good fellow and you all know it. He could have turned me in when he found that wanted poster. He could have brought the law and turned me in for the reward."

Knut stood and went off for some air.

Hanne watched her brother's vast bulk move through the woods. He seldom ventured an opinion. When he did, he was always right.

ROLF PRAYED for a quick death. The Germans had dug a proper well, with rocks fitted into the sides. It was deep and the water deathly cold. The water level was low—they had had to dig far.

He would have liked to see the sky again, but Ketil had closed the lid on him.

His back was scraped from his shoulder to his hip. It was surprising he hadn't broken a bone. He wished he'd broken his neck.

Shuddering with the cold, Rolf clutched the rune stone in his hands. He thought of Odin. Of the rune on the face of the stone he could barely feel in his fingers. He didn't want Ketil's sneering face to be the last image in his mind when he died.

The chattering of his teeth came louder and louder in the well.

Heilir Æsir, he prayed, calling on all the Gods. *Please take me now.*

His hands shook so badly he fumbled the stone, and it dropped into the water.

This seemed fateful. Odin had abandoned him. And then he heard a carriage approaching.

THE DOCTOR FROM Townsend managed, with the help of his horse, to drag Rolf out of the well. Rolf had screamed every time his wounded shoulder hit the side of the well, had screamed until he blacked out.

Now Rolf sat bundled on a cot in the back room at the Townsend General Store. He was next to a stove. They had removed his torn shirt, and a bandage for his back was wrapped around his rib cage.

The shopkeeper's wife had brought him a toddy of rum, tea, and molasses. He'd drained the mug, and now listened as the floor pounded with boots arriving into the main room of the store beyond the thin plank wall. With careful fingers, he felt the wound on his back. It was bandaged neatly, but the rough cloth of the bandage made his raw skin scream.

Rolf gave thanks over and over. He had lost his rune stone, or maybe he had given it as an offering when it sank away in the well. Either way, he had been saved by the favor of the Gods. His mission was clear—he must find the Nytteson and help them. He must protect them from Ketil.

The doctor was holding court in the front room, telling and retelling how he'd found the German couple butchered and Rolf down the well. Rolf had learned Gerlinger was the surname of the farmers from the cries of anguished disbelief coming from the next room.

The men began to organize a posse. Rolf listened carefully.

"I'm tellin' you, I saw the great brute from that wanted poster right here in town!" said a man with a gravelly voice. "He was suckin' on a candy stick. I remember it 'cause it looked so odd. A great big fellow like that, but happy like a little kid."

"We need to set out straightaway!" another man shouted. "We're wasting time."

"We don't know for sure it was him—" countered another voice.

Rolf banged open the door. Stood there shirtless, trailing a blanket, leaning on the door frame.

"He's awake!" said a stout farmer.

The men began shouting, asking Rolf to identify the killer.

The doctor shushed them all. Crossed to where Rolf stood and peered into his eyes.

"Do you know your name, fella? You had a bad fall."

"I'm Peter Kronen," Rolf lied.

"How's your back?"

A redheaded man pushed the doctor aside. "What's the killer look like? Tall? Short?"

Another man, this one with a big bushy beard, shone a lantern right in Rolf's face. "Was it a boy who threw you down the well? A great big blond boy? Like a giant, wearing horse blankets?"

"No. It was a man," Rolf said. "Tall and trim. Seemed well dressed. With a thick blond mustache."

"That ain't the kid I saw," the bearded man answered.

"He's very tall. A handsome man, some would say."

Rolf knew these men would die if they caught up with Ketil. The Berserker would relish the chance to fight so many men at once. He would kill them, then brag endlessly about it to the Nytteson back home. But if Ketil was busy fighting off a posse, it might give Rolf the chance to get to Wolf Creek before he did.

"Why did he do it?" the shopkeeper asked. "What could he have had against the Gerlingers?"

"I don't know," Rolf lied. "I was visiting with them, they are old friends of my family from Germany, when the man appeared. Mr. Gerlinger was playing the accordion for us—"

He broke off. He did not need to feign a shiver of horror as he remembered how they had been killed.

The men were convinced. They began to speak of organizing and provisioning the posse. They had many questions for Rolf about which direction Ketil might have gone.

"He did not seem the careful type," Rolf told them. "I imagine he left a trail."

The members of the posse gathered themselves up and headed for the door. The doctor was among their number.

Rolf stopped the shopkeeper.

"I need to get to Wolf Creek," he told the man.

"You'll want to catch the train to Helena; you can get a stage from there."

"Is there a train today?"

The shopkeeper eyed the bandages running around Rolf's chest to the padding on the back.

"There's a morning train and one in the afternoon. I guess you could catch it. But don't you need to rest a mite? You been whipped pretty solid."

"I need to buy clothing. And I'm hungry," he said. "But most of all, I must make the train."

He grasped the shopkeeper's hands. The man nodded.

Injured or not, Rolf had to hurry. He feared Ketil would kill the Berserker instead of recruiting her. And the siblings, too.

CHAPTER TWENTY-SIX

Wolf Creek was a busy, if lean-looking, town. The buildings were tall and skinny, as if drawn together against the wind that came down out of the mountains. Instead of a wide, flat thoroughfare, Main Street was pitted with rocks and gullies where the rain had washed away the soil.

Now that they knew Knut was being hunted, Owen insisted they take more care. Hanne, Knut, and Sissel stayed in a pine wood, a mile southeast of town, while Owen and Stieg went in to try to find out where Uncle Håkon's house was located.

Wolf Creek was a mining town, built all in a rush ten years before, when placer deposits had been found up the creek. There had been gold, and some miners were still having success panning it out of the water.

Owen and Stieg rode down the main street, searching for a general store, or perhaps a saloon, in which to make inquiries. It seemed like the only structure built to last was the jail. It was made of river rock and cement. The other buildings were clapboard, weathered near to silver. There was a three-story hotel and a school, a small one, where some children flocked in play around the building under the supervision of a prim-mouthed schoolteacher at the door.

The miners they passed seemed flinty eyed and suspicious to Owen, but he reckoned that might be because he was now traveling with a wanted man. Perhaps even the most friendly town might seem hostile when you were on the lookout for it. The sky was an ominous gray, with clouds looming overhead. That didn't help the impression.

Owen nodded toward a building, the Wolf Creek Outfitter and General Stores. They dismounted and tied their horses at the hitching post that ran along the front of the building.

Inside, they found it well stocked. There was everything to provision a small mining outfit, along with stores of dry goods and staples.

The shopkeeper was sitting on a stool by the door, polishing the glass bell for an oil lamp with a flannel cloth.

"Help you, gentlemen?" he asked.

"We could use some flour and some sugar, first off," Owen said. "Beans, too, if you got 'em."

Stieg met Owen's eye and seemed to understand Owen's thinking that they'd get better information out of the man once they'd made a purchase or two.

The shopkeeper went behind the counter.

"How much you want, say, a pound?"

"Two pounds of flour, two of cornmeal, and a half of sugar. Brown's fine."

"And do you have any dried apples?" Stieg asked.

"Nope. Got some raisins, though. You like raisins?"

"Well enough," Stieg answered.

"I got 'em in a sack like this. Five cents," said the shopkeeper. Owen nodded, and the man set the small brown bag on the counter.

"We're looking for a man who lives nearabouts," Owen said. "Wonder if you know him."

"Well, ain't but one way to find out," said the shopkeeper. "Ask away."

Owen smiled at that, but it didn't ease his wariness. "His name is Håkon Thorson."

"Hmm," said the shopkeeper. "He a Swede?"

"Pretty much," Owen answered.

"I think there was a Swede the name of Thorson working a little claim up the creek about three miles."

Stieg flashed Owen a smile.

"He bought it off another Swede named Peterson. Or might have been a Russian German. That claim's shifted hands a bunch of times."

"Just head up the creek?" Owen asked.

"Look for a little fork in the creek, about two miles up. Then follow it off to the left. It'll go up a ways, then you'll see a cabin in a clearing up there. Pretty enough, in a meadow. But not a lot of gold, from what I hear."

Stieg was grinning broadly. The shopkeeper's eyes flitted to his face, then back to Owen's.

"Anything else I can do for you boys?" he asked.

"I reckon not," Owen said. "And thank you."

"SIT DOWN," Sissel said. "You're wearing a path in the forest floor."

It was true. Hanne's footsteps had created a small furrow in the shrunken snow, revealing the soft pine needles and dry earth below. But she could not stay still.

She could smell the wood smoke drifting off the town. They were in the woods to the east, decamped just off the trail.

Owen had left Daisy with them, asked them to try to get her to eat. Hanne offered the dog some hardtack.

"I know," Hanne had told the dog in Norwegian. "It doesn't taste good, but you need to build your strength."

Daisy licked at the hardtack, but wouldn't take it into her mouth.

"She doesn't want it because it tastes horrible," said Sissel. "You want some meat, don't you, Daisy? Poor, sweet thing."

Sissel knelt down on the snow and pulled Daisy into her arms, cuddling the dog. Daisy allowed herself to be coddled and petted, though she did not seem to enjoy it much.

"Don't smother her," Hanne told her sister. "I'm glad you like her, but she's a working dog, not a plaything!"

"She's my friend, aren't you, Daisy?" Sissel said, snuggling into the dog's ruff.

Then Daisy growled. Sissel sat back, utterly surprised, fear ignited in her eyes.

The hair on Daisy's neck and shoulders stood up—her eyes focused on the trail behind them where two men came on horseback.

The men looked trail worn and weary. Their clothes were stained and brown. Hanne's chest tightened. Was this the threat she'd felt drawing near?

The man in the lead had a disfigured face. It looked as if he'd suffered a bite from an animal as a child. A dog? A horse? The second man was fat and had a ruddy face and red hair.

"Looky here, Barnabas," the bit-faced man said. "We got some young'uns. You ladies playing at rangers and Indians?"

Knut made a movement as if to rise, but Hanne made a motion for him to stay.

"We are waiting on our father," Hanne said. "You may pass us by."

"Oh, I may, may I?" the ugly man laughed.

He did not dismount, but took a good look around their small campsite. The second man had small, unsmiling black eyes set in his red, fleshy face. He was large set, but not so large as her brother.

"Why'dnt you head on into town, I wonder," the man asked. "You all shy or somethin'?"

Hanne stiffened her back and did not dignify him with an answer to his question.

"Move on now. We want no trouble," she said.

Hanne's eyes took inventory of all the available weapons: The men had a rifle on each saddle; the ugly man had a bowie knife in a leg scabbard; there were two big sticks in easy reach. There were rocks under the snow. She had her fingernails.

She forced herself to breathe. She put her hand on Knut's arm. It would look, to the men, as if she were restraining him, but what she was doing was grounding her energy into his. She breathed out slowly, pushing her anxiety into Knut's earthbound warmth.

"Oh, we're moving on, missy," said the one with the bitten face. "Don't you worry about us."

The men rode right through their little assembly, making them move out of the way. Knut had to step back so the first man wouldn't trample him.

The second man made Hanne's heartbeat spike. He looked at Knut, studying his features with beady black eyes. He kept his eyes on Knut as they passed by, rotating his head.

"Oh, I hate it here," Sissel said when the men were well away. "I want to go home already!"

"Come back, Stieg," Hanne prayed aloud. "Come back now."

"I wish we had never come."

"Get up," Hanne told her sister and brother. "Get on your horses."

"Why?" Sissel asked.

"We must go to meet Stieg and Owen."

"Why?"

Hanne glared at her sister. Limp, white-blond hair hung down around Sissel's peaked face. Her skin was sallow, but her expression fierce and obstinate.

"Because my Nytte tells me we must!" Hanne said severely. "It is hard enough to keep you alive! Do not make it harder!"

Sissel's gray eyes glinted with resentment. "We should have stayed with Frau Gerlinger!"

"And risk their lives?" Hanne snapped back.

"Girls, please do not fight," Knut said. "I cannot bear it."

He looked tired. Under his eyes were dark circles Hanne had not noticed before.

"We must head to town," Hanne said. "Come, both of you. We will meet Stieg and Owen on their way to us. I did not like the look of those men."

CHAPTER TWENTY-SEVEN

Rolf lay on his belly in a grove of gnarled scrub oak, not two hundred feet from the ramshackle claim deeded to one Håkon Thorson.

Rolf was praying all the time. He had no doubt that all of Æsir was listening to him. He finally understood a fragment of poetry that had always evaded him. *Golden-oiled swim on troubles.* Those favored by the Gods, anointed by their oils of gold, could surrender their worries and float past them.

He would have missed the train, but it had been held in the station, waiting on a bag of mail. Once he arrived in Helena, Rolf had met a trapper who was headed to Wolf Creek and had room to give him a ride in his wagon, which was empty except for a comfortable bearskin the trapper had decided not to sell.

Over breakfast at a broken-down hotel, Rolf had inquired

discreetly to the proprietor about a Norwegian named Thorson. He hadn't heard of him, but then a miner with teeth the color of moss bumped into Rolf when he was leaving. He knew Thorson. He told Rolf exactly how to get to Thorson's claim shanty, several hours up valley from Wolf Creek.

At the livery, the stable master had no stock for sale, but offered to rent him a horse. Every obstacle was surmounted even as it presented itself. Rolf felt favored indeed, the path golden-oiled.

The dead autumn grasses had overgrown the meadow around the house. The snow had melted away, except for patches near the knotty, gnarled scrub oak stands and a couple of lone pine trees.

There were no chickens or signs of other livestock. Everything was still inside the house. If it had not directly matched the description the miner had given Rolf, he would have thought he was in the wrong place.

All was quiet. He was ahead of Ketil, it seemed. And ahead of the Nytteson.

Rolf hid his rented horse in a stand of aspen trees nearby. He wanted to see what kind of a Nytteson this Håkon Thorson was before he made his move. So far, he'd seen no sign of the man.

Rolf's shoulder wound ached without reprieve. The skin was starting to scab, and when he moved, it broke open anew. Despite his discomfort, his eyes closed.

* * *

WHEN HE AWOKE, it was late morning. Noises came from the path leading to the meadow from the creek. It was the Nytteson. Rolf gave a silent thanks to Odin.

First in the party was an American cowboy, identifiable by his hat and poncho, and the rifle protruding from its scabbard. He must be acting as their guide.

Next came the Norwegians. Rolf was grateful for the opportunity to study them unobserved. He had much to learn about these youngsters if he was to help them.

In front was the tall, thin young man. He must be the Storm-Rend who had built the ice cave. The young man's eyes were bright as they took in the sight of the little house.

"Hey!" he called. "Hey! Uncle!"

Next came a small, pallid-looking girl. Yet to come into her gift, Rolf theorized, if she had one at all. Her face was thin, her expression miserable. Children so sickly seldom received the Nytte.

And then came the Oar-Breaker accused of the murders. He was so much an Oar-Breaker, wide shouldered and barrel chested.

Last was the Berserker. She was on edge. Her body was so tense in the saddle, it looked like she might launch herself out at any moment. Her light blond hair was whipping around her face, but Rolf could see how intelligent and alert she was. And how untrained.

"Uncle!" the Storm-Rend called again.

The Nytteson came close to the house and dismounted.

The American guide took the reins to the horses. He led the stock to a nearby tree to tether them, and the siblings approached the front door.

THE MEADOW THEIR uncle's home stood in was very pretty. Mountains rose behind the yellowed grasses. A waterfall could be seen cascading down a gulch. It could almost have been Norway, except for the clumps of dwarf bushes and the sage.

None of that put Hanne at ease. She felt as if her nerves were being drawn out of her body. Every part of her jangled with alarm.

As they drew up to the homestead shack, she saw the boards were weathered and uneven. Between the boards were great gaps and cracks. The backside of paper could be seen through the gaps. Shingles blown off the roof littered the dead grass around the shack.

"Uncle Håkon," Stieg called. "It is your nieces and nephews, come all the way from Øystese!"

There was no answer.

"He is not here, Brother," Hanne said.

"Then we will wait," decided Stieg.

She dismounted, and Owen took the reins of her horse. He did not look into her face, but she could read from the thin line of his pressed lips that he was not encouraged by the looks of the place.

"I'll keep watch," he said.

Owen had not liked the sound of the men from the woods near town when Hanne had described them, especially once she described the man with the bitten face.

Stieg knocked on the door and found it unlatched. He looked over his shoulder at Hanne and offered her a weak smile.

She felt a deep pang of love for her brother at that moment. He had led them to America to find this man. The only one who might help her. She patted him on the shoulder and tried to return his smile.

Then Stieg pushed the door in. It grated on the floor, hanging unevenly in the frame off leather hinges.

The inside of the cabin was very dim. Smelled dark and foul. There were no windows and the walls had been papered thickly.

There was a form in the corner. Horror crawled up from Hanne's gut through her veins. It was the desiccated form of a body.

"No," she gasped.

A shotgun lay on the floor, near the body. The wall behind was splattered with dark, dried blood and bits of tissue.

Stieg grabbed Hanne in shock and dread.

"No!" Stieg said. "This cannot be. This cannot be! We have come too far!"

"Where is he?" Sissel asked, stepping in with Knut. "It's awfully dark," she said.

Then Sissel saw the body and moaned. She cried out.

Owen was standing at the door. "Dear God," he said.

Sissel sank to her knees near the door. She put her forehead on the earthen floor.

"He shot himself!" Hanne said. Despair was choking her throat.

"Stieg," Knut said. "What does it say?"

And Hanne saw Knut had his hand on the wall. His fingers grazed over a word written on the wall. *Håpet*, it said. *Mistet håpet*. Lost hope.

Hanne then saw, as her eyes adjusted, that the walls of the shack were covered in writing. Every inch was scratched with inky scrawl or pencil marks.

I will not kill.

How can I distinguish between the good and evil? Only God can. Then how does he allow me to live?

Jesus, remove this affliction.

Hanne spun in a circle, taking in the words her uncle had scrawled over every inch of the heavy cream-colored paper covering the walls.

Death comes. I cannot hide. How can I hide from myself?

I am a monster and I wish to be a monster.

Into society I can go no more, for I wish to kill all I see.

Large and small. Sane and disturbed, the handwriting told a grim tale.

I hunger. I hunger.

Lord, help me! Help me or kill me!

Jesus, do not let me pass from this house. I pray. I beseech. I beseech you from my knees.

And over and over was written: *My blood for their blood.*

It was written a thousand times. Two thousand times. Small and large. In ink and graphite and blood.

Hanne stumbled. She had to get out.

She fell into Owen, who was guarding the door. He helped her out into the cold air. Her chest heaved and strained. She couldn't breathe.

Owen had his arms under her arms. The golden grass and the sky were swimming.

"It's over," she said. Owen helped her down to the ground. A chipped shingle lay by her foot.

"No," Owen said.

"There's no hope. We're doomed. I'm doomed."

"No," Owen said. "You're gonna be all right."

"He was my only hope."

"Shh," Owen said. He cradled her head to his chest. His arms felt so good around her. She pressed her face into his poncho and let her tears sink into the wool.

"Don't cry. You're such . . . you're such a good person, Hanne. You don't need him. You don't need to learn anything from anyone, do you hear me?"

"No, no," she wept.

"You're good," he told her. "You're good inside. I know you are. I know it in my soul, Hanne."

Then there came an unmistakable metallic *CLICK-CLUNK*—a rifle being cocked.

"I hate to interrupt," the man with the bitten face said. "But we're here for the Norwegian."

He and his redheaded partner were stalking toward them through the meadow. A third man, considerably younger, stood off to the side with the horses, near a stand of scrub oak. A tin star was pinned on his jacket.

Owen pulled Hanne into the house and kicked the door closed.

"Yeah, go on in the house. That's just fine with us. We know you got that Norwegian brute in there with you," called the bounty hunter. "Now you send him out and we go away. This here's a dead-or-alive situation, so don't be cute about it!"

Hanne felt herself inside a rising tornado.

Sissel's eyes were wide with panic.

"Who's that?" Knut asked.

"Shhh!" Stieg said.

"We got a deputy out here, too," called the voice. "Official and everything, if he is a mite on the young side."

Hanne's hands were clinging to Owen's arms.

"I don't want to—I don't want to," she begged. She saw her reflection in Owen's deep brown eyes. Her face was distorted and terrified. Tears were streaming down her face.

"I have my gun," Owen said to her. "I'll try to scare them off."

The power, the rage was flooding her now.

"Oh please," she called out, falling to her knees. She grabbed her head. "Please! I don't want to kill!"

"Hold her!" Stieg called to Knut. "Help her!"

Knut grabbed her. Around them, the words of her uncle taunted her. *My blood for their blood. My blood for their blood.*

And then bullets blasted into the wall, up near the ceiling. Four shots. So loud!

Hanne's brothers and sister clutched at their ears. Dropped clumsily to the floor.

The bullets punched stars of daylight through the dark shack.

"We mean business out here. Got rifles and pistols trained on you and ain't but one door. Come on out now, one at a time."

Light came streaming in through the bullet holes, illuminating the dirt floating in the air, and Hanne was no longer herself.

She saw Owen looking at her, drawing back as her eyes went black. Hanne twisted easily from Knut's large hands. A rusty knife was stuck in a cutting block and fit beautifully into the palm of her hand.

"Hanne, you don't have to go!" Stieg cried.

But she had the door open and was out.

OH, THE JOY OF IT!

The joy of the air and the sky and the quarry.

The men were so slow. She was halfway across the yard before the ugly man even pulled the triggers on the two pistols he had pointed at her.

The bullets came crashing through the air, and Hanne ducked them, one and two. Then she came within his arm's reach. She smiled as she brought up the knife into his gut. She twisted it, through bowel, belly, and lung.

Her senses sang. The creek water smelled good. She was alive with the rocks and the chickadees and the cold water. Now the hot pistol was hers, but she threw it away.

She heard Knut call out to her, "Stop, Hanne! Stop!"

She vaulted over the horse to where the beefy man cowered. He had a gun in each hand but moved so slow. He was so slow she could laugh.

She flew up and brought her leg straight around, kicking him on the side of the head. He went down to hands and knees. Now she punched him in the kidney and he fell facedown into the dirt.

"Hanne!" cried her sister.

The man had his hand out, scrambling for his pistol, which was just out of his reach.

This was dull. Hanne reached for the gun and blew the man's face away.

There was one left, the little one with the tin star pinned on his coat, and he was puking in the bushes.

"Hanne, STOP!" shrieked her sister's voice, but Hanne pulled a thick, sharp knife from a leather sheath at the dead man's leg and she leaped over the hedge. She drew the deputy to her and inserted the knife elegantly, softly, kindly, into his rib cage. She wiggled the knife, just a little, between the rib bones, and knew it had punctured the heart. The deputy fell, and she saw he wasn't very old at all.

Hanne's eyes flickered over the horses, the brush. Oh, how she wished there were another enemy to kill.

A keening rose from behind her. She saw her sister bent over the body of her brother Stieg, bandaging his arm. Something in the sprawl of his body, some extra sense she had, told her he would be fine.

Now Owen, her cowboy, was walking, running to his horse. He was not a threat. Hanne watched him with her head cocked.

He made his crippled dog sit with Hanne's siblings and went off at a gallop.

She recorded only the fact of his movement. The meaning did not settle until a few moments later.

SHE BECAME AWARE of the sticky feeling of her fingers.

And her brother Knut talking to her.

He was telling her he was going for a doctor for Stieg.

* * *

Hanne felt a terrible gnawing in her gut. She blinked, looking around her.

She was in the middle of a terrible, bloody battleground. Three men lay around her. Her hands were covered in blood, the cream-striped sleeves of her rose-colored coat splattered with it.

"No," she mumbled. "Please, no!"

She rose and saw her sister sitting against the wall of the cabin. Stieg's head lay in her lap.

"What happened?" Hanne asked. "Oh, Sissel, what happened?"

"You killed them. They shot their guns into the house, and you killed them all."

"Where's Knut? And Owen?"

"Knut went for help. And Owen . . . Owen just left."

Hanne brought her hands to her face but could not bear to touch her own skin. Her stomach was roaring, demanding to be fed.

Hanne walked away from the shack. She waded into the knee-deep grasses of the meadow, crossed a patch of snow in the shadow of a lean pine tree.

"Where are you going?" Sissel called.

But Hanne started to run, tearing through the grass, then down to the creek. She plunged into the shallow water, falling to her knees. Her fingers scraped up coarse sand and mud from the streambed, and she scoured her hands and the sleeves of her coat. She scrubbed and scrubbed until her skin was red, chafing.

There was no choice for her. Hanne put her face into her icy hands and wept. She could not control the Berserker within, so she must put an end to it the way her uncle had. Such was her loneliness and her misery.

She would not eat. She would deny the bellowing of her stomach and let her body burn out.

Hanne curled into a ball on the banks of the stream and tried to shut out all sensation. She was prepared to wait a long time.

ONLY AFTER NOT very much time had passed—ten minutes? an hour?—she felt a terrible pull. A flooding of clear, direct energy.

Someone she loved was in danger. She was on her feet and away from the creek in two seconds. The danger was a magnet, drawing her near. Her feet could barely keep up with her rib cage.

She got flashes of images in her mind. A stand of aspens. A wicked knife. The images shook free with the jarring of her footfalls. Ropes binding wrists and that knife again. Blood! She crashed through brambles, and her feet flew over rocks. Water shook from her clothing as she ran, freezing in the air.

She had a rock in her hand as she came to the aspens she recognized from her vision. And there—there was *Owen*.

He was bound to a tree.

Bleeding from a gash to his lower arm.

He had a cloth in his mouth and was trying to speak. He was calling to her.

Hanne came closer.

Where, where, where was his assailant? Slaughter awaited. Her senses were all honed to the point of a knife. She was waiting to smash and murder. Her pupils were dilated, wholly black.

"Hanne!" came a voice. Not Owen's voice—the enemy.

Where was he?

"Listen, listen to me. I know what you are. I know the state you're in. Just listen."

She could smell him, but where was he hiding? There were so many trees.

"I'm here to help you."

Up. He was up.

Her head tilted and there he was. He was hiding up in a space where two aspens laid their trunks together.

She strode to the trees and shook the trunks. She would shake him down.

"I mean you no harm!" the man called down. He had a pocked face. She knew him somehow, but he was not beloved, nor of her tribe.

"I only cut him to draw you here. I can help you!" he yelled. She could not shake him down so she began to scale the tree.

Now he climbed down, stumbling away. He was old. So old and weak she might as well have killed him already.

"Hanne, I have studied the old texts and here is what they say. Stop fighting the Nytte. Let it flow through you. Can you hear me, Hanne? Open your heart to it."

Hanne grabbed up the rock and advanced on the man.

He fell back, one hand raised. "Breathe, Hanne! I am no enemy. See me with your heart!"

Then he began to say some words.

"*Heill dagr. Heilir dags synir,*" he said. "Hanne, *heill nótt ok nift.*"

She had the rock up to brain him, but the words were so beautiful. They were an old map, calling her down a road she long remembered.

"*Ásáheill!*" he shouted. "*Nyttesdotterheill!*"

She drew in a breath.

"Daughter of Odin. Daughter of the Nytte. I am no enemy," he said. "I promise."

He laid his forehead onto the frozen earth. His breath steamed up from where he pressed his mouth to the ground at her feet.

"*Heill nótt ok nift.* Hail to the night and the daughter of night."

Hanne came rushing back into herself. The fresh cold air came in her lungs and she gasped. Colors and sparks swirled and receded in her vision. She knew, again, who she was.

"What were those words?" she said in Norwegian. "What is that? And who are you?"

The man looked up at her. He rubbed his head with a shaking hand.

"I am Rolf Tjossem," he said. "I was sent here by the Baron Fjelstad. I want to help you. That is all I want to do. And that was Old Norse. A rune poem dedicated to the Æsir—the ancient Norse Gods, the Gods who gave your family the Nytte many thousands of years ago. The Gods who protect and love you now."

Hanne stepped back, and the man rose shakily. He went to Owen and cut away the rope that held the kerchief in his mouth. Owen spat out the cloth.

"Hanne, are you all right?" Owen asked, his voice coarse from shouting.

Hanne bowed her head in shame. Owen had left her, she remembered it now. He had tried to leave them, once and for all, and this man, Rolf, had captured him.

Rolf cut Owen free from the trunk. Then Owen punched Rolf square on the jaw.

"Damn you!" Rolf said. "I am here to help!"

"You got a funny way of showing it!" Owen shouted. "You jump me and cut up my arm. And if you saw those men attack us, why didn't you help?"

"I knew the girl would finish them. I would have only been in the way."

Hanne rose. She found herself very weak. Hunger was consuming her. She stumbled a few steps to a fallen log and sat on it.

"I had to get her away from the uncle's shack," Rolf said. "The best way to do it was to put someone she loves in danger."

Owen's eyes ricocheted to Hanne's.

Oh, the shame of it! She felt her cheeks bloom red. Now he knew, he knew without a doubt, that she loved him.

"You can go," Hanne told Owen. "I know you meant to leave us. Please just go and say no more."

"Hanne," Owen said. "You got it wrong."

He walked to Pal, who was tied to a tree near the edge of the wood. He removed something that was slung over the saddle.

It was a big jackrabbit.

"I went to hunt you some food. You told me . . . you said you could die if you didn't eat."

Hanne felt the blood drain from her face.

"What do you mean?" she said.

"I can't leave you," Owen said. "I wouldn't. I can't. And I don't want to, damn it."

"You must go!" she shouted. "Do not care for me, Owen Bennett! It is dangerous to care for me! For you and for others! You see how he used you as a weapon against me?"

Hanne staggered. The hunger was flaring up, eating her from the inside out.

"You must go," she said to Owen. "Please."

Rolf crossed to Hanne and pressed three crumbling biscuits into Hanne's hands, and a hunk of hard cheese.

"Eat!" he urged her.

She turned her back on the men and shoved a biscuit into her mouth.

"I'm not leaving," Owen said to her back doggedly.

"We have no time for this argument," Rolf said. "There's a man hunting you. A very dangerous man. A Berserker of power greater than yours. He's trained and he's vicious."

"See," Owen said. "How could I leave with a man like that hunting you?"

Hanne rounded on him. "Do you honestly think I need your protection? After what you saw?"

Owen gritted his teeth.

"I'm not leaving."

Rolf interrupted again, pointing to the cheese. "Eat that, now. We need to gather your siblings and leave right away."

"But first, she must eat," Owen said.

Rolf nodded in agreement, though it seemed to pain him. He took the limp rabbit from Owen.

"I'll prepare the meat," Rolf said. "Please go for the others and bring them here."

"That okay with you?" Owen asked Hanne. She nodded. "Then I'll be right back."

"Owen, we will pay you and you will leave us. You must leave us," she said.

"Not today I won't," Owen said.

CHAPTER TWENTY-EIGHT

Knut felt bad for the dun-colored gelding. He pitied any animal he rode. They'd eye him warily when he approached, sizing up his bulk and heaving great sighs.

He was in a hurry, though. He had been thinking since he'd learned that there was a reward out for him—he ought to turn himself in. He'd thought about it for many miles, yesterday and the day before. He would do it in Wolf Creek. Today.

It was the only way to make things good for his siblings. Otherwise, the law would keep hunting them and Hanne would have to keep killing.

Knut knew that every time she used her Nytte, it pained her. He saw how she suffered. He felt it.

It didn't hurt him when he used his Nytte, but he'd never tried to explain it to Hanne. Maybe he should have. When he used it, he felt good. Like he was a part of the world and doing the work he was meant to do.

Sometimes his body shimmered when he used his Nytte. Only no one else seemed to see how his hands shone or how the blood pumping through his heart gave off a pattern of light under the skin, like a lantern. So he'd kept it to himself. A private happiness. It made him laugh. His family thought he was dull, and he knew he was dull about many things. Because the letters Stieg tried to teach him would not stay fixed in his mind, and he sometimes couldn't remember the beginning of the question by the time the end had been reached, but there were some things his brother and sisters didn't know. And how pretty the Nytte could be was one of them.

Knut wanted Hanne to be happy. She was happy with Owen Bennett. Owen Bennett had got his sister dancing. She had not danced since their mother had left. With Owen around, she could go on with him and keep dancing.

Knut did not think of what would happen after he confessed. He was scared to imagine the rest. All he allowed himself to think about was entering town with his hands up.

He prodded the horse with his heels, asking it to go faster, and it did.

Knut shivered as he rode into town. The town was rowdy and mean looking. Lots of people, but no one friendly. It was a rocky, hardscrabble place.

He headed for the squat stone structure with barred windows that he knew must be Wolf Creek's jailhouse.

Knut's great body began to shake, as if beset by palsy. He had known an old man in Øystese with palsy.

He tried not to think about the fact that at any moment someone could recognize him and shoot him for the reward. Stieg had told him the poster read "dead or alive."

Knut tried to remember Hanne's advice to him, that when he was frightened, he ought to try to think back to a pleasant time.

He thrust back in his memory in a panic. His mind raced quickly past moments of fishing in the glacial rivers, of laughing through a mouthful of boiled potatoes at a tale Stieg told, of watching the sunrise over the haycocks. He settled down on a memory of Hanne reading to him at the fire. Reading out from the illustrated collection of fairy tales that Stieg had brought home. The fire golden on her face. Her bright eyes twinkling as she read of trolls and billy goats and berries collected in a basket. He loved his sister. He kept that warmth in his chest, stoked his heart with the image of his sister, as he dismounted.

He loved her enough to turn himself in.

Knut tossed the reins over the hitching post and held his hands high over his head.

A voice came from inside the jail, near the door.

"Hell if I know where Ruben is. He went for supper and never came back."

Then the man the voice belonged to came out to stare at Knut. He wore a tin star on his chest and a slack expression on his face as he regarded Knut and sought to place him in his recollection. Then he scrambled to draw his pistol. He leveled it at Knut.

"Sheriff!" the deputy hollered, his Adam's apple bouncing as he gulped. "You better come see this!"

CHAPTER TWENTY-NINE

Owen watched Hanne as she paced, eating. The rabbit had been consumed by the time he'd returned with Stieg and Sissel. He suspected she might have eaten it raw, but he wasn't going to dwell on it. Now she ate johnnycakes as fast as Owen could fry them up.

Sissel had done her best to bandage Stieg's shoulder wound—luckily, the bullet had merely grazed his shoulder.

"Knut should have been back by now," Stieg said as Sissel put away the supplies. "Something has happened. Why did you let him go?" he said, turning to Sissel.

"I was to stop him?" Sissel asked, incredulous. "You were shot. Hanne was in a trance, and Owen had run away!"

Owen flipped a johnnycake while the siblings argued in Norwegian. He knew they were concerned about their brother, and he was, too.

The man named Rolf said something to them in Norwegian that seemed to irritate Hanne.

"What'd he say?" Owen asked.

"Speak English, Mr. Tjossem, so our friend can understand," Stieg said.

"I said that they need not be concerned about Knut," Rolf said. "If he were in danger, Hanne would sense it."

"But town's over a mile from here," Owen said. "Can she feel him so far away?"

Hanne stopped eating and seemed to pause as if searching for a feeling inside herself.

"Yes, and farther," Rolf said. "I knew a Berserker who sensed his brother being attacked on a battlefield, a country and a half away."

"I am feeling better," Hanne said. She brushed the crumbs from her hands and rose. "I will go for him."

"No. We must leave, right away," Rolf said.

"We must all go after Knut," Stieg said. "If something bad hasn't happened already, it will soon."

"Listen," Rolf said. "Listen to me. You will not like to hear this, but we should send the cowboy for Knut, and the rest of us should go into hiding."

"I'll do it," Owen said.

"What?" Hanne cried.

"If Ketil senses Hanne's presence—"

"We'd never leave our brother behind!" Stieg said.

"But! But! Consider. The cowboy is no relation to Knut. The Berserker will not know him or sense who he is. We can send word when we get somewhere safe and secluded—"

"You are as well as sentencing both Knut and Owen to death!" Hanne said.

"We should leave," Stieg said. "I don't want to hear any more from this man—"

"Please, be calm. Listen. We must keep your sister safe from the Berserker Ketil," Rolf said. He turned to Hanne. "If he is waiting for you in Wolf Creek, he will provoke you, Hanne. If you try to fight him, he will kill you. You cannot win against him!"

"I would rather die than leave my brother behind," Hanne said through her teeth.

"Very well," he said.

"Do not try to separate us again," Stieg said. "We have little enough reason to trust you as it is."

"Yes. Why are you helping us?" Hanne asked. "You have come very far. Why are you turning against your partner this way? Why should we trust you?"

"I heard you speak to the boy there"—Rolf nodded toward Owen—"back before the killings at your uncle's home. I heard you say you did not want to kill. Believe me, that is rare for a Berserker."

"You did not answer my question. Why should we trust you?"

"I have given all my adult life to serving and protecting the Nytteson. It's as simple as that."

"And why are you turning against your partner, this Ketil?" Hanne demanded.

Rolf bent down to the fire, poking it with a stick.

"Ketil is not my partner. He is a fool, a dangerous one. I was persuaded to take him with me on this journey by my employer and friend, the Baron Fjelstad."

Owen saw the siblings register this name—they knew of this Baron.

"Fjelstad is a good man. I do believe it. For years now he has been gathering the Nytteson and offering them protection. That has been our work . . ."

"But you have doubts about him," Stieg said. "They are written on your face."

"Perhaps. Ketil said some disturbing things, but he was trying to goad me—"

"It doesn't matter now. We must go for our brother," Stieg said. "Hanne, should we take Mr. Tjossem with us? What do your instincts say?"

"There is no one who knows more about the Nytte than I do," Rolf said simply. "You need me."

Hanne eyed the Norwegian, her arms crossed. "I think he's harmless enough," she told Stieg. Owen privately agreed.

"Then let's go find our brother," Stieg said. "It will be early evening by the time we get back to Wolf Creek."

Owen watched as Rolf bent, grimacing from the pain at his shoulder, and picked up a dark piece of ash-covered charcoal from the fire. Rolf tossed the charcoal from hand to hand while it cooled, then pocketed it.

He was a strange man, for sure.

HANNE WAS GRATEFUL for the rhythm of the horse's gait. She must think. She must calm herself enough to think and to recover. Knut was in danger; she knew this not with her gut-sense of the Nytte, but with her reason.

She thought of the men she had killed at the shack. They were enemies. They were bounty hunters and she did not mourn their deaths, but when she recalled the joy she'd felt, the delight of the slaughter, she felt hot shame.

The stranger Rolf could say she was different from other Berserkers, but she was not.

She tried to force herself to settle down. She must not go into town with a fluttering heart. She would be more likely to lose consciousness to the Berserker within if she did. It was as if there were a membrane keeping the Nytte from her bloodstream, and that membrane had gotten thinner and thinner. The Nytte was pulsing under her heartbeat, eager to be set free in her body.

A horse drew along, and Hanne was displeased to see it was the stranger, Rolf. She imagined he was about to give more warnings about this Berserker, Ketil. Or he would try to persuade her to stay out of town.

"I believe there is a way to direct the rage that comes into you when the Nytte overtakes you."

Hanne's knuckles went white on the pommel. She sat rigid with attention.

"How?" she said.

"The ancient poems allude to a mastery of the Nytte that has long been dismissed," Rolf continued. "There is a way for you to inhabit the Nytte, to become one with the power."

"How?"

She turned to stare at the scarred man. He made a little half shrug. "I don't know exactly how. Through prayer, possibly, or singing sacred songs."

Hanne snorted.

"I can teach them to you. We can work until we find the way—"

"I don't want to become one with the power. I just want to keep my family safe," Hanne said.

"Yes. I know," Rolf said. And he had the good sense to let his horse fall back and leave her alone.

To calm herself, she planned.

Once she found her younger brother, she would take him away, and leave Sissel with Stieg. Hanne could keep Knut safe, and they could go far away from Stieg and Sissel, to draw danger away from them. Knut would do as she said. They could flee to another country. Canada was only a few days' journey to the north, if she was remembering the maps she'd seen accurately. Or perhaps they could go to the Indian lands. It was very wild there. They might do well.

Stieg and Sissel could go to Chicago, as Stieg had once meant to do. And Owen, he could find a normal girl to settle with. Anyone would want to marry such a hardworking boy. Not to mention handsome. And kind.

He would have no trouble at all. Hanne forced herself to imagine him with a pretty, plump wife on a homestead.

After a few moments, Owen's horse appeared alongside hers. "Are you okay?" he asked. He had ridden up on her, as if she'd called him with her thoughts, and now his fine bay horse was right beside hers.

Hanne nodded tightly. "I am fine."

"I saw you talking to Mr. Tjossem. I think he means right by you."

Hanne did not answer. She wished Owen would go away. She needed to be quiet and focus on the task ahead.

"I wanted to tell you. Damn it, Hanne, don't shut me out."

Hanne turned her head, shocked that he would curse at her.

"You're taking it all on your shoulders, taking all the responsibility and the blame. Look, those were bad men. They got what they had coming—"

"Please be quiet!" she snapped. "I am not grieving for those men."

Hanne fixed her eyes on the trail ahead, as if by force of concentration she could make Owen go away. The line of the creek descended through the boulders and the scrub cottonwoods, bringing them closer and closer to town.

"You think you're a bad person, but I know that's not true," Owen said.

"I cannot bear to hurt anyone else," Hanne erupted. Her knuckles were white on the reins. "You must leave me and forget me, Mr. Bennett! It is hard enough knowing I have ruined the lives of my three siblings. I will not ruin anything else."

"When you move like you did back there at the cabin—"

"Don't!" Hanne said, and she felt herself in danger. Owen swam in her vision, becoming red, a threat.

"It's beautiful! It's like watching an angel fly! Like water flowing over a rock. Like, I don't know, like something God made. Something perfect and right."

Her hand was at her knife.

"Be quiet!" she hissed.

"If I had what you had, I'd be thankful."

"Thankful?" Hanne said. How could he be so stupid? "You have no sense—"

"You got family and they love you," Owen said, his eyes sparkling with feeling. "You belong to them, and them to you. That's something worth defending, Hanne. If you'd ever gone without it, if you'd ever known what it was like to be alone, miserable, and . . . unloved in the world, you'd understand."

Owen's face was twisted with emotion he was clearly trying to master. He turned Pal away from her.

Tears welled up in Hanne's eyes, making the trail waver in front of her.

She thought about Owen's upbringing, family life, and how little she knew of his history. He was fully immersed in the drama of their lives, and she knew next to nothing of his life.

Everywhere Hanne looked, she saw her own failings. She had failed to be a good friend to Owen, and she had failed to check her feelings for him, and now he was in danger.

She was a menace to those she loved, and she must separate from them. She would flee them, flee from loving them.

Hanne tried, very hard, to forget what Owen had said. She tried to make her mind empty and her heart cold.

FINALLY WOLF CREEK presented itself through the trees down the mountain. It looked like a long brown scab, crusted in the crook of the valley floor. At this end of the frost-packed street, there were only a few battered buildings, their false fronts leaning past right angles.

On the front steps of one such building sat an old man wearing a tattered buffalo-skin coat, his own skin wrinkled and withered by exposure. He eyed them with one squinting eye, taking care to aim his tobacco spurt away from their horses' hooves.

They dismounted and walked their horses past.

"Hanne," Stieg said low, flanking her, "are you sure you must go into town? Ought you not wait here?"

Looking ahead down the street, Hanne saw people. Townspeople crossing the street. Miners and a few women. Children accompanying their mothers on errands.

Hanne drew in a ragged breath. Her rib cage was tight, and she felt prickly in her palms and the soles of her feet. What might happen down where strangers would be around?

"Perhaps it is best," Rolf ventured from behind, "if Stieg and Owen go ahead simply to see if they can find information about what has happened to Knut."

"It is too dangerous for us to be separated," she continued. "We must stay together."

"Well, I cannot go with you," Rolf said. "If Ketil has managed to survive and he sees me with you, he'll know who you are. Your great advantage is that he does not know what you look like. He thinks the Berserker is a boy. He will think it's you." He nodded to Stieg.

"I'm glad we have an advantage, then," said Stieg. He was feigning confidence, but Hanne could see he was anxious and scared.

"Hanne, remember, you must not fight Ketil," Rolf said. "He is trained—"

"I do not wish to fight him or anyone, just to get my brother."

"Daisy, stay," Owen told his dog. She lay down, panting. She had kept pace well. The wound was healing.

"Keep Daisy here, will you?" Owen asked Rolf. "And if we don't come back . . ."

Rolf nodded. He sighed. "Hanne, let me give you a gift. To protect you in town. In case Ketil still lives."

Hanne looked to Stieg. He shrugged.

As Rolf dismounted, he reached into his vest pocket and took out the piece of charcoal he had pocketed from the fire.

"Give me your hands, please," he said.

Hanne extended her hands to the man. He pressed the bit of charcoal into the palm of her right hand, drawing a shape that looked like an arrow.

Hanne snatched her hand back.

"What is this? A rune?"

"Yes," he said. "It calls to Freya, goddess of war and love. It will focus your power and heighten your senses."

"Heighten my senses? No. I do not want that. That is the very last thing I want!" She rubbed at the sign with the fabric of her skirt.

"But Freya can help you, if you call to her. The old Gods watch you, Hanne. They are with you and within you."

"The old Gods are long dead! And we are their final joke upon mankind!"

"No! What you are is sacred and special."

"What I am is a monster! All of us are!" Hanne swept her hand out at her siblings. Stieg looked away, stung. "We are cursed."

"The more you fight who you are, the less control you have," Rolf told her. His face looked terribly sad. Sad and haggard, like the face of a failed man. "I beg you to accept the Nytte as the gift it is. Say it with me, '*Ásáheill! Heill Odin. Heill Freya . . .*'"

"Let's go," Hanne said, refusing to meet his eye as she climbed back into the saddle.

She kicked her horse and charged into town, rubbing her hand against her skirt to make sure the rune was smudged away. She would never accept the curse of the Nytte. It had stolen everything good from her.

CHAPTER THIRTY

In front of the jailhouse was a sight that confirmed Hanne's worst fears: Two carpenters were fortifying the gallows with extra timber. They meant to hang her brother.

"He's in the jail, then," Stieg said to her, trying to look nonchalant. Hanne nodded.

The afternoon was turning to evening; blue shadows drew long across the pitted main street. She was possessed by fear for Knut's well-being, but it came from her anxious mind, not from the gut-sense of her Nytte.

Across from the jail stood a three-story hotel, clapboard and painted white. It was the most handsome structure in town by far. Some ladies sat visiting on the porch, watching the carpenters reinforce the scaffold, as if waiting on a parade.

Owen nodded toward a stable down the street from the jail, on the opposite side of the street.

They dismounted and tied their horses to some hitching posts outside the stable. All around them, the sounds of a busy town echoed—voices calling, wagons bouncing over the rocky streets, and the sound of hammering. Hanne's senses prickled at every hammer hit, yet the Nytte did not kindle, so she knew Knut was not in danger. Yet.

"I'll create a distraction to draw out the sheriff and his men," Stieg suggested.

"What will you do?" Hanne asked.

"Leave it to me. What you and Owen must do is get the keys to Knut's cell from the sheriff or from his men when they come outside. Can you do that?"

Hanne and Owen both nodded. They glanced at each other, both trying to disguise their anxiety.

Stieg turned to Sissel.

"Sissel, you go into the street. When you see smoke rising from the hotel, call for help."

"Stieg! What do you mean to do?" Hanne repeated.

"I'm going to set a fire, but I'll be safe. You two will have to figure out how to free our brother."

"We will," Hanne said.

"Be careful," Owen said.

"Owen, thank you," Stieg said. "For everything you have done for us. We would have been lost many times over without your help. I am sorry for not bringing you into our confidence sooner."

Owen nodded. He clapped Stieg on the shoulder and shook his hand.

"We will meet here," Stieg said. "Or, if things go wrong, back where Rolf is waiting. Yes?"

They all agreed. Hanne reached forward and hugged Stieg, then turned to her sister. Hanne brushed a thin lock of Sissel's hair behind her ear, then drew Sissel's wrap more snugly around her head. Her sister's eyes were big and shining with fear.

"Get out of harm's way once you've helped Stieg. Promise? Come back here and wait for us."

"I will," Sissel said. Then suddenly Sissel hugged Hanne fiercely. "I'm sorry for all the times I was horrible."

Hanne put her arms around her sister's thin form and held her tight. She could feel Sissel's heart pounding through her ribs.

"I could have been more gentle with you," Hanne apologized.

"No," Sissel said, shaking her head. "It was all me, and I'm sorry for it. Do be careful, Hanne!"

"I will," Hanne said. "And you, too."

Owen took Hanne by the elbow.

"Come now," he said. "We'll go to the mercantile next to the jail to wait. Better if we go first . . ."

HANNE AND OWEN walked arm in arm across the hard-packed street, stepping over the ruts and rain gullies. Everything in the street stood out in clear detail to Hanne, her heart pumping hard with excitement and dread. She was glad for Owen's steadying hand laid over her forearm. The warmth helped.

They stepped onto the wooden plank stairs outside the mercantile. Three steps. Hanne noted them, trying to memorize their dimensions for later, when she knew she would fly down them and into the jailhouse next door.

The jail was squat and stone, the walls thick. Iron bars protected two tiny square windows set high on the side of the building.

"You talk," Hanne said. "Lest they hear my accent."

Owen nodded, and they stepped into the store.

"Afternoon," said a young woman shopkeeper. She had her hair up in the bun of an older woman, but had a youthfully shy, winning smile and a pert, upturned nose.

"May I help you?"

"Let's see," Owen said. "We need supplies. But might just first have a look around."

"Are you new to town? I must say, I hope so! There are few people our age hereabouts and we've undertaken a Bible study group."

"Bible study, eh?" Owen said. Hanne pretended to browse the glass cases closest to the window, but her eyes were on the street.

"Yes, we're starting with the Psalms, isn't that lovely?"

Hanne's eyes darted up and down the street. A peddler stopped his cart right outside the window, blocking her view. She strained her neck a bit to see around him.

"It there something to see?" the clerk asked. "What's happening?"

"Oh, nothing," Hanne said. She shook her head.

The girl came to the window nonetheless. Twilight was falling, and the light through the window was tinted a dusky blue.

"I like your coat," the clerk said, not unkindly. Hanne folded her arms, not wanting the girl to see the stained sleeves. "Such a pretty color of rose. Unusual."

The girl's eyes met Hanne's. They were hazel with a ring of brown at the pupil, and for a moment Hanne wished that she could have been

Owen's young wife, come to settle a claim near Wolf Creek. Wished she might be friends with this girl, who was her age and who wanted a friend. Wished they could study psalms together in a room with a fire at the hearth and mugs of strong coffee. Confide secrets to each other and laugh together.

"Thank you," Hanne managed to whisper, but the girl's eyes flashed away from Hanne and out the window. "Smoke," she cried. "Smoke! From the hotel!"

Hanne turned and looked, and there was smoke rising from the third-floor window.

A chair crashed through the panes of glass.

"Fire!" a girl's voice shouted. It was Sissel, and she was close, though not standing where Hanne could see her from the window. "Fire! Oh, help!"

Hanne darted through the front door, followed closely by Owen and the shopgirl.

There was Stieg, standing at the broken window! "Help!" he shouted, smoke billowing out from behind him. In the next window, the smoke was darker, and tongues of flame began to lick at the window panels.

Stieg ducked away from the window, and Hanne knew suddenly what he was doing. He was blowing the fire away from him with icy breath every time his face disappeared from the window so that he would not burn up.

Hanne saw Sissel dart into the sheriff's office and return, pulling at the sheriff's arm to show him the fire. He had the ring of keys in hand!

Hanne moved toward him. All around her, people were calling and shouting about the fire. Owen came to her side, and they moved in tandem toward the sheriff.

But the sheriff swore and pulled away from Sissel. He stepped back into the jail and then returned without the keys.

"The keys," Hanne said to Owen.

"Inside," Owen finished.

The sheriff started shouting directions to the men gathering quickly on the street below. Patrons began to stumble out of the front door of the hotel, coughing.

A bucket brigade was assembling down the main street, and as the sheriff began directing volunteers, Hanne and Owen slipped, unnoticed, into the jailhouse. Owen turned, and shut and locked the door behind them.

There was a boughten wooden desk, highly varnished, paired with an old Windsor chair. There were papers on the desk, and the wanted poster for Knut was at the top of the stack. But there were no keys in sight. And none in the shallow front drawer of the desk, either.

"He must have locked them in the safe!" Hanne gasped.

"I'll work on it," Owen said.

Hanne opened the door that led into the cell area. It was so dark Hanne felt blind for a moment.

"Knut?" she whispered.

Most of the room was the jail cell, but there was a small entrance area, a square cut off from the rest of the space by iron bars and the locked gate. The two small windows set high in the stone walls each showed a square of twilight blue. Low benches ran along the sides.

There was a great slope-shouldered figure on one of the benches.

"Hanne? Is it you?"

"Yes," she said. "Knut! We've come to free you."

"Oh, Hanne," her brother said. He rushed into the light. "I'm so glad. I can't tell you how glad!"

"Are keys kept in here, Knut?" Hanne began to pat along the wall, hoping to come across keys on a hook. It was so dark in the room.

"You must meet my friend, Hanne. I've met the nicest man."

"We have only a moment," Hanne said.

"But he's from Norway, too! And he wants to take us home, to a very safe place, don't you, Ketil?"

Hanne felt her blood turn cold and leaden.

"Indeed, I do," came a voice from the shadows. "You must be Hanne."

A blond man stepped out of the dark and rested his forehead against the bars. He was very handsome. His sly smile dazzling.

"Your brother told me all about you," he said. "A female Berserker. You are a rare creature, Hanne Amundsdotter. I have such wonderful things to show you."

Hanne's heart was in her throat. She gulped and gulped again.

"He's a Berserker, too, Hanne!" Knut said. "He came here to find us and bring us home to protect us!"

"There's no time for such talk, Knut," she managed to say. "We must get you out of there. They mean to hang you."

"They can try," Ketil said. His voice was low, like a purr. "But, Hanne, we could take them all."

He was terribly handsome. Hanne felt a thrill she did not want to feel, a tightening in her center, like he was pulling her to his side.

Owen came into the room, standing behind Hanne in the entrance space.

"It's no use," he said to Hanne. "We'd need dynamite to get that safe open."

Hanne fumbled to reach Owen's hand. She squeezed it hard, telling him to be wary.

Owen brought up his shotgun.

"Knut," Owen ventured. "You all right?"

"Yah," Knut said. "Hello, Owen! This is my friend Ketil. He's good."

"A Nytteson does not need a key," Ketil said in Norwegian. "Knut can smash down the wall."

He turned to Knut. "You can do it if you only try."

"The wall?" Knut asked.

"Oar-Breakers like you, there's no limit to your strength," Ketil said. "You'll see; it might hurt your body, but it will feel good in your soul."

"I think maybe I could, if my sister says so . . . ," Knut said.

"Yes, do it," Hanne said. She had to force her voice to be calm. "Because the sheriff may be back at any moment."

Knut touched Hanne's fingertips on the bars and smiled, then he lurched away, throwing his shoulder into the rock wall.

"OOF!" he exhaled. The whole building shuddered, but the wall did not give an inch.

Knut staggered back. Hanne could see the flesh of his shoulder through his torn shirt. There was rock dust in his hair.

"Again," Ketil commanded. "Harder this time, you can do it!"

"Raah!" Knut shouted, hurling himself at the wall.

"Good!" Ketil cried.

This time the stones moved, bowing out.

"Hurry!" Hanne urged her brother.

A banging came from the other room.

"Knut, hurry!" Hanne shouted.

Knut staggered to his feet. His arm hung at an angle that was all wrong.

"Again, boy! Now!" Ketil shouted.

Knut let out another inhuman roar as he threw himself against the unbudging stones. This time he did not relax after the charge but plowed his weight into the wall until the rocks began to move. Grating and grinding, the rock wall continued to bow outward. He dug his feet into the earthen floor of the jail and pushed on, finding new purchase when his feet slid, until the rocks fell outside. The early evening light shone through the hole he'd made. Hanne could see his shoulder was bleeding and battered, the bone jutting under the skin in the wrong place.

"Are you all right, Knut?" she cried. Another bang rattled from the room behind them. The sheriff might knock the whole front door in.

"Come, little brother," Ketil said to Knut.

"He's not your brother," Hanne said. "Knut! You must wait for us outside."

Ketil started to push Knut toward the hole.

"Stop!" Hanne said.

"Hold it right there!" Owen said.

"Lower your gun or I snap his neck," Ketil said.

Knut cried out in pain. Ketil had dug his fingers into the torn flesh of Knut's dislocated shoulder.

"You're hurting me!"

"I know. And I'm sorry for it, but I am taking you and your family back to the Baron. And I want your sister to know I mean business."

"Let him go!" Hanne cried. "I'll kill you!"

Ketil laughed. "Come, try."

Knut let out a cry of anguish as Ketil forced him out the gap in the wall.

"Knut!" Owen called. He damned the jail and the bars that kept them from following. "Wait for us!"

"Hanne!" called Knut, outside the jail now. He sounded confused and hurt.

The Nytte came roaring into force, like a flash flood ripping through a gorge. Hanne's grip on the bars tightened; her neck strained as she tried, without thinking, to pry the bars apart.

In the room behind them, the sheriff rammed the front door.

"Come on out, little girl. Let's see how much of a Berserker you are," Ketil shouted back into the jail through the broken wall.

Hanne roared in fury.

"Calm down, okay? He'll be okay—" Owen said.

Hanne pushed past him, stalking out into the jail's front office. Owen followed on her heels.

Then she grabbed Owen by the collar and threw him to the floor as a gunshot, and then another, came firing through the front door, sending the handle and lock into splinters. The door was flung open, smashing into Owen's knee. He grunted in pain.

"What the hell are you two doing?" shouted the sheriff, red faced and spitting with fury. He stood looking down at them, smoking six-shooter in his hand. Hanne sprang to her feet, grabbing the pistol by the barrel. It seared her palm. She did not feel it.

She swung the weapon, struck the sheriff across the temple with the handle, and felled him.

Hanne prowled out into the street. It was chaos, townspeople running and calling to one another. The fire had spread, engulfing the hotel in its entirety. Flames exploded through the glass, showering the street with shards that shone yellow and orange into the night.

The volunteers had stopped trying to quench the flames, and were now wetting down the buildings around the hotel, trying to keep the fire from taking the whole town.

Hanne scanned the crowd. Where were Knut and Ketil? *Where were they?*

With a wrenching jolt, Hanne felt them, behind her in the street.

"It's the killer!" she heard a man shout. "The Norwegian from the jail!"

There was a scream and more shouting.

Ketil was dragging Knut toward a livery stable, jerking him by his injured arm. The townspeople put down their buckets and wet blankets and surged toward Ketil and Knut. There was a deputy with a pistol. And a dark-faced rancher with a shotgun. A gap-toothed farmer with a rock in his hand.

"Get that boy!" the rancher cried. "He busted out of the jail!"

The farmer rushed to smash Knut on the head.

Hanne jumped forward, snatching the rock from his grip with one hand and grabbing the farmer by the throat with the other. His eyes bugged out with surprise, at her sex, at her strength, at his own feet lifting off the ground. She threw him into the crowd, crashing his body onto the deputy, who lost his footing and fell heavily.

Ketil laughed. Hanne rushed to Knut's side. Ketil still had hold of him.

"Very nice," Ketil said. "Let's see what else you can do." Knut was pale, moaning. He sank to his knees, and the crowd surged at them.

They wanted to kill her brother.

Time slowed as the Nytte unfurled around Hanne, counting heartbeats, locating weapons.

She felt every cell of her anatomy come alive, down to the strands of hair braided around her head like a crown.

Two brawny carpenters sprang forward together from behind Knut to try to drag him to the ground. Hanne felt the farmer's rock leave her hand. It hit one of the carpenters on the head. She heard the crack as it punctured his skull.

"Hanne, don't!" someone yelled.

The other carpenter was now under her, his weighty hammer ripped from the leather work belt at his waist. She placed the prongs underneath his throat. The man's unshaven neck strained as she pulled his greasy hair back. He eyed her, gasping and terrified. She saw her reflection in his eyes. A fierce, feral face. Mouth grim. Eyes narrowed.

"Stop, Hanne! Breathe!"

Her hand faltered. She just needed to drive the hammer up. She felt stillness around her. The crowd had drawn back from her.

"Don't do it. *Heill nótt something!*" It was a voice near her side. One of the townspeople? No. Warmth came to her. Oh, she knew that voice. She loved the sound of it.

"*Heill nótt the nift!*" It was her own cowboy, Owen, speaking to her. He was kneeling near her, his back to hers. He had his rifle up and trained on the crowd. He was protecting her.

The hammer wanted to plunge the prongs into the man's neck, but Owen's voice called her off. "*Heill nótt the nift*, Hanne."

He was saying old words, trying to speak the old language. Owen reached out his hand and placed it on her shoulder. Warmth rippled through Hanne's body. She shuddered, and she was herself again.

Hanne tossed the hammer aside and pushed off the carpenter, sitting back hard onto the frozen ground. Her breath steamed into the dark night.

"Everyone just stay calm," Owen said loudly. "This isn't what it looks like!"

All eyes were on Hanne as she regained her senses. There must have been at least fifty people gathered around. The firelight from the hotel glowed in their eyes. They looked angry and confused. She and Owen stood about three feet from where Ketil had regained his cruel hold on Knut. Knut whimpered in the momentary lull.

"I like your style," Ketil said low, to Hanne, from the side of his mouth, in Norwegian. "Vicious and quick."

Hanne took in a deep breath. She rose to her feet.

"Get back!" shouted a voice in the crowd.

"She's dangerous!"

"Someone go for the sheriff!"

"Shoot 'em all down!" called another.

"Please don't shoot! I am the murderer," Hanne announced, holding up her hands. "It was me who killed the people back in Norway. And you saw what I did just then. It is me the police are looking for. My brother does not belong on that poster. He is innocent!"

"She killed my Thomas!" a young woman screeched from the side of the fallen carpenter. Blood soaked her dress—the dead man's head in her lap. "She killed him with a rock!"

"Hanne!" came Sissel's voice. She pushed through the crowd.

"Hanne! Knut!" Stieg cried. He was right behind Sissel. His clothes and face were covered with char, and there was blood on his collar, but he seemed all right.

"Stay back!" Hanne shouted to Stieg and Sissel. "Please! I've already confessed. I will go to jail. You all can go free!"

"Put 'em all in jail!" someone shouted.

"No! Please," Stieg shouted. He tried to argue with the crowd, insisting that everything could be explained.

Meanwhile Ketil hissed to Hanne in Norwegian, "If you want your siblings and your beau to stay alive, you'll help me kill our way out of here. Follow my lead!"

Ketil released her brother's arm and raised up his hands, as if innocent. It was a ploy. Knut fell to the ground, moaning.

"I surrender!" Hanne yelled, her arms raised high. "Please, hear us out!"

But a man came pushing through the crowd. "The sheriff's dead!" he exclaimed. "Brained! With the butt of his own gun!"

"She did it!"

"Get her! Get them all!"

As the mob closed in, Ketil threw his head back and laughed.

WITHIN SECONDS—

A man had a gun at the back of Knut's head and another held Stieg by the arm. The young clerk from the shop tried to pull Sissel away to safety, and Sissel screamed. A stocky miner raised a shovel to strike Owen on the back of the head.

Hanne watched the mayhem all round. She loved her sister and her brothers and Owen so much.

But she did not want to kill. She would not kill any longer.

"Oh, please." She clasped her hands together. "Please, Freya. I do not want to kill!"

Beside her, Stieg pressed his fingers to his temples and began to blow an icy wind from his pursed lips. The man holding him stepped back, screaming, as frost bit into his chest. Sissel broke away from the clerk and came to huddle behind Stieg. Stieg turned the breath toward the man with the gun raised to Knut's head, and frost exploded the gun into icy metal shards.

"I beg you, Freya! Hear me!" Hanne raised her arms into the air.

Ketil, with a bloodthirsty scream, had seized the shovel from the man behind Owen and spun it in the air. He used the blade of the shovel to sever the man's arm.

324

Owen wheeled and shot at a deputy who was coming up on him from behind. The deputy's leg was blown away in a cloud of blood.

"Help us!" Hanne prayed.

Knut used his good arm to grab a man who was charging him and threw him into the fire. The man stumbled out, clothes burning. His screams tore the night.

Tears were coursing down Knut's frightened face, but he turned again, ready to fight for his family.

"I surrender!" Hanne screamed, even as a mud-stained miner grabbed her by the hair and tried to throw her to the ground. The man's mouth was contorted in a sneer, and his eyes were wide-open.

Then his grip went slack. Blood vomited out of his mouth, and his eyes went dead. Ketil had stuck him through the throat with a bowie knife.

"Come, girl! Show me what you can do!" Ketil goaded. Grinned. "Fight beside me, you proud Viking bitch!"

He was using words to gall her to action, but Hanne pushed them from her mind. Ketil turned to slay again, and Hanne sought desperately the words Rolf had said.

"*Ásáheill*," she burst out. "*Heill Odin*, hear me. Hear me, Freya! *Heill Freya!*" Hanne made the sign of the rune Rolf had shown her in the air, drawing with her finger. "*Ásáheill!* I surrender to the Nytte!"

Ketil had her by the coat collar. He shook her. Slapped her face.

"You are a Berserker! You were made to kill, so kill!"

"*Ásáheill! Ásáheill! Ásáheill!*" she hailed the Gods, reaching out with all her being.

Hanne's chest was drawn open as a giant breath filled her lungs. A golden light surged through her body, coursing through her blood.

Hanne looked around her and was amazed. Ketil struck her again, then threw her away from himself, disgusted.

All the people, the people fighting and hurting each other, were so beautiful. Hanne could see the light within each body. The soul, a heart-ring of sunshine, within each body's form. She knew the humans as the Gods saw them—all of a one, kept separate only by their own constructs. She could see how desperately they loved each other and how they hated themselves, for all their hearts were illuminated to her.

She saw her own heart. The meager, bitter stories of shame she had created and so clung to cracked and fell away like shards of broken crockery.

"Did you hear me?" Ketil screamed.

She looked at him with disinterest, then compassion. He, too, had a divine spark within his constricted, misshapen soul.

"You are made to kill!" he repeated.

"No," Hanne said, and her words echoed with the voices of Gods unseen. "I am made to live."

Her body began to emit light. Glowing softly from within, like a cloud illuminated by the sunrise.

She turned her eyes toward Ketil and found her hand reaching toward his chest.

"Stop," he said. "What are you doing?"

"I'm coming for you now," Hanne said. "It's your time." She saw her words, her breath itself, had shape and form. Ah! She saw breath streaming out of the mouths of all the people fighting, all their breath mingled together. Every breath a prayer.

Hanne laughed. She stepped toward Ketil.

"Stop!" Ketil shouted. He backed away from her, treading backward into the people surging to fight him.

He lashed out, whipping the knife toward her throat. She batted it away.

Ketil grabbed a shotgun out of a farmer's grip. He aimed the barrels into her gut and pulled the trigger, but Hanne stepped up lightly into the air, moving backward in time. Just a heartbeat backward.

She stepped on the gun, driving it into the ground. When it fired, the barrels exploded. Ketil released it, smoke billowing around him.

He swung at her, and she caught his fist in the air. She smiled at him, then she used her great, easy, fluid strength to twist his wrist until he was forced down to his knees.

With his free arm, Ketil shielded his eyes. She was shining so brightly now.

Hanne looked over her shoulder, at her brothers and sister. Each of them stopped fighting and stood gaping at her. Sissel held up a thin hand to shield her eyes from her sister's blaze.

Hanne's eyes fell next on Owen. Her beloved. His expression was awed and unafraid. Yes. The Gods wanted them together. Hanne and Owen as one had already happened and was yet to be and was all at the same time. She smiled.

Hanne turned her gaze back on Ketil. He shrank from her, arms covering his head. "Don't!" he pleaded. "Don't kill me! I beg you!"

"Don't be afraid," she said. She spoke in the old tongue. "You are going to meet the Gods."

Then the third story of the fiery hotel collapsed, crashing through the second, down to the ground. The heat surged, and everything grew wavy.

Hanne leaned down to Ketil, as tenderly as a new mother. She reached into his chest and snuffed out the light.

CHAPTER THIRTY-ONE

Owen hoped people would explain it away. Think what they had seen was a trick of the light—firelight shining on the girl when the hotel caved in, making her seem as if lit from within.

After Hanne had killed the Berserker, she crumpled unconscious to the ground. With both her and Ketil fallen and the fire leaping out to the nearby buildings, the fight was abandoned.

Those townspeople who could dragged themselves back to wet the buildings around the hotel. The building's foundation was still burning. The embers would likely last until morning.

Owen crawled to Hanne's body. It looked like a war had broken out on the main street of Wolf Creek, Montana. There was blood from the men who had been slain or injured in the fight. Everything was covered in ash and grime. Only Hanne lay there clean. Her skin was as fresh as if she'd just washed up, and her clothes were free of soot. Even the pink coat, which had been bloodstained, looked immaculate.

"Hanne," Stieg called. He staggered to his sister. Sissel came, too, and fell to Hanne's side.

With his good arm, Knut pulled Ketil's lifeless body away from them, toward the gutter of the street. Then he walked back to kneel at Hanne's feet.

The siblings and Owen gathered around Hanne while Stieg pressed trembling fingers to his sister's throat to search for a pulse. The smoke wafted around them. It seemed to Owen like a scene from hell, with Hanne a fallen angel.

"She's alive," Stieg said with a sob. Sissel took her sister's hand and wept onto it.

An old woman stalked forward.

"Devil take you all!" she screeched. "Murderers!"

She spat on the leg of Knut's trousers.

"We must go," Stieg said. "We must get away. Owen, can you carry her?"

Hanne opened her eyes.

"Oh," she said. "Are we alive, then?"

"Yes," Stieg answered. "We're alive. Barely."

"Hanne," Knut said, and then, overcome, he pressed his face to her belly. Hanne put her hand on her brother's back.

"It's all right, Knut. We're going to be all right," she said.

"Are you magic now?" Sissel asked. "Are you changed?"

Hanne took a breath. Owen watched her as she stretched her arms and hands.

She bowed her head. "I'm cold, that's all."

Owen put out his hand to help her up. He was a little afraid of her. But when she put her hand into his, he recognized it.

It was the hand of the girl he'd come to know on the trail. And the smile she offered gave him the same warm, heart-stopping thrill it had before.

"I know a place we can winter," he said, loud enough for the others to hear. "Up in Great Falls. I think they'll take us in."

Hanne took his hand into both of hers. She was standing close to him. She took his hand and held it to her heart, on top of her coat.

No, that did not suit her. She rearranged his hand, slipping it through the gap between the buttons on her coat, so that his hand could rest atop the very fabric of her shirt and feel the warm skin underneath and her heart beating for him.

HANNE FELT LIGHT in the saddle, almost giddy with relief. She kept smiling around at her siblings, following in single file on their tired horses behind her. Owen was leading them around town now, cutting a wide circle to return to where Rolf would be waiting for them with Daisy.

The guilt and dread had been removed from her. It was a strange feeling, to ride, in the dark, fleeing the scene of a terrible crime, and be joyful.

And she was not hungry.

She was not hungry in the least.

It meant that she had come somehow to peace with her Nytte. She had opened to it, surrendered and accepted the power. If she could do that and not suffer the punishing hunger, then perhaps her brothers could also find a way *out*. Perhaps with Rolf's help, they could find a way to live a long life with the Nytte. Perhaps Knut could learn to stop his growth. Stieg might not lose his eyes.

They went through the trees, the barren branches above hung with stars.

"He said his sister has a big place and needs help running it," Owen was telling Stieg. "My friend Hoakes is trustworthy, that much I know."

"We can pay for room and board," Stieg said. His voice was hoarse from the fire. "While we figure out where to go next."

"There's plenty of wild places in America," Owen said. "If we keep Knut out of sight. Maybe we should go to California come spring."

"I would like to see San Francisco," Stieg said. "They say there is gold in the streets. You can brush it up with a broom!"

Knut's head jerked awake. He had been dozing in the saddle. Hanne had reset the shoulder, with Owen's help; then Owen had made a sling out of some canvas. As for Stieg, blood from his bandaged shoulder had bled through the gray cloth of his coat. And Rolf did not complain, but it was clear there was something wrong with his back.

They all needed time to rest and recuperate.

Hanne hoped they would find that in Great Falls.

What they needed now was a place to hide for the winter, and time to form a new plan. Rolf would teach them all he knew. And if his predictions were true, more Nytteson would be coming for them. The Baron himself might come.

Knut was still a wanted man, in America and Norway both. They were not out of danger by a long sight.

But Hanne trusted that there was a plan for them. The Gods had brought her to a shining new clarity; they would not abandon her and her siblings now.

They found Rolf where they had left him. Daisy was tied to an aspen tree. Perhaps she had tried to follow. She began to whine, then bark, as they approached, wriggling with joy.

Rolf had his head down, his posture one of defeat. He did not look up, even as they approached. He was rocking to and fro, muttering. He seemed not to hear them.

"Rolf!" Hanne cried. "Mr. Tjossem!"

She slid off the horse and crossed to stand next to him. He was in a trance.

Hanne saw he had drawn runes all over his face and hands with charcoal. The designs shouted to Hanne. She understood them, each one a poem, many words and images compressed into line. They danced before her eyes, as if written in firelight.

Rolf was praying in a steady stream of Old Norse. "*Óreiðum augum lítið okkr þinig ok gefið sitjöndum sigr.*" He was praying for the Gods to see them, to look kindly on them and grant them victory.

Hanne knelt at his side. She put her hand on his shoulder. At Hanne's touch, he stopped chanting, opened red-rimmed eyes to take in her face.

"You were right," she said. "The Gods came when I hailed them. They were within me, as you said."

The old man's eyes shone with joy. Joy and relief.

Hanne embraced him. The soot from his face marked her clean clothes.

HOURS LATER, after they had ridden and made camp, Hanne awoke in the tent. Sissel was asleep, next to her in the bedroll. Their coats and mufflers were laid atop the bedroll, for added warmth.

The tent was dark, the only light a dim glow near the flaps from the campfire outside.

Hanne crawled to the entrance, her body immediately shivering, though she was sleeping in her dress. Outside she saw Owen poking at the fire. All else was still.

Hanne took her coat from the pile atop their bedroll. Sissel did not move. Her face, asleep, was much younger. Asleep there was none of the protesting and the dissatisfaction that made up her personality. Hanne smiled with love for her difficult sister.

Hanne shrugged on her coat and stuck her bare feet into her shoes. The worn wooden soles fit her feet perfectly, but Hanne had made up her mind to insist Stieg buy her and Sissel proper American button-up boots. She was finished with the heavy, clunky shoes—they were burdensome relics. It was time to walk lighter.

She slipped out of the tent.

The tent where Stieg, Knut, and Rolf were sleeping was humming gently with snores.

Owen had a tin mug in his hands. He sat staring into the fire as if it were telling him a story.

"Are you well, Owen?" Hanne whispered.

Owen looked up. His face warmed into a smile when he saw her. Daisy lay at his feet, asleep.

"I'm good. Couldn't sleep."

"Something woke me up," she said. "I'm not sure what it was."

"Maybe I made too much noise."

"Maybe," Hanne said.

"Want some coffee?" he offered.

"No, thank you."

She had some fleeting thought of propriety but let it go. Her skirts swished as she went to sit next to the cowboy.

He shifted on the rock he had pulled up to the fire, giving her the spot he had already warmed with his body heat.

She sat down. Their arms brushed.

She leaned into him, ever so softly inclining her head toward his.

"Are you thinking about today?" she asked.

"Naw," he said. "I guess I was thinking about the future."

A log spat and cracked in the fire. Hanne watched the orange flames dance against the empty night sky.

She wanted to know what Owen was thinking, but she did not speak. The experience she had had in Wolf Creek, the beautiful light, lingered in her still. She only wanted to sit in it, be still, and marvel.

After a long while, Owen cleared his throat. "I like dogs," he said. "As you well know."

"Yes."

"I'd like to train them and sell them. I think cowboys would pay top dollar for a trained working dog. I do."

Hanne agreed, but he rushed on before she could say so.

"I'd like to have a ranch, just a small one. A good, big garden and some livestock, but I don't want to farm wheat or corn or sorghum. I'd train up the dogs. Breed them and train them. For a living."

He looked at her. Hanne felt his eyes on her face.

She knew he was looking for her response, and that what he was asking her was important. Her response mattered. She took a breath.

"If we do not have cattle," she said, "we must live near someone who does. For the dogs will need to practice with a herd, don't you think?"

A grin broke out on Owen's face.

"I was thinking about that," he said. "We'd better do just that. A small flock of sheep might be helpful, for training pups."

"I like that idea, because I can spin and weave," Hanne offered. "Not as well as my aunty Aud; you should see the weavings she makes. But I can do it well enough."

"I don't doubt there's much you can't do," Owen said.

"Wait," Hanne said. "I believe that was a compliment, but I must untangle the grammar."

Owen laughed, then checked the volume of his voice.

Hanne leaned in just as Owen moved closer.

His eyes were big as he drew near. The embers of the fire glimmered in his pupils. Hanne leaned farther still. She closed her eyes and felt his mouth on hers. His lips were rough and soft at the same time.

He put his hand to the side of her face. Hanne's pulse thrummed, her whole body yearning for Owen, all that wanting expressing itself in their kiss.

Hanne drew back, her face and neck on fire. Though the air was biting cold and her breath frosty, she was heated through.

Hanne slipped her hand into Owen's. His skin was cracked and tough, and she loved it. She wished he would never let go of her hand.

Then came a sound in the bushes—crackling, and the huffing of a horse drawing nearer. Hanne and Owen both stood.

"Who's there?" Owen asked. He reached backward for his rifle, grabbing it from inside his bedroll.

Hanne felt no internal alarm and saw that Daisy, who had woken and sniffed, was also unconcerned. She lay her head back on her paws, covered her nose with her tail, and went back to sleep.

The figure drew nearer. "It's just me," came a voice.

It was Rolf. He came into the clearing of their camp, riding Joyful.

"But, Rolf, where have you been?" Hanne asked.

Rolf swung his leg over the horse and dropped to the ground. He looked tired and frail. Hanne crossed the campsite and went to his side.

"I had an idea," he said, leaning on her. "To get us a bit of time." He reached into the saddlebags and removed some tattered clothing.

Hanne helped Rolf over to the warm rock. He sat, clutching the clothing in hands stiff with cold. Owen poured him a cup of coffee from the kettle, which was set in the outer coals to keep warm.

Hanne sat beside Rolf and put her arm around him. He was shivering.

"The Baron will expect to hear from me soon," he said. "I will telegraph him and tell him a story. I will say that Ketil perished in a storm. Or a landslide. Something natural. And that I'm still looking for you."

"I'll have to go back, though. In the spring. If I don't come back, he will send people looking for me."

Rolf leaned toward the fire for its warmth.

"I don't understand. Where did you go, Rolf?" she asked him.

"I went back to Wolf Creek."

No wonder he was so cold and tired. Wolf Creek was three hours behind them. He had not slept at all, then.

"The town was quiet. Still in great disorder. I found Ketil's body. It was lying in the street."

"What'd you do with it?" Owen asked.

"I changed the Berserker's clothes for Knut's horse blankets."

Rolf held up the clothing he had brought from the saddlebags. It was the jacket and vest that Ketil had worn. He tossed the clothes into the fire. The flames flared and devoured the fine fabrics.

Hanne shot a glance at Owen. "But no one would take his face for Knut's—"

"Then I rolled him into the remains of the fire. The embers were still hot in the foundation. They melted his features away."

Hanne shivered at the thought.

"You think it will work?" Owen said.

Rolf shrugged. "I pulled his body to the jail and pinned the wanted poster for Knut onto the blanket. I thought it worth a chance. He was as tall as Knut, if not as stocky."

"Oh, do you think it could work?" Hanne asked. "Or will they chase us forever?"

Rolf sipped from the tin mug of coffee. He grimaced at the bitterness of the brew. "There is an old line of Eddic poetry that says, '*The thrumming of one strand alters the web. The blood of one heart poured out changes the line. One cannot predict the journey ahead as one cannot predict the way sparks will dodge, as they rise dancing from the fire.*'"

A log in the fire crackled and sparks drifted up, as if to illustrate Rolf's verse.

"Which I guess is my way of saying that I don't know," Rolf finished.

Hanne watched the sparks wink out against the black, starry sky. She sighed. He was right. There was no way to know what would happen next.

"You're shivering pretty bad, Mr. Tjossem. Think more coffee would help?" Owen said.

"I just want to sleep," Rolf said. "I'm too old for this kind of business."

Hanne and Owen helped him to his feet.

"Next time, tell me, and I'll go," Owen said. "We look after each other."

"Very well," Rolf said.

Without thinking, Hanne hugged Rolf and kissed him on the cheek. He looked at her, and she was surprised to see tears glimmering in his eyes.

Rolf said nothing, only bobbed his head. He shuffled off to the tent where Stieg and Knut were sleeping.

"That was good thinking on his part," Owen said. "I suppose we're lucky he found us."

"We are," Hanne said. And her heart leaped with happiness—Owen felt himself a part of the *we* of her family.

"What are you smiling about?" Owen asked.

Hanne dropped to sit back down and Owen settled next to her. He put his arm around her. Hanne pressed her face into his neck. The smell of him—smoke, leather, salt—was intoxicating.

"Well? Say something," Owen said. There was a smile in his voice.

"Will you stay with me always?" Hanne asked.

"I been askin' to do that for days now," Owen told her softly.

She raised her face and kissed him, the firelight warming her knees, his arm warming her back.

In the future there might be a ranch under the vast Montana sky, dogs to train, sheep to shear. It was a life so simple and so lovely she could not have dreamed it for herself. Hanne would fight for it, for she meant now to live and live fully.

ACKNOWLEDGMENTS

I wish to thank my agent, Susanna Einstein, for her support during the many drafts I wrote of this novel. Without her confidence in me, I'm not sure I would have made it. Susanna, I could not imagine a better advocate or friend.

I am indebted to Liz Szabla, my editor at Feiwel and Friends, for her passionate and thoughtful work with me on this manuscript. I absolutely loved collaborating on the final pass with you, Liz. I can't wait to sit down and pore over the sequel!

The magnificent cover for this book still thrills me every time I look at it. Greg Ruth, thank you for the perfect illustration. Liz Dresner, thank you for the design of the cover and the interior.

Thank you, Jean Feiwel, for your support of my work and for the strong and vital publishing imprint you have created—I love being a Friend. Thanks to fellow Friends Alexei Esikoff, Ilana Worrell, Kim Waymer, and copyeditor Pat McHugh for all your work to make this a better book. Thanks to my friend Anne Heausler for liberating *Berserker* from a great many "hads."

I am tremendously lucky to be represented in the entertainment industry by Eddie Gamarra of the Gotham Group. Eddie, your guidance and excellent advice is invaluable—thank you. I also thank Sandy Hodgman for representing this book, and all my books, so wonderfully in the worldwide market.

I am so grateful to have Lauren Festa, Amanda Mustafic, Katie Halata, and my dear friend Molly Ellis working to market and publicize this book. I am humbled by all you have done to promote this book. Thank you.

Kristin Bair, thank you for your beautifully detailed notes on the outline and *first* draft of *Berserker*—and for your notes on the outline and *second* draft of *Berserker*, which had almost nothing in common. Then you gave me notes on the rewrite! Your generosity knows no bounds and I'm so glad for it.

I am grateful to Linda Peavy for her excellent work helping me to check the facts of life in Montana, 1883. It was a pleasure to collaborate with you, Linda. I'd also like to thank my cousins Kim and Wayne Stenehjem for the tour of Cass County, North Dakota. Kim, you gave me such a great overview of the time period and the challenges the homesteaders faced. Many thanks!

I have a wonderful fellowship of author friends and plain old friend friends that gave me encouragement and advice along the way with this book—heartfelt thanks to Cate and Evan Baily, Anna Banks, Leigh Bardugo, Jessica Brody, David Conway, Kevin Hammonds, Mallory Kass, Jaqueline Kelly, Jennifer Kelly, Vicki

Larson, Ed Manning, Jennifer Mathieu, Donna Miele, Danielle Paige, Joy Peskin, Wendy Shanker, Kerry Tatlock, and Greg Cope White.

Libba Bray and Aaron Zimmerman, a special thanks to you two for helping me to cheat on *Berserker* just enough to keep things spicy. And thank you to Kriss Seco for taking such exquisite care of my kids while I was dreaming up blizzards and Norse poetry.

The love and support of my family is my greatest asset, and I treasure it above all else. Thank you to my husband, my children, my parents, my brother, and all my beautiful in-laws.

THANK YOU FOR READING THIS FEIWEL AND FRIENDS BOOK.

The Friends who made

BERSERKER

possible are:

JEAN FEIWEL, Publisher

LIZ SZABLA, Associate Publisher

RICH DEAS, Senior Creative Director

HOLLY WEST, Editor

ALEXEI ESIKOFF, Senior Managing Editor

KIM WAYMER, Senior Production Manager

ANNA ROBERTO, Editor

CHRISTINE BARCELLONA, Editor

KAT BRZOZOWSKI, Editor

ANNA POON, Assistant Editor

EMILY SETTLE, Administrative Assistant

LIZ DRESNER, Senior Designer

ILANA WORRELL, Production Editor

FOLLOW US ON FACEBOOK OR VISIT US ONLINE AT FIERCEREADS.COM

OUR BOOKS ARE FRIENDS FOR LIFE.